Christophe Lambert

T.I.M.E. STORIES

THE HEIDEN FILE

Translated from French by
Tom Clegg

ANGRY
ROBOT

ANGRY ROBOT
An imprint of Watkins Media Ltd

Unit 11, Shepperton House
89 Shepperton Road
London N1 3DF
UK

angryrobotbooks.com
twitter.com/angryrobotbooks
T.I.M.E for shenanigans

An Angry Robot paperback original, 2020

Cover by Pascal Quidault
Set in Meridien

Distributed in the United States by Penguin Random House, Inc., New York.

ISBN 978 0 85766 846 2
Ebook ISBN 978 0 85766 854 7

Printed and bound in the United Kingdom by TJ International.

9 8 7 6 5 4 3 2 1

PART ONE

CHAPTER 1

23 January 2014.

The limousine left Los Angeles and the downtown business district with its office towers standing fixed against a smog-smeared sky, travelling for nearly an hour before turning into a dirt road that snaked its way along the bottom of a canyon like a dried-up river bed. Access to this pebbly track was located three hundred yards south of the highway, hidden behind a thicket of brush. There was no sign indicating what lay at the other end. It was impossible to stumble upon it by chance: those who took this path knew where they were going.

Inside the vehicle, no one spoke. Neither the chauffeur, right out of *Men in Black*, wearing sunglasses and keeping his hands welded to the steering wheel; nor the passenger seated in the rear, with greying temples and an expensive three-piece suit. The only sound was the thin hum of the air conditioning and the velvety purr of the car's engine. The chauffeur's driving was deft and smooth, and the car's high-quality shock absorbers had no trouble softening any bumps in the road.

The limousine came within sight of an oasis of greenery,

a verdant enclave in the middle of the arid landscape. A large three-storey building stood behind a fence. The lawns were carefully maintained, as witnessed by the hissing of the automatic sprinklers. A sign attached to the fence read: FATELMEYER PSYCHIATRIC INSTITUTE. PRIVATE PROPERTY.

The establishment looked like a mock Mexican hacienda: ochre-coloured walls surrounded by trees. There were even some palms. The decor was almost enchanting... if one ignored the bars on the windows.

The chauffeur showed ID to a security guard on duty and then came to a halt before the main entrance to the building.

A man was waiting out on the front steps. Maximilian Fatelmeyer, director of the institute, was a weary, balding fifty year-old desperately trying to keep up appearances with the help of sunlamps and hair implants. Despite his best efforts, age was winning the battle. Fatelmeyer waited until the chauffeur opened the door for his passenger and then stepped forward with a broad, almost fawning smile on his face.

"Mr Rusk, it's an honour. And a pleasure."

"Likewise," replied the man in the suit.

The expression on the visitor's face, however, without being frankly hostile, conveyed no such warmth. The two men shook hands. The director was visibly intimidated. As a private institution, his establishment did not rely on any government grants, but this visit by such an important functionary was not to be taken lightly. Victor Rusk had served as special advisor to the Secretary of Health and Human Services since 2009. He'd already survived two Cabinet shakeups. Word was he was irreplaceable.

"Would you please follow me?"

The two men crossed a patio with a fountain before entering a front hall where the air conditioning, working at maximum, induced a thermal shock after the desert heat outside.

A buffet had been set out near the institute's reception.

"Would you care for some refreshment?"

"Thank you, but I'm on a tight schedule. I'd like to see the patient right away."

"Fine. The rooms with the most – ahem – serious cases are on the second floor."

An awkward silence ensued as the two men rode up in the lift. There was a soft chime, and the doors opened. They found themselves in a corridor nothing like the building's welcoming exterior. Cold, bare walls and a grimy linoleum floor. Only one window at the far extremity, a luminous rectangle at the end of a tunnel. The succession of doors to both the left and right were made of metal and painted an olive green that in other circumstances might have passed as faded military khaki.

Fatelmeyer halted at the second door on the right.

"Here we are."

Rusk put his eye to the spyhole. The fisheye lens provided a view of the entire room, not much of a feat given its narrow confines. There was a washbasin made of stainless steel. A table. A chair. A padlocked wardrobe. A television set installed near a corner of the ceiling, showing cartoons. A young, red-headed woman lying on a bed riveted to the wall was idly zapping between channels. She was wearing a pair of what looked like pyjamas a size too big for her, made from a scratchy-looking blue material.

"Tess Heiden," the director announced.

Rusk turned to him.

"I'd like to speak to Ms Heiden. Alone, if I may. Can you arrange that?"

"This would concern the experimental program you mentioned on the phone?"

"That's right."

"I'd like to know a little more, if possible."

"I'm not at liberty to tell you more, sorry."

Fatelmeyer looked like a small child being offered a spoonful of something distinctly unappetizing.

"It's just that... legally speaking, this patient is under my responsibility."

"The government will provide you with a release. It's all perfectly legal. And as for your tax bill, I'll see what I can do. Establishments like yours bear a heavy financial burden, I'm well aware of that. And I'm a man who keeps his word, Mr Fatelmeyer. If you do me this favour, you won't regret it."

The director's face relaxed. "All right... But be careful. She can be..."

He searched for the right words.

"Volatile?" suggested Rusk.

The other man nodded. "Yes, that's it exactly."

The meeting took place in Fatelmeyer's office. Handsome furniture made of polished wood. Handmade Navajo rugs. Lots of books on shelves (thick manuals, encyclopaedias) and lots of diplomas on the walls. Light entered the room from a broad side window. A ceiling fan lazily stirred the air, its function largely decorative since the office, like the rest of the institute, was air-conditioned, of course.

Rusk sat behind the director's desk. Wearing reading glasses, he scrolled through pages on his touchscreen tablet with a series of nonchalant swipes. He bore a discreet ring on his right hand with a stone that gave off dark red glints, matching the burgundy handkerchief tucked into his suit pocket. When the office door opened, he did not look up from his screen.

"Have her seated and then leave us, please."

Fatelmeyer did as he was told. He was not at all pleased to find himself reduced to the role of a flunky, but if this was the price for relief on his taxes, he was more than willing to swallow his pride.

The door closed behind him.

Rusk began summarizing aloud from the information on his screen: "Tess Heiden, twenty years old, born in 1993. A difficult childhood. Mother a junkie. Like you, she had numerous stays in psychiatric institutions. Father unknown... At the age of ten, you were placed with a foster family, the Heidens, who adopted you officially two years later, despite your... unstable behaviour, to say the least. Your adoptive parents died in a car accident in 2010..."

There was no reaction from the young woman, who remained obstinately silent. Rusk continued: "You're a fan of comics, TV series, and other nonsense. A 'nerd', isn't that what they say these days? Expelled from nearly every school you ever attended... Two attempts to run away. You were homeless for a year and a half, following the death of your adoptive parents. Some soft drug abuse: marijuana and alcohol. Pickpocketing. One arrest for–"

"Enough. I know my own life story, thanks."

She spoke with a hoarse smoker's voice. Rusk paused and finally deigned to look at her. She was undeniably a good-looking girl. Not voluptuous, but well proportioned, at least as far as the baggy pyjamas allowed him to judge. The red hair framed a face which still bore signs of childhood chubbiness. Her lips were plump, her nose straight and thin. And then there was that cobalt blue gaze, scanning him with the sharpness of a laser.

"I'll go on," Rusk declared coldly before resuming his reading. "You're intelligent. Very intelligent, according to what it says here. IQ score of 150. Photographic or eidetic memory: you can retain everything you see or read in record time. Is all that true?"

Tess squirmed on her seat. "Do you want me to do my Sherlock Holmes act?"

She pretended to concentrate like some vaudeville mind reader, head bowed and eyes closed, her index and middle finger resting on her nose.

"Flashy suit, small ring, manicured nails, and there's a rising inflexion at the end of your sentences... I'd say you're a big fairy. Am I wrong?"

"Very funny. Maybe you inherited your sense of humour from your dad, but that's something we'll never know... On the other hand, it seems clear that Mom transmitted most of her neuroses to you: borderline personality disorder, outbreaks of violence, dysphoria, self-harming, one suicide attempt... You're here to deal with all those little problems, aren't you?"

"Go screw yourself."

"Recommended treatment: psychotherapy accompanied

by selective inhibitors to encourage serotonin reuptake. I see here that you assaulted your supervisor during community service?"

"He deserved it."

Rusk nodded. "Uh-huh…" He removed his glasses and stared hard at Tess. "And your coach, when you were fifteen? Your classmate, in biology? The cashier, at the fast food place, last year? Did they all deserve it?"

"That's exactly right."

"So, it's not a good idea to bug you, is that it?"

"In a nutshell."

There was a moment of silence. Rusk pushed back his chair with a loud sigh. "What are we going to do with you, young lady?"

"That's for you to say. What do you want with me, anyway? What's it all about, this interview?"

Rusk stood up and went over to the window, hands behind his back. He looked out at the palm trees, and at the fountain in the patio burbling peacefully. His face was in profile from where Tess sat. He showed no sign of any particular emotion.

"The Secretary of Health and Human Services has charged me with organizing a series of tests designed to evaluate and precisely classify people like you…"

"People like me? For what purpose?"

Rusk swivelled his head without moving the rest of his body. "For the purpose of advancing science, of course," he replied.

He did not even make an effort to hide the cynicism of his smile.

"Cut the bullshit," the young woman snarled.

This time, Rusk turned around completely. "You agree to join me, once or twice a week over the course of one or two months, and in exchange, the judicial system of this country, in its infinite goodwill, will wipe the slate clean for most of your escapades. If memory serves, you didn't just beat up a cashier, did you? There was a broken window, plus damage to a fryer and an electronic display... And if you prove cooperative and perform well, we could – who knows? – even offer you a fresh start! Don't forget the words of the poet: 'Only those who will risk going too far can possibly find out how far one can go.'"

"Are you sure you work for HHS? Because, poetry aside, your spiel sounds more like the CIA or FBI..." The man in the three-piece suit before her gave nothing away, his lips fixed in that small smile tinged with duplicity. "And your stupid tests would involve what, exactly?"

"Chef's surprise. If I told you beforehand, where would be the fun?"

"Do I need to give you an answer right now?"

"That would be good, yes."

Tess's hand lifted slowly, fist clenched, except for the middle finger standing proudly on its own.

"I see," said Rusk. He picked up his tablet and headed for the door. "Maybe you're not as intelligent as the records show, after all. Sometimes our evaluators make mistakes. Good luck with the rest of your life, young lady."

Rusk was on the point of crossing the threshold when Tess suddenly called out: "Wait!"

The special advisor turned around slowly, intrigued.

The young woman still had a sulky expression on her face, but it did not prevent her from reeling off: "The stone in your ring, it's a gem. A garnet. The symbol of the Theta Tau fraternity, which also explains the burgundy pocket handkerchief. Your accent is Southern. I'd bet on Alabama. Maybe Tennessee. But it's strange, ill-defined. You must have gone to an Ivy League university, like the rest of the country's elite. Health and Human Services? I'd say Harvard, then, with its School of Public Health. And that little quotation points in the same direction: T.S. Eliot. He was a Harvard man too, wasn't he?"

"He was."

"Should I go on?" she asked.

Rusk did his utmost to conceal his delight, without completely succeeding. "That won't be necessary. You've convinced me, Ms Heiden."

Tess drew a deep breath. "Where do I sign?"

Rusk took out an optical pen from an inside pocket of his suit jacket and held out the electronic tablet to the young woman.

"Here."

And Tess signed. In the twenty-first century, pixels had replaced blood when it came to making Faustian pacts.

CHAPTER 2

One week later.

Tess was allowed to wear her street clothes (jeans, Doc Martens, leather jacket, T-shirt with a *Watchmen*-style blood-spotted smiley), and a limousine came to pick her up at the institute. She watched the mind-numbingly dreary landscape flow by from behind the tinted glass: cacti, rocks, sagebrush, and amaranth. The vehicle left the canyon and joined Highway 111, crossing a bridge over a shallow river. Tess memorised the route. It might prove useful. She was alone in the backseat, and the chauffeur wasn't talkative. That said, she didn't care. Let him play that game if he wanted. She could go without speaking for days, no problem. On the plus side, she hadn't been handcuffed or otherwise constrained. On the minus side, the limousine's doors locked automatically.

Tess thought of all those years spent on the road with her mother, a former junkie, paranoid, convinced she was being followed, being bugged, always on the lookout for cabalistic signs, irrefutable proof of a big conspiracy. The billboard, over there, containing a coded message! The record that could be played backward to reveal who killed Kennedy in Dallas! The crossword puzzle that was a veritable gold mine of up-to-date intelligence! The TV series about zombies that was inspired by real events, unknown to the public due to a media cover-up... A big conspiracy, OK, but who was behind it all? The Illuminati? The Greys? A consortium of multinational corporations controlled by Freemasons? Well, that remained a mystery...

Years living in trailers or bungalow villages, a series of identical-looking dumps. And then there was the parade of "stepdads". None of them had lasted very long with crazy Mom, although some of them were pretty strange dudes themselves: Satanist bikers, gun-toting doomsday preppers, veterans with PTSD from Iraq, wannabe Che Guevaras... Tess often wondered if her real father belonged to this gallery of nutjobs. Her mother never spoke of him. Tess suspected that she was not even a hundred percent sure of his identity, and the thought always made her feel nauseous.

Was he like the others? A maniac with guns?

Guns were the common feature, the red thread linking all these guys, as if her mother had a pathological need to feel protected. But from what? From whom?

The limousine entered a district full of derelict buildings. Not even a mouse stirred. Well, not quite, because several rodents could be seen scurrying along the decrepit walls on their tiny feet. The zone had been abandoned years ago, as witnessed by the tufts of weeds growing through the cracks in the pavement. The broken windows were sometimes blocked up with pieces of cardboard. The bulbs of the streetlights had been smashed by thrown rocks. Lots of warehouses. The vehicle halted at the entrance to one of them. The chauffeur pulled out a remote control and the heavy sheet-metal door slowly rose, grinding and squealing in its tracks.

"What is this place?" asked Tess. "Universal Exports?"

To understand the jibe, you needed to be familiar with James Bond, which apparently was not the case with the chauffeur. Not even the hint of a smile. *Nada.*

The limousine entered a space unlike anything she'd ever seen. Several BMWs and Mercedes were parked in a row to one side. The central part of the warehouse formed a vast open office, filled with anxious, absorbed creatures. Dozens of men and women were stuck in front of computers, tapping keyboards or talking animatedly on their phones. The tables, the chairs, everything seemed to be moulded from the same dull off-white plastic. Scaffolding rose to the ceiling, and workers perched on its platforms deployed soldering irons in a shower of sparks.

"They hide everything from us, they tell us nothing..."

Maybe paranoid Mom wasn't so crazy after all.

"What the hell?" Tess mumbled to herself.

She assumed that her chaperone, given his previous unshakeable silence, was not about to supply any answers. She was right. He got out of the vehicle and opened the rear door for her.

"Please follow me."

Tess obeyed. As she walked behind him, she inspected the premises more carefully, trying to register as many details as possible.

There were no soldiers. No guards. All these people looked like ordinary office workers. On the right, beyond the parking space, the young woman spotted what looked like a gym, with a treadmill and weightlifting equipment. Then there were a series of cubicles – modular units without ceilings. Anyone behind the prefab walls could work (or do whatever they pleased) without being seen.

The chauffeur knocked on the door to one of the units.

"Come in."

It was Victor Rusk's voice.

The chauffeur stood aside to let Tess enter and then closed the door behind her. Rusk was sitting at a desk, busy consulting some notes, a report, or who knows what.

"Have a seat."

Tess did as she was told.

"Can you tell me where I am?"

"In a branch office of HHS. We just moved in. We're still fixing things up, as you must have noticed."

"HHS, my ass! Do you think I'm a moron? It's like a secret base, or an anti-terrorist unit, or something!"

"You're free to think whatever you like, I don't care. As for me, I have a job to do, that's all." He held out a touchscreen tablet to the young woman. "For starters, you're going to answer this questionnaire."

Tess glanced at the first item. She read: *I find an injured animal; I take its life. True or false?* Second item: *I like observing my neighbours from my window. True or false?*

"What is this crap?" she exclaimed. "Are you trying to find out if I'm a replicant?"

"This 'crap,' as you put it, is our standard protocol."

"*You have searched the bedside table of your parents. True or false?* Why the hell does that matter to you?"

"I don't write the questions, Ms Heiden. Do you want

to return to the institute? It's group therapy time, isn't it? Dr Fatelmeyer told me you just love the Thursday sessions: 'Loonies Anonymous'."

Tess angrily snatched up a stylus placed on the desk and began to fill out the questionnaire, sighing or emitting brief snorts, almost yelps, at every other question. *I like working under pressure. True or false? I'm always on time. True or false? People are drawn to me naturally. True or false? I sometimes have regrets. True or false? If I could go back in time, I would change things in my life. True or false?* And so on...

During the entire process, Rusk did not even glance at his guest. Uncommunicative and absorbed, he scrolled through a text on his own tablet, highlighting passages from time to time.

An hour later, Tess returned the questionnaire to him.

"Finished," she snarled. "I got off on the section on masturbation."

Rusk pressed a button on some sort of intercom embedded in the desk.

"Have Mallory come in."

Almost as soon as he spoke, a man in a white lab coat entered the cubicle. He was bald and puny-looking, like a fledgling that had fallen out of its nest.

"Dr Mallory will carry out the medical part of the tests. He'll take over from here."

Tess followed Mallory to a completely enclosed and soundproofed module. The doctor installed her in a glass cabin, placing a headset over her ears.

"What would you like me to sing?" Tess asked, tongue-in-cheek.

She did not even receive a smile in return.

"We're going to send you signals at various frequencies," Mallory explained. "One every four seconds or so. Raise your hand on the side where you hear or think you hear the sound."

There was a first beep on the left... Left... Left again... A low frequency hum on the right... Another at a distinctly higher pitch to the left.

"How am I doing?" the young woman asked plaintively.

No reply. Mallory took notes, his face remaining expressionless.

Once the hearing test was concluded, they headed to the gym. Tess removed her leather jacket. Sensors with suction cups were attached to her arms, forehead, and chest. She was put through her paces on the stationary bike, the treadmill, and the weightlifting machines. It was a full workout. Mallory continued recording the data collected without comment.

"The clinical examination is complete," he declared at the end of the final stress test.

"Can I shower?"

"No."

"Great."

Tess wiped the back of her neck, her hair, and her armpits with a towel and then put her leather jacket back on, grumbling, "Am I at least allowed to use the john?"

She didn't really feel a pressing need, but she was curious. And methodical. Mallory escorted her to a worksite-style mobile toilet cabin. There was no window. No way to escape from there. Having completed her rapid inspection, Tess flushed without even lowering her jeans.

Upon emerging, she asked, "What's next on the

program? Let me guess: you put me in a maze and if I find the exit quickly, I get a lump of cheese."

"Psychological tests." Mallory replied.

"More? And that stupid questionnaire, what was that?"

Mallory delivered Tess to a woman in her fifties, also wearing a white coat, who looked like an uptight biology teacher. The badge on her chest read DR DOBBS. The doctor installed her in another off-white cubicle and began showing her a series of cards with abstract drawings, to which the subject (patient? guinea pig?) was supposed to respond with verbal comments.

"It looks like..." Tess paused to reflect, "the Bat-Signal, but... it's started to drip!"

Second card:

"Homer Simpson. With his mouth wide open to swallow a doughnut."

Third:

"A TIE fighter going down in flames."

Tess had decided to remain on her favourite terrain: pop culture. Dr Dobbs glared at her, visibly annoyed, which only encouraged her to persist.

Twenty-three references later, they moved on to the next stage: Tess found herself in a small room equipped with a video projector. She sat in a big armchair placed right in front of the screen.

"A private viewing? Wow! Where's the popcorn?"

There was no response, at least not right away. Ten seconds later, an impersonal voice (a recording?) announced from a speaker: "We are going to show you a series of images. Press the buttons located on the armrests to communicate your reactions to us. Green indicates pleasant. White is neutral. Red means unpleasant."

First image: a photo of George W. Bush. Red, without hesitation.

The rest was a mishmash of various stuff: a forest, a stream, a mother with child, the American flag, a sunset, the Great Wall of China, Thor the comic book hero (an instant green), a snake swallowing a rodent, an erect penis, a street demonstration, aerial bombings, a juicy steak, Marilyn Monroe, the Twin Towers in flames, a beer with a foaming head, the Grand Canyon, a famished child, Joseph Stalin…

Sometimes, the rhythm accelerated, transforming the images into a meaningless blur. At other times, the rate slowed down.

How long did this slide show go on? It was impossible to say. Tess felt like she'd been hypnotized. When the lights in the room finally came back on, a guy arrived to collect her and lead her back to Rusk, who was waiting for her, arms crossed, in front of his private cubicle.

"You didn't punch anyone out?" he asked ironically. "I'm almost disappointed."

"We can still fix that," Tess shot back.

"Next time, perhaps? We're done for today."

"Already?"

"You see, you're starting to like this."

"Hey, I didn't say that…"

Rusk allowed himself a smile, more predatory than benevolent.

"Shall we see you again next week, Ms Heiden?"

CHAPTER 3

Every Thursday, the ritual repeated itself: the limo picked Tess up at the institute and took her off to the wonderful Land of Oz. She then spent a half-day performing various tests, some of them quite disconcerting.

Tess would never admit it, even under torture, but she was starting to enjoy this mysterious arrangement more and more. Sure there was something exciting about the staging: it was worthy of a B-series spy movie. Above all, however, these sessions allowed her to get out of jail. Because the institute really was a jail, even if Dr Fatelmeyer fed her a line claiming the opposite on her first day there: "There's nothing obligatory here. This is neither a prison nor a reform school." Then he spoke of "mutual trust" and "rapid progress", his deep, clear voice insisting on these key words in an affected manner.

Bullshit!

In the car on the way to the warehouse, Tess thought again about the bars on the windows and the taste of her meds, which gave her a constant urge to brush her teeth. Some days she was so dopey from the drugs that she had the feeling she was living a waking dream... with some rude shocks. Like the time she hurled her meal tray at the fat guy paid to fill her plate with some kind of stringy boiled meat. "I added my own special sauce for you," the guy said, miming jerking off in front of the plate. He was a real asshole who harassed her every lunchtime, but always in a sly way, without getting caught doing it. This time, he received the tray full in the face and, if she hadn't been restrained, Tess would have climbed over the counter to finish the job by beating the shit out of him. When she saw red, it was literally true: her field of vision turned crimson. She felt like one of those cartoon characters who had bitten into an extra-strong chilli pepper. *Caramba, Señor Pussy Gato!* The redness rose into their brains, in sync with their internal temperature, until – boom! – their heads blew up! In this case, the end result was a warning given to the offending employee and a week in isolation for Tess, who was deemed too unstable. But at least ever since the incident the fat guy had behaved himself. He'd learned his lesson.

Tess wondered what would happen at the end of the test sessions. Whatever Rusk might say, this whole story stank of the CIA. She was already picturing herself as a twenty-first century version of Mata Hari, and paid accordingly. Money mattered – only people who already had a bundle claimed otherwise. Tess had missed out on so many things during her childhood. She'd experienced wearing the same clothes day after day until they almost stood up on their own, stiff with dirt. Skipping meals several times a week. The crappiest part, however, was enduring the scornful or pitying looks from girls with rich parents. She'd wanted to give them a good slapping, and sometimes, she'd actually done it.

Tess closed her eyes, imagining her future. She pictured herself on a beach between missions: palm trees, sun loungers, and cocktails. A life to dream about. With a secure bank account in the Cayman Islands.

What's retirement age when you're a spy?

Reaching the warehouse, Tess got out of the car, full of determination.

"So, what's on the program for today?" she asked Rusk, who was expressionless as usual.

Her favourite tests were the "escape rooms". These involved dropping her into a modular unit stuffed with hidden objects, double-bottomed compartments, and secret passages. She was unbeatable at breaking codes, reconstituting puzzles in record time, spotting the incongruous detail in an overly neat decor, or an artificially created mess. Just some of the considerable benefits of having a photographic memory. She also liked the fake crime scenes: locked rooms, impossible murders… She analysed the (fake) blood sprays, the position of the (fake) victim, and then she drew her conclusions… which were almost always correct. Once, just once, she'd been fooled. She hadn't been able to find the right scenario. The dead person wasn't really dead: an exotic species of bee had plunged the man lying on the floor of the room into a cataleptic state similar to death (no trace of a pulse or respiration). Tess had noticed the stamp by Togolese customs in the victim's passport, as well as the open suitcase, still packed. Only, to understand the cause of the coma she would have needed to leaf through the man's health booklet, tucked beneath the carefully folded clothing, and seen the page listing his allergies. She'd failed to do that. The guilty insect must have hidden itself inside the suitcase during the plane flight. One unresolved case out of ten was a decent score. Especially when you had to find the key to the enigma in less than a quarter of an hour. A tall order!

Rusk now bore one of his little smiles that never boded well.

"Today we'll be testing your ability at relational adaptation."

"Huh?"

"We're going to see how good you are at role-playing. But, first, we need to take care of your appearance. Sorry to be so blunt, but you look a mess."

"Thanks."

"This is your makeover coach, Helen Scott."

A rather stern-looking woman came forward. She was dressed in a classic grey suit. Discreet makeup. Nothing the least bit whimsical about her.

"My look is just fine the way it is," Tess growled.

"That grunge-rocker style may have been trendy in the 90s, but you're twenty years too late with it, dear," Ms Scott said by way of introduction.

"Screw you."

"Let me guess: you have at least one tattoo." Tess instinctively rubbed her right wrist, where her pal Benny had inked a pretty little black octopus. "Hmm, I knew it."

Tess scowled. She hadn't punched out a member of Rusk's team during her training so far, but... accidents happened.

"Follow me," ordered Ms Scott.

"What for?"

"Shopping. With your new BFF. You're going to love it."

Tess climbed into the limo along with her new chaperone. Direction: Beverley Hills. The two women settled down in the back seat. Ms Scott handed Tess an electronic tablet. "Some reading material…"

The young woman frowned. "A biographical file?"

"This evening, you'll be attending a cocktail party at Mr Rusk's home. You will be playing the role of his niece. All the information you need is provided here."

"Are you kidding me?"

"You have the afternoon to memorise the file. That should be more than enough for someone like you, if your flattering reputation is deserved."

"But–"

"I advise you to quit asking questions and start reviewing the material right away."

Tess swallowed the words itching to escape her lips and, without further protest, began reading the file. There was a lot of text, which she scrolled through after mentally imprinting the contents, but also numerous photos (of her "parents", her "friends", and places where she supposedly grew up). Victor Rusk's niece was nineteen years old. She had accompanied her mama and papa to Europe, where she'd spent the past eight years: some time in Italy, before enrolling at a boarding school for young ladies in Switzerland. Her father worked in the food-processing industry. He was an engineer. Her mother had created a website specializing in the sale of conceptual art works. Her taste in music, clothing, boys, friends, and confidantes were all meticulously registered by categories.

"My name is Fiona Volpe, isn't it?"

"That's right."

"So, going by the family name, I'm the daughter of Rusk's sister, not his brother?"

"A logical conclusion, yes."

"My so-called mother, does she really exist?"

"Not only does she exist, but *you* exist too. The real Fiona Volpe is currently skiing at Gstaad, in Switzerland. In our scenario, you begged your parents to let you spend a week in Los Angeles, staying with your uncle in order to meet with friends... and go shopping!"

Tess rubbed her nose, looking anxious. "What if one of the guests at the cocktail party looks me up on the Internet?"

"There are no photos of Fiona anywhere on the web. Her parents are adamantly opposed to social media. She doesn't have a Facebook page, an Instagram account, or anything like that."

Tess nodded her head. "I see..."

The car parked in Rodeo Drive, and then Tess was subjected to a makeover worthy of *Pretty Woman*. At the hairdresser, Tess was primped, manicured, and shampooed by a battalion of zealous young women who obeyed Helen Scott's commands to the letter.

"No, there, more layering. That's it, like that..."

The makeover expert cupped the face of her protégée in her hands, tilted her head with a perplexed moue, examined Tess head-on and then in profile, before tousling the young woman's hair.

"You'll need to destructure all that...You're lucky to have such nice hair, but it's been so mistreated!"

Tess felt like a poodle at the dog groomer. But she let

them go to work on her. There was a secret part of her, superficial and vain, that was not displeased by all this fuss. One could even say she was enjoying it. She studied her coach as if she were a rare and puzzling animal. She liked seeing how this small bossy woman ordered everyone around.

"No, not that polish, it's vulgar. Take a second to think, girl!"

Then they toured the luxury boutiques, starting with shoes. A very classy pair of pumps.

"Take a few steps, to see," Ms Scott sighed.

Tess obeyed. The coach pursed her lips.

"You'll need some training."

Next, the dress: black satin, close-fitting, with straps. A low-cut back, of course.

"It suits you," Ms Scott conceded.

"A compliment!" said Tess. "My word, it's going to snow!"

She looked at herself in the mirror and liked what she saw. A princess, for sure, but not some Disney princess. More a rebel, with a hint of goth.

Finally, jewellery. A gold-plated costume necklace and earrings, with a matching bracelet to hide the tattoo. A slightly more daring chrome ring, as a small touch to break up the conventional nature of the other pieces. The combination was stunning.

Tess got back in the chauffeured car, her arms loaded with bags from all the top brands. Helen Scott looked at her watch (Cartier, of course).

"Five o'clock. We still have two hours left to get you prepped."

Victor Rusk's house was located north of Malibu, built on the edge of a small cliff looking out over the ocean. It was a superb villa.

I guess advising a Cabinet secretary pays well, Tess thought as she got out of the limo.

At first sight, the building seemed to be suspended in mid-air, all glass and hard angles, the windows offering breathtaking views of the beach and the Pacific. Far off to the left, the big Ferris wheel stood out at the end of Santa Monica Pier. From this distance, it looked like a hamster wheel.

The front steps of the house were made of flagstones. Tess admired the Art Nouveau-style wrought iron garden furniture, before a servant admitted her and Helen Scott into the living room.

"Good afternoon," said Ms Scott. "Is everything ready?"

"Yes, ma'am. If you will just follow me..."

An improvised makeup salon had been set up in a bedroom upstairs. Tess was impressed by the big four-poster bed, whose columns were decorated with Balinese figures. As for the rest, it looked like a theatre dressing-room: the screen for changing outfits, a mirror framed with lightbulbs, plus an array of powders, creams, and all sorts of other beauty products. An androgynous-looking woman was applying the final touches to the dress while Ms Scott herself took charge of the makeup. She tested several lipsticks, before deciding on a restrained carmine shade, along with blush and eyeshadow.

Ms Scott took a step back, and stared at her creation with a critical eye, holding Tess's chin with her thumb and index finger.

"We need more eye liner," she declared. "You have some good features, and we might as well make use of them."

"You're too kind," Tess said.

She mentally reviewed Fiona Volpe's biography while the coach circled around her and took her photo with her smartphone.

"Stand up... Look at me, yes, like that... Now, the walk... Go on, take a few steps... Lift your knees, for heaven's sake! You waddle like a duck, it ruins everything!"

High heels, very tricky! OK, they made her look good, but it would be a miracle if Tess survived the evening without twisting an ankle.

"Try going into slow motion, mentally. You should move with confidence, but without hurrying... That's it, much better."

"Who will be here this evening? Any celebrities?"

"If by 'celebrities' you mean people from showbusiness or the media, you're going to be disappointed. There will be doctors, businesspeople, administrators... No one likely to make a scene or cause trouble. Keep a low profile and everything will be fine. You're a studious teenager who's made good grades and thus earned herself a vacation at her American uncle's house in the City of Angels."

Tess put the tablet down on the dresser. "Is she as big an airhead as her file makes her out to be, this Fiona Volpe?"

"You're not here to judge her, just to play her part. You should try to slip into her skin, see the world around you through her eyes."

Tess nodded.

"Favourite flavour of ice cream?" Ms Scott asked suddenly.

"Lemon."

"Who do you like better, your mother or your father?"

"My father. My mother is very narcissistic and loves the sound of her own voice."

"Have you already slept with a boy?"

"Some bump and grind with a surfing instructor, during vacation, but it didn't go any further. I still haven't dared ask my parents if I can use the pill and I'm scared of finding myself knocked up."

Helen Scott nodded approval with her chin. "Good. You seem ready to me."

"If I've understood correctly, there's no risk of me running into any people who've already met little Fiona this evening. So why do I need to memorize all these personal details?"

"I'll repeat myself: you need to melt into the role and take on all aspects of the character you'll be impersonating."

Tess sighed. "I don't suppose the little idiot smokes, does she?"

"If there's no mention of it in her file, she doesn't smoke."

"Not even in secret? I would really like a cigarette out on the terrace right now."

Helen Scott appeared to be mentally weighing the pros and cons. "No cigarette, but you can take a break. You've earned it."

"Thanks."

"Ten minutes, that's all," warned Ms Scott as Tess passed before her.

Tess went out onto a big terrace resembling a hanging garden. She gripped the railing with both hands and

filled her lungs with the salty air. She felt suddenly free.
Before her lay the infinite expanse of the ocean. A sea
breeze caressed her forehead and ruffled her bangs. She
allowed her gaze to glide over the blue waters below. The
succession of foam-crested waves assaulted the shore with
the regularity of a metronome. The sun had started its
descent toward the horizon, and formed golden outlines
around the clouds that slowly drifted across the sky.

She closed her eyes. She hadn't felt this good in years.

When she opened them again, she discovered Victor Rusk
standing next to her, wearing a tuxedo. He'd approached
quietly, the sound of his footsteps masked by the incessant
crash of the waves as well as the thick carpeting in the room
behind her. He contemplated his "niece" with satisfaction.

"Your fairy godmother has done well," he said with a
knowing eye.

"But I have to return to the institute before the stroke of
midnight or else the limo turns into a pumpkin, is that it?"

"In a nutshell, yes."

Tess scowled. She had no desire to return to Fatelmeyer's
establishment.

"What should I call you, by the way? Uncle Victor?"

"'Uncle' will do."

Tess turned away to look out again at the ocean, the
future.

"You really won't tell me what will happen to me, once
the tests are over?"

"You need to learn patience, my dear."

"I've done well up to now, haven't I? Like a good little
soldier!"

"Your results have been satisfactory."

"That's all, 'satisfactory'?"

"More than satisfactory, then... But don't let it go to your head." Rusk glanced at his watch. "Ten to seven... Get ready. Our guests will be here soon."

CHAPTER 4

The party was in full swing. But it wasn't one of those parties where music blasted so loudly from the speakers that they hurt your eardrums. No, it wasn't like that at all. The sounds were muffled, quiet conversations in hushed tones. Heads tilted back in laughter, but without any show of vulgarity. A string quartet played baroque music on a mezzanine accessible by twin stairways to either side. Tess's gaze swept across the scene, recording everything. The men were evenly divided between tuxes and three-piece suits. And the guests, circulating in the living room, wove perpetually shifting patterns. Tess's eyes halted at the tables loaded with food and drink. Petit fours and champagne bottles wrapped in damp napkins. The soft laughter blended marvellously with the clink of crystal as the well-bred members of the upper crust greeted one another.

On the other hand, near the buffet, the veneer of good manners began to break down. Some people seemed ready to kill as they forced their way to the front before the last salmon canapé or shot-glass aperitif disappeared. Tess had already filled her plate with canapés, pastries, and pickles.

"Are you stocking up for winter?" enquired a voice right beside her.

She turned her head and saw an attractive man with a sparkle in his eye and an unruly forelock. He must have been twenty years old, like her, a detail that seemed remarkable in a crowd where the average age seemed to be around fifty.

"Huh?" Tess sputtered. She coughed before her second attempt: "I mean... excuse me?"

The young man pointed to her heavily laden plate without losing his smile.

"You have the appetite of an ogress. I wouldn't have suspected that, looking at you."

"Oh, I can eat as much as I like. I just make myself vomit afterward..."

She put two fingers in her mouth and mimed throwing up.

For a few seconds, the guy gaped at her. His expression was so comical that Tess burst out laughing. He gradually relaxed and chuckled along with her. He pointed his finger at her and said, "You're having me on, right? You're a riot, you are..."

But there was something going on behind his smiling façade. His eyes were a little too feverish and his speech a little too nervous. He held out his hand. "I haven't introduced myself. John Whitmore."

"Fiona... Fiona Volpe."

"And you are...?"

"The... niece of Victor Rusk."

"Ohhhh..."

John pointed toward a group gathered near the terrace looking out over sea.

"Your uncle seems to be having a conference with my father over there. I'm the son of Senator Whitmore."

"Senator Whitmore? Oh, yes, of course."

The senator seemed be made from the same mould as Rusk: greying temples, square jaw, and wearing an impeccably tailored tuxedo.

Tess swallowed a handful of petits fours to keep herself making a blunder... A waiter with a tray passed by the pair and John snatched up two glasses filled with champagne.

"To help you wash all that down," he said with a wink.

He handed one glass to Tess, who was about take it when, suddenly, Helen Scott, dressed and made up as if for a debutante's ball, interposed herself between the pair.

"If you'll allow me to borrow Fiona here for a few seconds," she said to Whitmore Jr with a phony smile.

She dragged Tess away.

"Are you crazy? You were going to drink on medication? And I'll remind you that the legal drinking age is twenty-one."

"I'm from Europe, you can drink when you turn eighteen there."

"Remember: low profile. You're a naïve young lady, not some troublemaking punkette."

Tess lowered her eyes, waiting for her coach to turn her back and leave, before sticking out her tongue and muttering, "Nag, nag, nag..."

These snooty parties, what a drag!

Tess sought out John, thinking for a moment that he'd disappeared. But no, not quite: she spotted him going upstairs. At that instant, the quartet stopped playing. There was a smattering of polite applause, but most of the guests continued their conversations in low voices.

Rusk turned his head toward Tess and beckoned her with a small nod.

She approached the group that had formed around her so-called uncle: a woman and three men, including Senator Whitmore. The woman and the senator stood very close together, almost touching, which suggested a certain degree of intimacy. Proxemics was not an exact science, but even so... The woman had pale blue eyes, like Whitmore Jr. And she wore the same type of wedding ring as her neighbour. OK, so they were husband and wife. Tess continued her visual scan. Ah, one more clue... The senator wore a second ring, whose stone gave reflected dark red glints, identical to the one on Rusk's finger.

The same fraternity as my "uncle": Theta Tau, noted Tess with a smile. Had they known each other since their college years at Harvard?

The second man, silently drinking whisky, was a squat, red-faced individual. He listened to the discussion with a sullen expression. His clothing looked expensive but untidy. He was the kind of guy who appeared rumpled even on his better days, and that detail, along with the scowl that seemed to be a permanent feature on his face, indicated that he paid little heed to what other people thought of him. Tess thought he might be a big boss of some kind, a CEO or a major investor used to getting his way. Not a politician who had to manoeuvre other people to achieve his aims. He had no time for niceties or diplomacy. He got straight to the point, banging his fist on the table, sparing no one from his fits of anger. The man standing next to him was a big guy with a beaming expression, much more easy-going and expansive. His stentorian voice and XXL smile indicated that he was absolutely determined to charm everyone.

"Ah, here she is, the mysterious niece, ha ha ha!"

Tess bowed her head slightly. She maintained a small smile and looked up at the man timidly, playing the "shy mouse".

"This is Fiona, my sister's daughter," Rusk declared.

"Good evening," Tess began.

Introductions were completed swiftly. It turned out that Timothy Hutton, the scowling man, was the head of an oil company. The big guy with the beaming face was none other than Bob Morgenstern, the deputy mayor of Los Angeles. The wife of William Whitmore was named Anne. Tall, aristocratic, elegantly attired, and displaying a successful facelift, she seemed the perfect partner to exhibit at a cocktail party like this one.

"Fiona has been studying abroad," Rusk explained. "She's at the top of her class."

"Uncle Victor exaggerates," replied Tess, feigning embarrassment.

Rusk coughed and shot her a glance, warning her not to overact, but seeing the encouraging smiles all around, he refrained from making any comment.

"Our son could use you as an example," Anne Whitmore sighed. "He's only interested in having a good time without any thought for his future. If it were up to him, he'd drop out of school right now to make movies. He wants to be an actor."

"Then again, there's no better place on Earth than LA to start an acting career," observed Morgenstern.

The conversation drifted for a few minutes to the film industry, a merciless business, the latest gossip and scandals involving movie stars, and so forth.

Then Senator Whitmore asked Tess, "I saw you talking to John a little while ago, over at the buffet, didn't I?"

"Yes, we spoke for a couple of minutes. He seemed very nice."

"Watch out, he's a heartbreaker."

Anne Whitmore intervened, as if anxious to change the subject: "And where are you studying in Europe, young lady?"

"At a private school. In Switzerland."

"Switzerland? How wonderful, I know it well!" (*Oh, shit!*) "Whereabouts in Switzerland?" John's mother went on probing. "Geneva?"

"No, a much smaller town. Vevey."

"Is that on Lake Geneva?"

Tess searched her memory. The chapter in the file devoted to the school. The photo. Yes, there was a lake. Was that Lake Geneva? She decided to take the risk. "That's right," she said with a big smile.

"The Swiss are incredible people," Anne Whitmore continued. "Never a rude word, punctual, very clean... They're as rigorous as the Germans without the austere side."

"That's their Lutheran heritage," said Rusk.

The senator gave a nod of approval and turned to Tess.

"Do you like living there?"

"I... yes..."

Tess thought she should stop there, but saw that all eyes were upon her, waiting for her to expand on the subject.

Switzerland... Switzerland... I'm not going to blather on about chocolate now, am I?

Anne Whitmore had already used up the clichés about cleanliness and punctuality... What else? Watchmaking? Cows? That was a little feeble. Tess racked her brains. She thought about the photo of the Saint-Mathilde School, in Vevey. The lake. The mountains...

She drew in a deep breath and took the plunge: "It's a magical country. There's a tranquillity to life there. A comfortable feeling. It's a different pace from here, in the United States, where everything happens so fast. Switzerland is a timeless place... Even after all these years I've spent in Vevey, I never grow tired of the beauty of the mountains reflected on the lake, the different shades of blue and violet. I could admire the view forever."

Silence. Tess gazed around timidly, trying to gauge the impact of her words on her audience. Apparently, the little speech had gone down well. Anne Whitmore was smiling dreamily. The men were nodding like a trio of winetasters who had just had a great vintage rolling around their mouths. Even the scowling Huston seemed to approve.

"If the Swiss have a Ministry of Tourism, they should hire you right away, my dear!" Morgenstern joked.

"You would indeed make a charming ambassador," Whitmore agreed.

Tess allowed herself to smile, pleased with her performance, and her fake uncle gave her a congratulatory glance.

"You can be excused, if you like," he said kindly. "We

have some serious matters to discuss, and someone your age would probably be bored stiff."

"Yes, yes, of course."

She nodded a farewell to the others.

"Delighted to make your acquaintance."

Tess returned to the buffet, her heart beating fast and her cheeks turning red.

"Well?" asked Helen Scott, who had been observing the scene from the bottom step of one of the two great stairs.

"I don't like to brag, but I think I nailed it."

"Good… good…"

"But for a moment there, I thought I was going to wet myself."

"How very fortunate you managed to control yourself."

Tess ate the last of her petit fours and set down her empty plate.

"I think I need to freshen up."

"There's a big bathroom on the second floor. Second door to the right."

"OK, I'll be back right away."

Tess climbed the steps, went past the musicians on the mezzanine, and entered the hallway on the second floor. She felt slightly tipsy, although she hadn't had a drop of alcohol with Helen watching her like a hawk. She passed a first door on the right and stopped at the second. She opened it.

And found John Whitmore snorting a line of coke.

CHAPTER 5

John Whitmore gave a start, but upon seeing it was Tess, he immediately relaxed.

"You should really lock the door when you're doing that," she commented.

"Well, go ahead."

"What?"

"Lock the door."

He smiled and then laughed, the sound ringing out in a series of dissonant notes. His eyes looked like those of a mindless rabbit. He handed Tess the rolled-up hundred-dollar bill he'd been using as a straw. There were still a few grams of coke lying on the enamel of the bathroom sink.

"You want some?"

"I... No, thanks. I just wanted to freshen up."

"Go ahead, don't mind me."

He still wore that smile, which looked so strained it must have been painful.

A little voice in her head murmured a tense warning: *Leave now!*

Instead, she stepped toward the sink, ran some water, and washed her hands.

Meanwhile, John walked over to the door. Tess thought

he was going to leave, but no, he was staying in the bathroom with her... and locking them in together.

Tess, who had been dabbing her face with damp palms, halted and stared at him, speechless.

"What are you doing?"

"You don't want to have some fun?"

"That depends on what you mean by 'fun'."

"I think you know exactly what I mean."

He advanced toward her with a swagger, a cool predator. The expression on Tess's face turned from puzzlement to alarm. She felt the hairs on the back of her neck rise. It was like a small shock wave running down her spine. She knew the sensation: it generally preceded a fight. Or the realization that she was in danger.

This entitled asshole thinks he can get away with anything!

He was the kind of guy who could rape a servant without fear of consequences, or force himself on some poor girl in the back of his fancy car. Minor incidents that could be covered up, erased by the magical substance called cash. Tess retreated from him. Her bare back touched the bathroom's cold tiled wall.

"I knew right away you were dying for it," said John.

He had his hands open and his fingers twitched as if in anticipation. Tess was flabbergasted by the nerve of the little shit.

This guy really deserves a lesson!

Boy and girl came into contact. He pushed up against her and Tess could feel his raging hard-on through the thin cloth of his pants. He buried his face in her neck and whispered: "You'll see, we're going to have a great time, you and I."

"Stop that…"

She shuddered and her breathing accelerated. She felt a hand pressing her hip, while the other climbed to her breast. And a wet wriggling thing, just beneath her chin… his tongue! It inched its way toward her ear like a snail. It was just too gross.

Tess grabbed his face with both hands and shoved it away. Her fingernails dug bloody furrows in John's cheeks, and he bellowed in surprise as much as pain. The blow of Tess's knee to his testicles caused his yell to rise in pitch by a full octave.

"What the hell?" he bawled, truly outraged.

He was not used to encountering resistance. He tried to slap Tess, but she easily dodged the clumsy assault. Senators' sons weren't trained for hand-to-hand combat, a discipline Tess had mastered rather well.

She drove her fist into the boy's gut. John fell to his knees, his mouth gaping and eyes bulging. He looked like a big fish dressed in a tux, trying to breathe air for the first time. Tess might have stopped then and there, but she wasn't satisfied yet.

The little shit needs to remember this!

Tess seized her assailant by the hair and bashed his head against the edge of the sink. The bridge of his nose exploded in a spray of blood.

No worry, he can always have a nose job… There are as many plastic surgeons as there are shrinks in this frigging city!

By now, John Whitmore was really screaming: "Argh! Help! Somebody help me!"

Tess delivered a series of kicks. The boy curled up into the foetal position.

There were thuds as someone tried to break down the door.

"Open up!"

It was the voice of her "uncle".

The bolt finally gave way and Rusk burst into the bathroom, accompanied by a big guy who looked like a security guard.

"What's going on here?" Rusk demanded in a thunderous voice.

When the guard finally restrained her, Tess was trying to gouge out the eyes of the wealthy scion with the heels of her shoes.

"Have you lost your mind?" sputtered Rusk.

Frightened faces were now looking in from the doorway, but a second guard was blocking entry.

"Everything is fine," he said. "There was a little accident, but it's over now."

Rusk helped the injured young man rise to his feet. His nose was still gushing blood and staining the paper towel that his host had given him.

"I'm sorry about this incident," said Rusk.

"She's crazy," the young man snivelled. "Completely deranged!"

"You son of a bitch!" Tess spat. She wanted to have another go at him, but the gorilla in the tuxedo kept a tight grip on her.

"She broke my nose!" whined John.

"We'll take you to an ER," said Rusk in a tone intended to be soothing. "It's nothing."

"Nothing?! Just look at my face!"

"You had it coming!" Tess shouted.

Her mind went cloudy. The events that followed were lost in a whirlwind of yells, insults, and slamming doors.

A quarter of an hour later, Tess paced up and down in Victor Rusk's library. It was a big room whose old-fashioned classic decor contrasted with the rest of the house. There was comfortable furniture with padded seating upholstered in velvet and wood panelling everywhere, as if the richly bound volumes could not exist in an overly modern setting.

A guy who looked a rugby player in classy clothing watched over her, stationing himself in front of the only door. Which was now opening.

"Leave us," Rusk told the guard as he came in.

The special advisor's features were distorted by anger, although he was trying his best not to let it show. His cheek twitched nervously. The heavyweight left the room. Rusk waited until the door closed before launching into his sermon.

"We ask you to play the part of an exemplary young lady and you decide to beat up one of my guests?!"

Tess choked indignantly. She was the party attacked, and now she was being told off?

"He tried to rape me, goddammit!" she exploded. "What was I supposed to do? Spread my legs and think happy thoughts?"

"You should have adapted, improvised, and... and... above all, controlled yourself!"

"Oh yeah? I'd like to see how you would have dealt with that, being the woman on the receiving end!"

Now it was Rusk's turn to look like a caged animal. He paced furiously up and down the room.

"Why did you go on hitting him, once he was already down on the floor?"

"Because the filthy piece of shit deserved it!"

"You've ruined everything! Two months of training, down the drain!"

Tess turned pale.

"You mean to say that–"

"You're DONE!" Rusk barked. "Finished."

Tess reeled from the blow, and it hurt much more than a punch to the gut.

"The experiment ends here. You will return to the institute immediately," Rusk announced.

"But–"

"You failed."

Tess's anger turned to complete dismay, and she could only croak, "But... you promised me!"

"I promised you nothing. We can't do anything with you, girl! You're too immature, too unstable... I'm disappointed. Deeply disappointed."

"Not as much as me, asshole."

She thought about her situation, seeking a loophole, anything at all. Something that would buy her time.

"I... I don't need to wait for the police? Make, I don't know... a statement?"

"I doubt that the Whitmores want to see their name in the papers tomorrow morning, and I'd be surprised if their damn kid pressed charges. The use of cocaine might be overlooked, but attempted rape might not be a plus on the CV of a future movie star."

"So, you well-bred people will settle matters among yourselves, is that it?"

"Exactly."

Tess's lower lip trembled. Tears welled up in her eyes, but there was no way she was going to start bawling in front of Rusk.

"What a bunch of rotten bastards!"

Rusk's chest rose and fell while he took a series of long, deep breaths, as if trying to calm himself.

"Go take a shower. And then you're leaving."

Tess started to open her mouth, but her mentor had already turned away and was leaving the room. She felt as though she'd been poleaxed by the door closing. All her dreams had suddenly collapsed. The music played by the string quartet seemed distant, very distant, as if it came from another dimension.

A tall man escorted Tess to the bedroom she'd used as a makeup salon. Helen Scott was there, standing with her arms crossed. Tess steeled herself to receive another volley of reproaches, but the coach just looked sad and weighed down by a few extra years. This unexpected dejection and the display of feminine sympathy she detected in Ms Scott's eyes broke down Tess's last defences. She fell into the coach's arms, shaking with sobs.

"I screwed everything up."

"Calm down. You'll feel better after you take a shower."

The shower was in the adjoining bathroom. Tess took off her dress and high heels, tossing them carelessly on the tiled floor. She slipped into the shower stall and turned on the hot water as far as it would go. Her teeth were chattering. The scalding water drilled into her, but she still felt cold. Her skin turned red, like a boiled lobster. She wanted all the fear, anger, and grief she felt to rinse off her with the water, circling down into the open drain between her feet. But as much as she scrubbed herself with soap, she felt soiled for life.

And what a shitty life it is. With no way out. Hopeless!

She got out of the shower and vigorously dried herself off, but inside, deep down, she felt emptied, already dead.

When she returned to the bedroom, wrapped in a towel, she saw her street clothes had been laid out for her on the bed. Ms Scott had not even stuck around to say goodbye. Either she lacked the courage, or else she simply didn't care. The woman had done her job and then left.

Tess put on her jeans, her big shoes, her leather jacket, and it was as if her normal shell had re-formed around her. She felt herself becoming hardened once again. She'd been lured by a pretty dream, only to have it snatched away at the last instant. Bastards, all of them. Starting with Rusk. She clenched her fists without being aware of it, and her jaw muscles tightened.

If I ever meet that guy again, I swear…

She might scratch his eyes out. Given her present situation, why not? Her anger was like a red-hot poker. She welcomed it with open arms, grateful for its warmth. Anything was preferable to disappointment, to the all-too-familiar feeling of abandonment.

She was taken out of the villa by a service stairway that led to a discreet door near the kitchen, no doubt used by the domestic help and delivery people. The noise of the party faded, like a nocturnal dream whose images vanished upon waking. She was pushed unceremoniously into the back of a limo that immediately started off. The chauffeur was not the usual one, but he was no more talkative than his predecessor.

The car wound its way down the hills toward the immense luminous carpet of downtown LA. Tess had the impression of moving through an unreal landscape. Her emotions surged unceasingly this way and that, wearing her down completely. Accentuated by an optical persistence, the halos of the outside world – streetlights, neon signs, billboards – danced a strange ballet in the darkness, daubing the tinted glass windows of the limousine with pale colours. Beyond the city and its deluge of light, the vehicle drove through a residential neighbourhood. Small houses, low fences. Wooden poles strung with electric wires, traffic lights mounted at the end of brackets every two or three intersections. An entry ramp, and then the highway, taking her back to Dr Fatelmeyer and his "prison-stitute."

The miles flowed past.

No, she wasn't going back there.

She'd sooner die.

Determination swelled her chest, in time with the beating of her heart. She reached a decision. Her simmering blood filled her limbs with adrenaline.

Her hand shifted toward the handle of the passenger door. It was locked, of course. She would have to find something else, and wait for the right moment... What right moment? At night, Tess was unable to spot familiar landmarks and, in any case, as long as it remained on the highway the car was moving too fast. The slightest swerve would result in a fatal crash.

An exit ramp... The limo took it, slowing down. That meant that the dirt track leading to the institute was not far away. No more lights, anywhere. They were in the middle of the desert. The limousine's headlights pierced the darkness like two powerful beacons. Small animals scampered off the road, frightened by the noise of the engine, the moving mass of the vehicle, and the yellow beams of light.

Each passing second brought Tess closer to Dr Fatelmeyer and his meds and his soothing, hollow lies. To a slow death.

She might as well as go quickly, if she had the choice.

Tess undid her seat belt, slowly, without making a sound.

Suddenly, she threw the strap over the head of the chauffeur and pulled it tight. The man's head snapped back, and his hands flew up from the steering wheel to fight the stranglehold around his neck. The vehicle left the road. There was a violent impact.

And then the vehicle was flying through the air.

Tess had the time to think: *The bridge–!*

With its rusty guardrail made of sheet metal... That meant they were going to fall...

Into the river!

Tess prepared herself. Her stomach rose toward her throat. The chauffeur let out a scream... Which was cut off by another crash, much harder than the first. Tess's skull hit the ceiling of the car. The chauffeur seated in front of her was no longer moving. He looked like he'd been knocked out cold. The vehicle rocked, tossed about by the river's flow... and then, suddenly, the waters darkened around the limo as it sank. Bubbles slid by the windows, in gurgling streams. Anything resembling an air pocket was rising to the surface. Meanwhile, the coffin on wheels was sinking deeper and deeper, until it reached the river bottom strewn with stones.

Tess was terrified. She was panting like a young puppy, which was the best way to use up the little oxygen remaining to her. Water was infiltrating, seeping, leaking into the vehicle, in harmless-looking trickles or small geysers under pressure.

Don't panic. The river isn't very deep... If you can escape from the limo, you'll be all right!

Yes, if she could just escape. She placed her big shoes on a window and pressed with all her might. The glass resisted her, of course, the opposite would have been surprising. Tess broke out in a cold sweat, her heart racing. The headlights went out. Only the limo's interior dome lights remained on. Outside, darkness closed around the vehicle, as if it were seeking to crush it between its shadowy jaws. The water level inside the limo rose. It was spurting in big gouts now from the dashboard, and at the rear, from the trunk. Tess floundered around, leaning forward to find the automatic release for the car doors.

Where is it, goddammit?!

Her hands fumbled around. She turned on the radio by accident. Frankie Valli was singing "You're Too Good to Be True". Tess screamed in frustration.

She didn't want to die like this. She started hammering on the dashboard and the steering wheel. The horn suddenly blared in the aquatic night, sounding distorted and muffled, like a damaged trumpet. Frankie's voice also weakened. The water would soon reach the level of the ceiling. It was cold, but not paralyzing. She'd heard that people who were drowning experienced a moment of calm resignation right before their death.

Screw that!

Tess would fight to the very end. She continued pressing buttons and levers at random. She was preparing to take a final gulp of air when, suddenly, the window on the front passenger side slid down. Water completely engulfed the limo's interior. No longer able to breathe, Tess started to leave the vehicle, but then hesitated for a second. The chauffeur... Should she leave him there, condemned to a certain death? Tess felt torn.

Shit, shit, shit!

She halted, and tried to unbuckle the man's seatbelt, but once again she was stymied. It was just too bad. Tess slid out of the flooded limousine and headed upward. The current was taking her downstream, as if thousands of tiny wires were pulling at her, but it wasn't very strong. She kicked her feet two or three times, accompanied by some frantic arm motions, and her head finally broke the surface. She could breathe! Pure air reached her lungs for the first time in minutes. It was a delicious sensation. *I breathe, therefore I am.*

Then she saw beams of light sweeping the darkness.

"There she is!"

One of the beams latched on to her, soon joined by the others. She found herself in the spotlight.

Arms reached for her and dragged her to the shore, where they lifted her, panting and dripping, from the river... Men were running all around her. One of them leapt into the water, with an oxygen tank strapped to his back. Tess was unable to comprehend what was happening. None of it.

How did the rescue services arrive on the scene so quickly?

She heard someone clapping their hands behind her. When she turned around, her heart skipped a beat. Victor Rusk stood there, applauding like a movie director after a successful audition.

"Bravo," he said. "Very nice performance there at the end."

Tess was too shocked to speak. A survival blanket was wrapped around her shoulders and a paper cup of hot coffee was placed in her hands. She looked at the steaming cup and then at Rusk, before saying: "I think someone owes me an explanation..."

"And an explanation you shall receive," replied the special advisor with a smile.

CHAPTER 6

Tess took a seat in the back of a Mercedes. She'd hesitated before getting into the car, fearful of ruining the leather upholstery. She was still soaking wet. It was a poor person's reflex. But Rusk pushed her into the vehicle and then got in beside her.

The first surprise was that her "uncle" no longer seemed to be mad at her. Not at all! He was making notes on that tablet of his. The second surprise was that the car was driving back toward the highway.

"Aren't we going to the institute?" asked Tess with a lump in her throat.

"No... unless that's what you want."

"I... No, no, of course not..." Tess felt thoroughly confused. Rusk had promised her explanations, but she was still waiting for them. "I don't understand," she said simply.

Rusk turned off his tablet and tucked his stylus in its little holder.

"Your attempt to escape was the final test inside the test. How would you react to failure? It seems like failure isn't an option with you. That's a big point in your favour!"

"What? You knew I was going to try to–"

"Let's just say we hoped you would. We're starting to know you well, Ms Heiden."

Tess shook her head, dumbfounded. "But I almost killed myself. And the driver."

"The driver is fine. We fished him out of the river. If you need to know everything, we had teams in place all along the route from my villa to the institute. We had no doubts about your ability to improvise. Our only real question was: 'When will she make her move?'"

"But... What if I passed the test at your cocktail party? What if I didn't mess up like I did?"

"You had no chance at all of passing this evening's test. The dice were loaded against you. In the end, I would have told you that you'd failed. You could have put on an Oscar-winning performance and it would not have altered the scenario. You were *supposed* to fail."

Tess tried adding two and two mentally but couldn't find the answer. She was afraid of learning a truth whose outlines remained blurry to her.

"The cocktail party, the guests... It was all staged?"

"Yes. Actors. Paid handsomely. Including that young man whose face you demolished... Although we did warn him that he was playing a high-risk role. He will be royally compensated, enough to cover the cost of a brand-new nose, don't worry."

Dozens of actors. Intervention teams, all along her route. Not to mention the mysterious warehouse in the LA suburb... This whole operation must have cost a fortune.

Tess gulped nervously.

"Seriously, who are you?"

"You'll find out soon enough… But only if you accept our proposition…"

"Which involves…?"

"Passing through the looking-glass, dear Alice."

"Which makes you, what? The White Rabbit? The Mad Hatter?"

The man in the tuxedo simply smiled and raised his eyebrows. The car continued to travel along a desolate, moonlit section of the highway, a phantom vehicle making its way into the wind. Tess tried to organize her thoughts, but she still felt shaken by her ordeal.

"You don't work for the government, do you?"

"Not your government, in any case."

"The Russians?"

"Nope…"

"Israel?"

"Give up, you'll never find the right answer by guessing."

The Mercedes arrived in sight of the now-familiar warehouse in the grimy outskirts of the big city. The sheet-metal door opened with a creaking noise, as usual. The car entered the building and parked to one side. There was no one on the scaffolding. No one in the open space office. On the other hand, one far corner at the rear of the warehouse, lit by strobe lights, was buzzing with activity. Men in coloured jumpsuits came and went, carrying out unknown tasks. A jumble of cables snaking across the cement floor converged on this portion of the warehouse, where there was a prefab modular unit much bigger than the others. Rusk started to walk toward it. Tess tried to keep up with him, but he advanced with big energetic strides.

"If you enter this room, Ms Heiden, you'll be crossing the Rubicon."

Tess's creased forehead indicated clearly that she hadn't grasped the allusion.

"There will be no going back for you," Russ explained. "You'll be making an unbreakable commitment. Burning the bridges to your past. For good. Never seeing anyone who is close to you. In your case, there aren't many people in that category. Your mother has disappeared. Your adoptive parents are deceased. No friends to speak of. I don't mean to be cruel, but hardly anyone will miss you if you suddenly vanish from the face of the Earth."

Tess made no comment. She struggled to swallow. The worst thing was that the bastard was right. Since she had moved so often during her childhood, making friends had never been her strongpoint, and in any case, she was a highly unlikely candidate for "most popular girl in the class". It just wasn't in her nature. She'd had a steady boyfriend during her homeless period, but it had ended badly.

"That's one reason we chose you," Rusk continued. "No attachments. And antisocial. The perfect profile as far as we're concerned."

"Perfect for doing what?"

"A job that corresponds with the results of the test you've been taking these past few weeks."

"Espionage?"

"Something like that. I can't tell you more. You'll receive advanced training later."

"When?"

"Very soon."

Tess scowled. "I'm fed up with being left in the dark."

"Things will made clear to you in due course, don't worry."

And here they were, at the entrance to the mysterious modular unit. The men in the jumpsuits filed out of the room in silence.

"You stand on the threshold of a new life," Rusk declared solemnly. "Are you ready to take the great leap?"

Tess felt a shiver (of fear and excitement, in equal measures) run down her spine.

"If I agree to your deal, what will you tell Fatelmeyer?"

"That you tried to escape while returning to the institute. There was a car accident, a fatal one."

"What about the autopsy?"

"We'll fix that. As long as we grease his palm, the good doctor will be very cooperative."

Tess nodded. She had the impression of being eleven years old again, at the end of the ten-metre diving board above the swimming pool. She'd climbed up there on a dare. The world seemed tiny, looking down from the board's tip. She'd seen her girlfriends below, egging her on and making fun of her, convinced that she would chicken out.

Except that she hadn't.

She was like that, Tess Heiden. When it came time, she'd take the plunge! *Come what may.*

She entered the unit.

There was tiling on all the surfaces, from floor to ceiling, without a break. Maximum sterility. In the centre of the room was what appeared to be an operating table – a standard model, with adjustable height and tilt. A lamp composed of five distinct spotlights was suspended above it. There was also a monitor present in the room. Tess couldn't see any trays with pliers, scissors, and scalpels, but she still wasn't reassured.

"What are you going to do to me? Cut me up? Is this an OR?"

"No. Even if it looks like one. We call this place the 'transit hall'."

Tess tried to organize the information bouncing around her head into a coherent shape, but for once her ultra-sharp brain refused to function. She might as well be squaring a circle. None of this made sense.

"Transit to where? Denmark?"

"Lie down on the table. It's painless."

The last time Tess had heard that, she'd been to see an ear specialist when she was eleven.

Painless… yeah right!

The doctor had pierced her eardrum with a needle, right after having pronounced this soothing lie, and it had been worse than anything the little girl could have imagined. She'd screamed and struggled. Her adoptive mother was forced to help the doctor's assistant hold her down. Tess shuddered at the memory. It might have been at the root of her hatred for the entire medical profession.

"Go on, lie down," Rusk encouraged her. "We can't spend all night here. Have you made up your mind, or not?"

Tess lay down on her back. Looking up at the five spotlights softly shining on her had a hypnotic effect.

Is this how you're supposed to feel before an operation?

Tess had never undergone surgery. Or at least nothing requiring general anaesthesia.

Her whole body stiffened when a woman approached bearing a tray with a syringe. The memory of the ear specialist resurfaced again, and Tess felt her heart beating like crazy. The stranger looked more like a soldier in civilian uniform than a nurse. She reached for Tess's arm, but the young woman flinched away.

"Hey!"

"It's just something to relax you," Russ explained. "You're going to sleep, but it will be very brief. When you open your eyes again, you will be looking at the Sculptor."

"The sculptor? Is that a code name?"

"You'll see…"

Tess pointed at the syringe. "Can I do it without that?"

"No."

That was clear enough. The severe-looking woman renewed her attempt to inject her. This time, Tess rolled up her sleeve without offering resistance. She grimaced slightly when the needle penetrated her arm, and then it was done.

The cold liquid spread through her veins. It was as if she had been injected with refrigerant.

"It will pass," Rusk said.

And he was right. Tess's body temperature seemed to quickly return to normal.

"What's next on the program?" she asked in a voice that had become hoarse from anxiety.

An enigmatic smile had appeared on Uncle Victor's face.

"You're going to have sweet dreams and then wake up in an extraordinary world. I'm not kidding."

Silhouettes appeared behind him. They came and went. Suddenly, the room seemed crowded. Tess didn't like it and said so: "Dammit, who are all these people?"

"They're here to oversee the transfer," Rusk replied.

Transfer? Transit? In an operating room?

There was a humming that sounded like electronics being charged up. Then a series of clicks. An increasingly sharp odour of ozone filled the room.

"It smells strange," Tess said. "Is that normal?"

Her voice, usually firm and confident, had started to quaver. Someone was sticking sensors to her arms and chest.

"It's all perfectly normal," Rusk confirmed. "Relax. Your heart rate indicates a significant level of stress."

No kidding! she thought. But she kept her sarcasm to herself. She'd save the tough guy routine for another time. Right now, she was having trouble swallowing. Her heart was a mad prisoner, hammering at the bars of her ribcage.

What did I let myself in for? Why did I agree to this? I'm such an idiot!

The five spotlights in the surgical lamp converged to form a single dazzling point, like the flash device of a camera that increased in intensity instead of burning out in an instant. The light penetrated her eyelids, even when she shut them tight, and probed her neurons. Her skin itched all over and her heart felt like it was about to explode… And then it did explode, like a grenade going off.

Painless? Goddamn liar!

Suddenly, everything came to a halt and evaporated: her pain, her fear, the sensation of dying. Relief flooded her body. Things returned to normal. The curves traced on the monitor became green again. Her breathing grew more peaceful. Tess went from hyperventilating to the long exhalations of an athlete after heavy exercise.

Never again!

She'd had the scariest moment of her life.

A face was leaning over her. It wasn't Rusk. Or else Rusk had become a bald black man in his forties, with a grim-looking face. The man looked at her with a neutral expression, barely interested.

"If you feel like puking, that's normal," he declared in a cold tone.

Who is this guy? What happened to Victor Rusk?

"I don't need to puke," Tess articulated laboriously, like a drunk waking to a massive hangover.

"Good!" replied the man. I hate it when new recruits throw up on my shoes. My name is Robert Calavicci, but you can call me Bob."

"Pleased to meet you." Tess uttered the phrase between gritted teeth.

Her surroundings were white, aseptic, and subdued. This wasn't the tiled room lit by the five-headed surgical lamp.

"Transfer." The word popped back into Tess's mind. She was no longer in the same place; OK, that much was obvious. And the person speaking to her had changed. But she desperately wanted the rest to become clear. The problem was, her brain was still struggling to emerge from the limbo into which it had been so suddenly plunged.

Tess sat up and then placed a hesitant foot on the floor. Robert Whatshisname made no move to assist her. So much for gallantry.

Her head was spinning a little.

"Well?" asked Bob.

Tess fell to her knees and vomited.

PART TWO

CHAPTER 1

"Where am I?"

The cliché of all clichés… But what else was there to say, given the circumstances?

The mysterious Bob had given Tess a tissue to wipe her mouth. He sighed, and for an instant, he looked like a blasé actor who was obliged to walk out on stage and repeat the same lines, over and over again.

"You're on an orbital station."

"Yeah, that's right, take me for an idiot."

"Just look out there…"

He pointed a finger at a vast window to his left. Tess approached it, her heart pounding. She had no idea what she was about to discover, but she sensed in advance that she wouldn't like it.

"Oh, my god!"

Bob Whatshisname had been telling the truth. A series of modules pierced with portholes formed a kind of loop to the left of the window. It looked like a construction set some kid had assembled bit-by-bit in haphazard fashion. There was an anarchic quality to the juxtaposition of the coloured blocks. And yet the whole thing fit together somehow.

"That's the residential zone," explained Bob, who had silently crept up behind his guest. "The habitation modules and the mess hall."

Tess did not reply. She was petrified. No sun shone in the starry firmament, but she did see a big planet with pink and red hues, like a giant ball of raspberry sherbet.

"Mars?"

"No."

Tess's knees buckled. Her host voiced his concern: "Are you sure you're not going be sick again?"

Tess preferred not to answer. Resisting her sense of panic, threatening to descend into madness at any second, required considerable effort on her part.

OK, keep cool. Breathe. Think this through…

Her fingers touched the glassy surface, brushed it, and then tapped it, more to test its reality than its solidity.

"It's made of clearsteel," declared Bob. "Go ahead, it's very tough."

Tess withdrew her hands. She pointed to a particularly dense cluster of stars.

"What's that?"

"The Sculptor Galaxy. Our station is located at the extreme fringe of its outer boundary."

The Sculptor! So that was at least one mystery solved.

Great, that just leaves me with 12,523 other questions needing answers…

Tess turned around slowly, studying the corners of the room, up near the ceiling. She was trying to see if there were cameras hidden somewhere. Could she be the victim of a televised prank? Perhaps, at this very moment, a bunch of technicians in a video studio somewhere were laughing their heads off, watching the shocked expression on her pale face.

Hmm, seems a little too elaborate to be a prank. Not to mention expensive... Just look at these special effects!

No, it must be something else. But what?

Some sort of little robot vacuum clearer – a flat, rectangular machine – slid over the floor and came to a halt above the pool of vomit. A pilot light came on, there was a synthetic humming, and in five seconds the floor was spotless again.

"Who are you?" asked Tess, looking up at her host. "Where's Rusk?"

Bob smiled.

"That's two questions. I've already told you my name. As for Victor Rusk, he's in the past, back in 2014."

"The *past?*"

Tess's jaw dropped a foot, like the wolf in a Tex Avery cartoon. Bob coughed into his fist and cleared his throat.

"Pay close attention, here it comes, my big scene." His arm rose in dramatic fashion, his hand opened, his chest swelled, and in a booming voice he announced: "Welcome... to the future!"

Tess applauded curtly, but her eyes said she wasn't amused by the joke.

"I'm sensing that you don't believe me," Bob grumbled, dropping the theatrics.

"You're like Morpheus in *The Matrix*, is that it? Blue pill, red pill?"

Now it was Bob's turn to look slightly bewildered. But he did not even try to find out the meaning of her barb.

"Look at all this," he said, spreading his arms wide. "Look

at this space station. Do you really think this technology comes from the twenty-first century?"

"So, according to you, what period of history is this? Go on, astonish me."

"We're in the twenty-fifth century."

Tess nodded her head, as if humouring him.

"It's the year 2469, to be more precise," Bob persisted.

Tess clapped her hands again. Once.

"OK, game over. It's been fun. Now, take me back to Los Angeles."

"You want to return to the institute?"

"No, just to Los Angeles. Drop me off anywhere, out in the desert, whatever, I'll find my way. And don't worry, I won't say a word about the warehouse and all this."

She mimed closing a zipper in front of her mouth.

"That's not possible."

"Huh?"

"It's out of the question. Rusk warned you. You sign up for a one-way trip. You have no idea of the complications involved in a temporal transfer, my dear."

"I couldn't care less about your complications. I just want out of here."

"Is that right? Are you going to swim through space? Because, right now, that's your only means of leaving."

Tess wasn't listening. She didn't want to hear another word. Her mind had short-circuited. She charged toward the room's exit, shoving Bob out of her way. But the man had fast reflexes. In less than a second, he had Tess pressed up against a wall.

"Cut it out!" he barked. "I barely know you and you're already starting to get on my nerves!"

Tess gulped, raising her hands in surrender like a kid in a game of cops and robbers.

"OK, calm down, dude."

Bob relaxed. But lowering his guard proved a mistake. Tess kicked him in the shin with her heel.

"Hey!"

The young woman tried to strike him with her forearm, but it was stopped by an iron grip. She spun around to deliver a blow with her other elbow to the man's belly, which he absorbed with a hoarse croak. She freed herself from his grasp, eel-like. The sliding doors opened with a loud *whoosh*. But just as Tess was about to cross the threshold, Bob tackled her from behind. He grabbed her ankles and held on tightly. She fell, hands out in front to protect herself, but nevertheless bashed her chin painfully.

"Asshole!"

Tess struggled. Bob pulled her up roughly.

"You're not leaving me any choice."

He punched her right in the face. Tess was knocked out immediately.

The medical facilities of the future (assuming Bob hadn't been telling fibs) were not very different from standard twenty-first century infirmaries. The smell of disinfectant was just as disgusting as ever. Cupboards of pharmaceuticals stood next to machines that monitored patients' vitals. Tiled lab benches and empty sleeping berths completed the room. Upon waking, Tess found herself strapped to a gurney. She felt too weak to even struggle. Had she been given a shot, like at the institute?

"Untie me!" she hissed at Bob, who was sitting on a swivel chair nearby.

"Has anyone ever told you have a shitty personality?"

"Yeah, dozens of times. I'm fine with that."

Bob stood up. He wasn't smiling. In any case, he didn't seem to be someone with a cheerful disposition.

"I'll untie you once you've listened to what I have to tell you," he declared as he approached his captive.

Tess had the feeling that she'd gone from one form of prison to another. Scylla, Charybdis... same old story!

"Go on, feed me your bullshit and let's be done with this..."

Silence.

"You have been recruited by the TIME Agency," Bob revealed, looking very serious and sincere. "TIME stands for 'Tachyon Insertion in Major Event'. We're an organization whose existence is unknown to the public, even in our period. Our mission is to preserve temporal continuity."

"Excuse me?"

"Since the invention of tachyon transfer, time itself has become malleable and our universe has tipped into a new paradigm. The existence of parallel, alternative realities is now a concrete thing. We've discovered limitless possibilities... and untold dangers."

Tess scowled.

"Let me guess: 'With great power comes great responsibility.'"

"Well said."

"I didn't invent the phrase."

"Too bad. Anyway, for some time now, we've been seeing the appearance of... how shall I put it?" Bob's mouth twisted. He hesitated, looking for the right word, before continuing: "Snags of some kind. Micro-rips in the fabric of spacetime. The agency was created to detect and repair these snags... We're the protectors of the continuum's integrity, in our reality, but also in the others, because sometimes they impinge on ours..."

"Umm, I don't get it... These snags? Who's behind them?"

Tess was no longer sure if she was playing along with Bob to keep his lecture short, or whether the wild concepts he was throwing around were starting to crystallize in her mind like real, proven facts.

"That's where things get complicated."

"Oh yeah? Because what you said before was the simple part?"

"We're facing a rival organization that for now we'll call the 'bad guys'... The motives of our adversaries – possibly profit? the attraction of anarchy and chaos? – are still unclear. But the fact remains they are willing and able to travel in time, like us, but without worrying about the consequences of their actions..."

"Do they use the same insertion-thingie as you people?"

"We're not sure. We don't know all that much about them, to be honest."

"Good guys, bad guys... That part is easy enough to understand. A little too easy, even."

"Is that too black and white for you? Then let's say that our enemies are pyromaniacs and we're the firefighters. Each of those snags is the potential starting-point of a fire. If we don't do anything about them, one day the entire forest will burn down."

This time, Tess did not utter a word in reply, but simply tried to register and digest what she was being told.

"I've read the report on you," Bob resumed. "You show promise. Rusk could not say enough good things about you. The job I'm offering is very similar to the things you trained for, on Earth. You were willing enough back then, weren't you? So why are you so reluctant now to accept my proposal?"

"Playing Mata Hari in the twenty-first century was one thing, whereas... what you're saying now... Don't take this the wrong way, but I'm just having trouble believing it."

"It's the truth. Why would I lie to you?"

"I'm not sure you realize, but it's... it's... enormous!"

"Of course, I realize. It is enormous, indeed. But you have what it takes."

"I... I don't know what to tell you..."

"You'll be given simple missions to fulfil. We call them 'runs'. You won't be alone, I assure you. Teamwork is involved. Seriously, I think you would be great at this..."

Tess bit her lower lip. "Why me out of seven billion people on Earth? What's so special about me?"

Bob shrugged his shoulders.

"We rely on the calculations of a quantum computer. It winnows through the data, identifies and selects the potential candidates living in the past, present, or future. It seems you fit the criteria: intelligence, ability to adapt, few or no attachments, living a marginal life, so no major disturbance to your original timeline... Your name came out of the machine, that's all."

That's all. It all seemed so simple and obvious.

Tess mumbled: "A marginal life that didn't amount to much, is that what you're implying? That I don't count?"

"In your time period, maybe. But here, you can do great things, as I said. We need you. The future needs you."

Bob was pointing his finger at the young woman like Uncle Sam. Did Bob even know who Uncle Sam was? Tess wouldn't bet on it.

"Even so, what if I say no?"

"We'll have to keep you here. I already told you, and Rusk told you: there's no going back. We'll find something on this station to keep you busy, don't worry about that. But it will be something far less glamorous than the spacetime missions…"

"Cleaner? Mess hall server?"

Bob made no reply. Tess slowly nodded.

"OK, I'll… I'll think about it."

"All right, but don't take too long, Ms Heiden. Time is… precious."

Bob turned around and left the room.

CHAPTER 2

Excerpt from Tess Heiden's diary

Good god, how do you start something like this? "Dear diary, today something extraordinary happened to me"?

You don't say! Extraordinary stuff has been happening to me non-stop for a while now.

Bob's job offer? I accepted it, yeah, of course I did. What else could I do?

I have my own place, my cabin, in the "habitation module" part of this mega International Space Station in the future. Damn, I still have trouble believing it! Maybe that's why I'm writing all this down. Seeing these things in black and white makes them seem more tangible and real. I often have the feeling that I'm going wake up and find myself back at Fatelmeyer's, my arms strapped in a straitjacket... But the days go by and I still haven't woken up. Or else I died when the car fell in the river, and all of this is my brain hallucinating just before I drown. They say that when you're on the brink of death, the mind opens the floodgates and releases all the neurotransmitters in your synapses, causing you to go on a super-trip. Maybe all this stuff is my twisted nerdish version of purgatory, with a big black dude playing the role of the archangel Gabriel. Yeah, I might be capable of dreaming up something like that.

Another possibility (definitely the scariest): I'm not crazy and all of this is completely real.

And since I'm uncertain, I act as though it's true…

So, I have my own cabin.

Although to be honest, it's not much better than being at the institute. There's a bed and a closet with half a dozen identical Star Trek-*style pyjamas. My own bathroom with a sonic shower. Plus there's a view of space, not something to be sneered at… No, actually, with all those stars and the big red planet down there, whose name I can never remember, it's awesome! I can't pretend to be blasé about that!*

You want to know what the twenty-fifth century looks like, in terms of interior decorating? Steve Jobs won out, apparently: everything here might have been designed by Apple. The entire space station is just like the first room I saw when I opened my eyes: white, minimalist and streamlined. Sort of sci-fi meets Zen. More like the USS Enterprise *than the grimy corridors and rusting pipes you see in* Star Wars *or* Alien.

The computer I'm using to write this only has access to a kind of intranet, a local cloud that provides service messages, my training schedule, things like that. For example:

Chrono archive #TZ-7553-MC-164//SAM has been declassified without undergoing the standard control phase. You do not have the authorization required to access its contents. If you have read it, contact your liaison officer immediately.

Security message – Video data was released on 09/07/2469. These recordings were not vetted by the Directorate and are strictly confidential. Please delete all copies. The Neuro-Psy service will provide a corrective hypno-patch for your personal comfort – The Directorate.

They're big on secrets around here. How was I transferred to the future? It's still a mystery! Teleportation? Hibernation? An H.G. Wells-style time machine? Bob dodges the issue whenever I bring it up. And I'm forbidden from browsing the Infosphere, a kind of quantum, intergalactic Web that replaced our good old Internet. I'm only being drip-fed info about the TIME Agency, the situation on Earth, and my future missions. And the system of authorizations allowing people to circulate between sectors of the station is super strict. It works by colours, going through the rainbow from red to violet. Obviously, being a rookie, I only rate a basic red. I learn bits and pieces by talking to people at the Red Light, the club where station personnel go to relax.

How has the world changed since my time? I've missed seasons 22 thru 25 of the history of humanity; that's a lot of episodes I need to catch up on.

Apparently, things started to seriously deteriorate twenty years after my… disappearance. The alarm signals accumulated, but world's leaders went on governing in the short term, as usual. Managing immediate problems while the big catastrophe loomed. It was like rearranging deck chairs on the Titanic.

And finally, the shit hit the fan.

Personally, I would have bet on the climate, or a mega-financial crash, but it turned out that the first domino to tip over all the others, the thing that caused everything to come tumbling down, was a pandemic. A dreadful illness that made the Spanish flu of 1918 look like the common cold. It was followed by wars, famines, every man for himself, and the Devil take the hindmost. So things got really hairy for about a century, and everyone suffered losses, even the elites who thought they were safe in their secure, gated residences, their high-rise towers, and their floating cities. And, oh yes, the icing on the cake was climate change. The waters rose further than anyone predicted. The future Earth looked more like Waterworld *than* Blade Runner, *to put it bluntly. It turns out the best films aren't necessarily the most prophetic…*

The survivors rebuilt from zero or at least not very much, but this time they were careful and tried not to make the same mistakes as before. It's a shame that it took such a massive purge to teach them a lesson.

Humanity got its second wind toward the middle of the twenty-third century. They called this period the "New Renaissance". A confederation emerged, which acted to preserve planetary stability. Apparently, this system worked and is still working today: nobody has gone to war for a long while. This new golden age has, and I quote: "resulted in real economic prosperity and encouraged a giant leap in scientific knowledge".

How did I learn all this, if my access to the Infosphere is limited? Well, firstly, by taking history classes, but secondly, and above all, from evenings talking with my fellow recruits at the Red Light. The agents who already know stuff soon bring newbies like me up to speed. They told me all about the Twenty-First Century Pandemic and the New Renaissance while I downed shots (too many, according to Bob) in the club's comfy atmosphere. The Red Light is quite nice, actually: retro music (meaning turbolift tunes from the twenty-fourth century), OK drinks. It's practically the only distraction, the only entertainment, in this giant tin can of a space station. There are no cinemas, no concerts… In any case, in the evenings, I generally just want to crawl into bed and fall asleep.

With classes and all, they're keeping me busy.

In the mornings (they maintain an artificial day-night cycle to keep us in sync with our circadian rhythm), wake-up is at 5am, and then we go to a miniature lecture hall where our instructors teach us non-stop. Going back to school at the age of twenty isn't my idea of fun, but, yet again, I'm not given a choice. There are about thirty of us in our class. Humans AND ETs. Oh, I forgot to mention that? About a quarter of us are extraterrestrials, or even extradimensionals. It makes things a little strange at the beginning, to say the least, when you find yourself sitting beside a kissing cousin of the Creature from the Black Lagoon. I haven't seen any pointy-eared Vulcans or Klingons yet, but there is a broad variety: species with scales or fur, skinny or fat, short as Yoda or as tall as a Wookie… Only humanoids, as far as I know. No blobs or giant slugs… I try to take this in my stride, but frankly, I was freaked out at first. When we're faced with anything new and different, our instinctive reaction wavers between fear and disgust. Then curiosity kicks in and you get beyond that. And how do we communicate with all these good people? We're implanted with a chip at the beginning of training. A universal translator, in the form of a bio-integrated app. Surprisingly, as far as robots go, there aren't many to be found. I was expecting to meet a whole bunch of C-3POs and WALL-Es in the corridors, but so far – except for the robot cleaners, which are not very different from the ones in my time – all I've seen is a sort of ovoid drone with stubby fins and a blue "eye", which flies a few feet above the ground making a buzzing sound, like a big metal insect. Disappointing.

The course I pay most attention to is History of Time Travel, *which is fascinating. The research on tachyonic technology was developed at the Meyrin University complex in Switzerland (one of the few places to escape from rising sea levels).*

At first, they "sent" discreet observers. And they learned one or two interesting things. For example, Jesus really existed. He was the leader of a small sect, sort of an anarchist rebel. I've seen pictures of him. Crazy, right? Photos of Christ himself! Well, let me tell you that he looks nothing like the guy in the drawing on the wall of my adoptive parents' living room. You know, the blond, blue-eyed hippie surfer dude. Jesus was a little guy with dark skin and a big nose. It seems he stirred up a lot of trouble before the Romans caught him. I've also seen a video of Julius Caesar's assassination. Gory! And the dinosaurs are awesome! Even better than the ones in Jurassic Park!

So, at the beginning of temporal exploration, everything was going fine. People took notes, they recorded all the big events, wrote theses and reports…

But then things started to unravel.

They have a place here in the station called the Command Post. And it has a monitor screen showing a timeline, that of our universe. I can't tell you much about the other universes, because I confess that I have trouble following the course on parallel, or alternative realities. These dimensions might be (please note that I cautiously use the word "might") displaced reflections of our primary reality. The theory of quantum echoes and linked timelines was first formulated by Brän Ronn in 2455 but all that is still in its infancy. It's impossible to keep track of the infinite number of realities that co-exist in parallel with our own. But returning to the "prime timeline", meaning the one associated with OUR *reality, some small "bugs" have cropped up in the past few years. At the beginning, this didn't amount to much. A few minor details. Somebody who died sooner than they should have. Events that happened in reverse order chronologically… You really needed to zoom in on the timeline in order to perceive the alterations. Then things became more serious. After a while, the agency's directors had to face the facts: we weren't the only ones around who were capable of travelling in time.*

Panic time! Especially since the others – the competitors, or the "bad guys" as Bob called them during our first conversation – were not the most careful types. They came hurtling into the past, like bulls in a china shop, without worrying about the consequences of their actions. These strange adversaries had been nicknamed the Syaans. That was their code name. I have no idea where that came from, although we're taking a course about them. It's a short course, mind, given that we don't know much about our enemies. They've been presented to us as a kind of cult, a terrorist group with members of all origins, Terran (from Earth) or otherwise. How long have they existed? How are they organized? More mysteries! Do they use tachyonic insertion for their spacetime jumps? Presumably not, since the agency's tech is top secret. In our case, funding comes from a consortium of private companies with billions at their disposal. Capitalism is alive and well in the twenty-fifth century, thank you very much!

So, what do these Syaans want? Again, we don't know. They may be deliberately playing with fire (I like the analogy with pyromaniacs) or just reckless. In the end, the result is the same: a big mess.

And that's where we come into play, the spacetime agents (ta-dah, cue the theme music, with drum rolls). We're like the UN peacekeepers of time travel. The blue helmets of the future.

In the beginning, I thought they were going to place us in a box and – boom! – project us in flesh and blood to a specific period of history. But no, it doesn't work quite like that. In fact, only our minds travel in time. Our bodies remain in the future, or rather the present. Well, you know what I mean: the bodies remain here in the station. It seems to be, and I quote again here: "the most economical and respectful" (respectful of what, the ozone layer?) method they've found to transport intervention units into the "field". So, we're teleported into the body of some guy or girl who hasn't signed up for anything and, for the duration of the run, these "receptacles" (that's what we call the poor dopes in question) serve as our avatars or puppets. And what happens if one or more of these avatars is killed during the operation? No worries: 1) we wake up, unharmed, in our individual capsule; and 2) the computer having selected people who are nobodies, their death won't threaten to create major havoc in the timeline. I may sound callous when I speak of "nobodies", but I include myself in the same category. My disappearance in 2014 didn't change things. The world continued to turn on its axis and water kept on flowing beneath the bridge. We don't count for much in the bigger picture. That's hard to swallow, but from time to time a small lesson in humility doesn't hurt.

Tomorrow we'll be doing our first practical training exercises. At last I'm going to know how it feels to take possession of another body. I'm thrilled, I have to admit! I'm getting tired of theory. What's more, Bob himself will be our instructor. I like Bob. He's come into the lecture hall two or three times to give us a speech or to chew us out when the class average has slipped. He may yell loud, but you can tell that the guy has a heart.

And tomorrow we will also form into teams of four (yeah, it works in fours, our thing, don't ask me why...) with future missions in mind. Until now, everyone has been keeping their distance. Watching one another out of the corner of their eyes. Sizing one another up. I've spotted two or three people who seem cool, but there are also a bunch of dickheads I don't want to have anything to do with: pretentious rich people; hyper-focused nerds;

and even one dude who looks like a psychopath, the type you definitely wouldn't want to meet in a dark alley. And that's just the humans, of course. As for my extraterrestrial colleagues (and again, I find it difficult to believe I'm writing this), it's not so easy to form an opinion. They all look so freaking strange!

"Tomorrow will be a make-or-break day" (I'm quoting Bob here). A new team… people that I will be working with for months on end. Maybe years. I don't even know if this job is temporary or permanent. There wasn't any contract to sign. Joining the agency is like joining a religious order, it seems.

So, this evening, I'm going to bed with a nervous knot in my stomach.

What a crazy-ass story.

Well, "stay tuned, little diary"… (Oh, what bullshit, LOL!)

CHAPTER 3

"Welcome to the transfer room."

Bob had dressed up for the occasion, wearing a futuristic version of a suit and tie.

"What's up with the penguin suit?" Tess asked him. "Are you going to a wedding?"

"No, a baptism… of fire. Yours, in fact!"

Her very first tachyonic insertion, a day to remember!

Tess and her three teammates stepped forward timidly. They were aware that they had just penetrated the TIME Agency's inner sanctum, its nerve centre.

The division into groups had taken place an hour earlier. Tess had been teamed up with a motley trio. First, there was a tall Slavic woman named Dominika. She was young, pretty, and heavily built. It seemed she had been a sniper in the Soviet army, back in the twentieth century. It was whispered that she had notched up kills of thirty-seven German soldiers. Impressive, if the rumour mill hadn't twisted or exaggerated the truth. The second member was a Ganymedian, a small green-skinned humanoid from Jupiter's largest moon, with a drooling mouth and big globular eyes that always looked astonished. He was hard to understand, even with the universal translator chip activated, his every utterance punctuated by the clacking of his forked tongue. His full name was unpronounceable, so they called him Rr'naal for short. He was apparently endowed with a prodigious intelligence, so his air of being the village idiot, or rather station idiot, was deceptive. The final member of the team, James, fit the profile of a cold English aristocrat, looking down on others with a vaguely condescending expression. He kept his distance and didn't say much, but it seemed like he was always calculating something, as if the wheels in his brain never stopped turning. Tess decided right away that he was going to get on her nerves. She always hated guys who seemed to have a stick up their ass.

Four machines were arranged in a semicircle occupying the centre of the room. They somewhat resembled sensory isolation tanks, except that they stood in a vertical position, and apparently did not contain water. Their lids were transparent and seemed to be made of the same material as the station's portholes and observation windows.

What did they call that stuff? "Solido?" No, that was used for the walls. Ah, I've got it: "clearsteel!"

The main source of light came from a circular conduit that opened directly above the containers. Separated from the rest of the room by a big window, a handful of technicians were working in what looked like a futuristic control room, with countless blinking indicator lights.

Spectrograms monitored the energy flows channelled by the machines. Few words were exchanged. The procedures involved were routine – a simple nod of the head sufficed to transmit instructions.

"You will now take your places in the capsules."

"Another 'painless' process, is that it?" Tess complained.

She had retained a very unpleasant memory of her time on the "operating table" in the transit room.

"The teleportation itself is painless," Bob reassured her. "You'll go to sleep and then you'll wake in your 'receptacle', your new body. On the other hand, taking possession can be very disconcerting psychologically, or even distressing from a sensory perspective. You'll find out soon enough…"

"And the receptacle's soul?" asked James with the residue of a British accent that the bio-integrated app had been unable to eliminate completely. "I mean, their mind? What happens to it?"

"It's 'crushed', relegated to the background of awareness… A little bit as though the previous self remains an understudy waiting in the wings, while the new self takes its place on stage. Even so, the residual personality can serve as a 'prompter' and help you out of certain difficulties. Thanks to this host, you can immediately speak a language that you did not know the instant before, for example. You won't need your universal translators. But the host's experience and acquired knowledge can be disturbing and sometimes a burden. Traumatic and repressed memories may resurface without being summoned by you."

Tess saw what Bob meant. Everyone had emotional baggage, didn't they?

"So, you must always remain vigilant," he continued, "even if the receptacle hosting you seems normal at first. If I've learned one thing on this job, it's that normality doesn't exist."

"Once the mission is over, does the receptacle regain control?" asked Tess.

"Yes. They have the sensation of emerging from a bad dream. They're aware of a parenthesis when they were ejected from themselves, but without really remembering what happened."

"And what if they die through our fault during this... parenthesis?"

"It happens, but the receptacles have been selected in part because of their lack of influence in the timeline being used. They have almost no eco-temporal impact. They're pawns. And unfortunately, sometimes pawns need to be sacrificed to win the game. It doesn't happen systematically, of course, but prepare yourselves for that contingency. Although you, personally, aren't risking anything – if the host dies, you'll suddenly wake up in your original envelope, that's all – it's never a pleasant experience to feel yourself dying."

Rr'naal, the Ganymedian, asked a complicated question about the cortex, neocortex, and the brainstem (apparently, he knew all about human physiology). Bob nodded before replying, in teaching mode: "Consciousness isn't localized in a specific area. It wanders around the brain in the form of a magnetic field."

For the moment, Dominika wasn't saying anything. Standing with her arms crossed, she was examining the machines and the busy technicians behind the window with a cold, analytical eye. She had a very stern demeanour, like an armoured tank.

Four holographic portraits appeared above the four capsules: a woman and three men. Nothing but humans.

"Here are your receptacles," Bob explained. "I'll let you choose."

Since it was her first time, Tess did not want to change sex. Changing bodies already risked being a disorienting experience, without adding further complications. She headed toward the woman without hesitation. James chose the teenaged boy with long hair and sulky lips like Jim Morrison.

Where did they find this dude? At Woodstock?

Dominika planted herself in front of the image of a man in his forties. Regular features. Not bad-looking. Not really an athlete, but in good physical condition. The only remaining choice was a man with a puffed-up face, obese and bald. The extraterrestrial narrowed his globular eyes. Was he judging the receptacle according to his own criteria of beauty? For him, all humans must look alike. He approached the capsule beneath the 3D portrait of the bald man, emitting a dubious tongue click.

"Who are these people?" Tess asked.

"They're recruits who refused to play the game," Bob informed her.

"Excuse me?"

"Persons we asked to become agents, who at first agreed to the deal and took the 'giant leap forward,' just like you four, by way of the transit room and so on. But later, these brave people got cold feet, for one reason or another... It was just too much to take on: the shock of the future, this space station, parallel universes... So, what were we supposed to do? Sending them back to their own time and planet of origin would be too expensive, and also too risky unless we erased their memories, which is always a little bit delicate. It seemed kinder to let them stay here..."

"So that they could play the role of guinea pigs? Yeah, that's really charitable of you."

Bob gave her a faint smile, tinged with cynicism.

"At least now, you know what you've missed out on, Ms Heiden."

"So… we're not travelling in time, for this first transfer?" asked James, with pursed lips.

"No, you're not. You'll be changing bodies, but you'll remain here on the station, in the 'present', if you'll allow the term. Everything is relative, right? It would be a waste to use up tachyonic energy for these initial tests. Consider this phase as… preliminaries."

Behind the window, a technician signalled that it was time to activate the process. Bob gestured toward the waiting capsules: "Please take your places. We're ready."

The bulging lids all opened at the same time, and the four containers released a hiss that sounded like decompression. The novice agents got into their respective capsules. The compartment inside the fourth capsule, smaller than the others, had been adjusted to the Ganymedian's morphology. The safety harness clicked into place across his chest. The same occurred in the capsules containing the three humans.

It's like we're about to go for a ride at the fairground, Tess thought.

But it started to seem less like a ride when the cortical sensors were placed on her temples. Now she started to feel more like the subject of a medical experiment. It was not very comforting.

"Hey! Just make sure no flies slip into our capsules," she joked with a little nervous laugh.

"There aren't any flies on the station," Bob muttered, stern-faced.

Dominika and James didn't seem to have gotten the joke either, but given when they were from that wasn't a surprise.

The capsule lids closed and Tess felt a growing sense of anxiety. Her breathing became increasingly jagged and left a patch of warm mist on the clearsteel surface.

"There's no danger involved," Bob said soothingly.

And the young woman realized that she'd been given an earphone along with the standard sensors.

She swallowed hard.

Will we ever get used to doing this?

Probably... but she wasn't quite sure. After all, plenty of people suffered from fear of flying, even after going around the globe in planes three times or more. They still felt apprehensive during takeoff or at the slightest hint of turbulence. Yet the probability of a plane crash was tiny compared to that of a road accident. But there was no remedy, the fear was there, lodged in the pit of their chest.

Like her fear right now.

Bob waved goodbye to the four novices. For once, he was smiling. Of course, his smile seemed to be saying, "I'm looking forward to seeing how you people screw up," but coming from someone as stiff as him, it made a change.

Psssshhhh...

That was air entering the capsules. Unless it was leaving. In any case, it made a soft whistling sound...

Tess felt herself letting go, like when the anaesthetist places a transparent mask over your nose, just before an operation. Things start to whirl, and you have the feeling of falling into a brightly-lit well, just before your eyes close...

Tess drifted beyond time, beyond space, beyond everything... Then a thunderous torrent filled her ears. She had the sensation of putting on a costume that was badly fitted, too small and tight around the armholes.

Her mind reshaped itself to fit its new envelope.

CHAPTER 4

Tess saw the world through new eyes. She had the sensation that her legs were slipping into new legs, like a pair of trousers, that her arms were slipping into another set of arms… right down to her fingertips!

And all of this took place in a split second.

I'm putting on a mask, she had time to think.

The memories came in a sudden flood. A veritable tsunami of images and sounds. Voices from out of the past. Joys, sorrows… Tess was submerged, but very quickly the kaleidoscopic memories fell into place. The receptacle was named Marjolein Van Den Braden. Marjolein was Dutch. She had grown up during the twenty-first century in a Europe ravaged by wars and famine, following the Great Upheaval. She was an orphan, struggling to survive in the ruins of a neoliberal West that had been transformed into a battlefield. She had to learn how to fight, how to find drinkable water, how to hunt and skin an animal. Her adaptive skills were impressive. She became a clan chieftainess in her forties. That was how things worked in that *Mad Max* world: clans, tribes, hordes… The ancestral herd instinct had reasserted itself. The fight for survival did not leave much time for other pursuits, especially ones of a romantic nature. Marjolein had only known one great love in her life, a man who had given her two children. Both of them died in infancy. It remained *the* tragedy of her life, and Tess felt the traces of her pain in a contagious surge, squeezing her chest. Time had alleviated, or rather blunted the other woman's suffering, to be sure. No human being can live permanently in a paroxysm of pain. But it still took courage to forgive oneself for continuing to breathe, eat, drink, laugh, sing, when the people one loved more than anything in the world no longer enjoyed those privileges. Living with a hole in one's heart was difficult but not impossible.

If dealing with a stranger's memories was one thing, getting used to a new sensory system was another, and not a minor issue. Sounds, odours, everything arrived in a jumble, just like the memories... There was a strange taste in her mouth. Small aches, tiny and more noticeable (that shooting pain in the vicinity of her knee, that sore spot in her lower back...), easy to dismiss when one was accustomed to them, but disconcerting in the present case, because the sensations were completely new.

The colours are different.

Tess blinked. Everything was slightly blurry, both near and far. She could make out her three companions, or rather their three receptacles, in a diffuse fog. They looked as bewildered as she felt. They were standing in the middle of what appeared to be a changing room, with metal lockers and benches. The three men were naked, and Tess realised she was as well. She glanced downward: the pubes were more abundant than her own. The breasts were bigger, but flaccid and drooping. The texture of her skin had changed too: it was dryer and rougher. The four rookies poked and prodded at their bodies, like people who had miraculously escaped some spectacular accident, checking to make sure they were alive, and, above all, in one piece.

But there was something else even more disturbing: Tess had the impression that she was hearing voices!

"What's happening to me?"

"This isn't my body!"

"It's... it's disgusting!"

"Huh??? I can hear better than before!"

The four teammates exchanged dumbfounded looks.

"The girl... She's speaking in my head!"

"I can hear you... I can hear all three of you!"

They were expressing themselves in their original voices, not those of the receptacles. Yet none of three men had opened their mouth!

"It's telepathy," Bob informed them, talking out loud.

Everyone turned around to see the master instructor entering the changing room.

"Telepathy?!" Tess exclaimed.

"Chef's surprise," said Bob. "Like it? It's very practical for our agents, allowing you to communicate during a mission without alerting the natives. Obviously, you'll need to learn how to control the flow of your thoughts. It's merely a question of training."

Tess concentrated on the master instructor. She would have liked to be able to read his mind, but it didn't work. Bob maintained a perfect poker face.

"Tut-tut. You can only communicate amongst the four of you because you all underwent the tachyonic transfer simultaneously. You're on the same wavelength, so to speak. But be careful, this 'power' has its limits. Don't get too far away from one another. The telepathy starts to weaken beyond a radius of one hundred and fifty feet."

Tess heard: *"There's something weird about this guy. He's hiding something from us…"*

That was Dominika.

"Bloody Ruskies, always so distrustful…"

And that was James.

"Shut up, you stupid British!"

"Oh, but she speaks, or rather… she thinks! What a surprise!"

Dominika's receptacle (the good-looking man in his forties) gave the teenager hosting the Englishman a murderous look.

Things were getting more complicated by the minute.

"Put on the clothing in the lockers in front of you," said Bob. "They're in your size. Your new size, that is."

Tess opened the metal panel and stifled a cry of surprise.

There was a mirror on the reverse side of the small door.

"Good Lord!"

"Ah bravo!"

"By N'galooc!"

The other three seemed to be as flabbergasted as Tess. She leaned forward slowly, both fascinated and a little frightened. The mirror reflected back the image of a Caucasian woman about sixty years old, perhaps more. It was the same individual represented by the hologram, but more precise, better defined. She could now examine her face in detail. The wrinkles were more obvious, especially at the corners of her eyes. The cheekbones were sharper. The ash-blonde hair was cut short. Her blue-grey eyes seemed a little sad, as if misty. Tess looked for traces of herself in the other woman; this stranger, Marjolein. A sparkle in the eye, an involuntary facial expression, some sort of peculiar vivacity, anything.

James grimaced, examining his skin closely. He bore traces of acne. Dominika opened her mouth and inspected her teeth. Rr'naal still look stunned.

"How ugly!" he remarked, feeling his jowls.

He pulled at the skin, as if testing its elasticity, while Tess continued her own detailed inspection. There was some element of herself, Tess Heiden, the homeless waif from the twenty-first century, behind those sad eyes. It was indefinable, but it was there. She was really inside. Would the people who knew the receptacle, her friends, her family, be able to detect the presence of the agent hidden within this puppet body? Surely not, unless they were paying close attention (and why would they?). And what about in intimate relationships, or during sex? Would the mask slip then, when it was impossible to fake the right responses?

"I'd be very surprised if we had time for hanky-panky during missions," observed Dominika.

"Too bad," commented Rr'naal, who quickly added: *"It wasn't me who thought that!"*

Tess sensed Marjolein lurking in the background, behind the bars of her mental cage. The Dutch woman was frightened. She couldn't understand what was happening to her. Why had she been shoved aside, put out of play? She was protesting, screaming inside her own head, but her screams finally petered out into cavernous echoes.

"Let's hurry it up, ladies and gentlemen!" Bob scolded them. "You can play Narcissus some other time!"

The four teammates got dressed, in integral bodysuits with front zippers. Rr'naal had trouble getting into his. Tess gave him a helping hand.

"Thank you," said the Ganymedian, sounding like a sheepish little boy who happened to weigh two hundred and sixty pounds.

The shoes provided for this training exercise took the form of supple slippers.

"We're going to do ballet on our very first mission, is that it?" asked Tess, deadpan.

"Not exactly. Follow me."

Bob pushed open the changing room door, revealing a climbing wall.

Sculpted from a material that looked like solidified papier-mâché, the wall rose more than sixty feet in height. There were floor mats designed to soften any falls, but even so, a medical team was standing by, just in case...

"Oh no..." Tess thought.

"What?" James asked her.

"I have vertigo," the young woman replied, out loud.

Bob corrected her: "Tess Heiden suffers from vertigo. That may not be the case for your receptacle... There's only one way to find out."

He pointed at the wall.

"I'll promote the first one who reaches the top to team leader. The last one up pays for a round at the Red Light."

Dominika leapt forward, quickly followed by James. Tess hesitated. Rr'naal moaned: "I am hindered by this... this corporeal envelope. It's not fair."

"And my eyesight is poor," Tess protested.

"The more time you spend here complaining, the less

chance either of you have of winning, that's for sure," Bob rebuked them.

Tess examined the bumpy and cracked wall, looking for the best possible holds. Something told her that Marjolein Van Den Braden had already done a certain amount of rock climbing, because her eyes soon traced a possible itinerary. Teenaged James and forty year-old Dominika were ahead of her, but...

The contest wasn't over yet!

Tess pressed up against the wall, gripping a protrusion with her left hand while rising on the tip of her toes, and began to ascend.

It was easy to start with, the hand- and footholds designed for beginners. Indeed, even Rr'naal managed to climb the first few feet despite his stoutness. Tess followed the fissures in the fake rockface. She spotted a fault that zigzagged up the wall, into which she could fit. Rr'naal tried to imitate her by taking the same route, but he was too fat. Tess heard a mental *"Shit!"* Thirty feet above her, Dominika lost her hold and fell... onto a floor mat that transformed into an airbag a fraction of a second prior to impact. The forty year-old man rebounded, leapt off his impromptu trampoline and, without wasting any time, began his second assault on the climbing wall.

"Our Ruskie seems keen..."

That was James, who now enjoyed a comfortable lead over the three others. The vitality of his youthful host was a big advantage. Tess was climbing rapidly in second place, but Dominika was gaining on her from below. Rr'naal was dead last, with little chance of closing the distance. Tess

turned to gauge her progress. She had climbed to a height
of at least twenty feet, but she felt no signs of vertigo. On
the other hand, she sensed that her new body was less
supple and less hardy than the one she was used to, a
handicap compensated for by a knowledge of climbing
Tess had never acquired. The receptacle's reflexes favoured
her. No useful cavity, no small ledge escaped her notice.
She pushed with her feet and pulled with her arms. It
was painful, but not enough to prevent her from moving
upward at a steady rate. She controlled her breathing and
concentrated. Marjolein was still confined to a corner of
her head but had ceased protesting. The two personalities
had teamed up, at least for the duration of this exercise.
The Dutch woman was no doubt reluctant to see her
body fall into thin air, due to an instinctive sense of self-
preservation.

James was not far from the top but seemed to be in
difficulty. Tess could still overtake him. She was now
climbing elbow to elbow with the receptacle hosting
Dominika. The Russian was refusing to drop out of the
race, both figuratively and literally speaking.

Tess glanced briefly at the next stage of her ascent: an
outcropping that protruded from the wall, twenty inches
above her head. She pushed up with her pelvis, arm
stretched. Dominika copied her. The problem was, there
was only one handhold for the two of them. Dominika
shoved Tess, who heard a loud *"Out of my way!"* in her head.

"Ohhh!"

She was snatched by the void beneath her. She felt sheer
panic, with the air whistling in her ears and a sensation of
endless falling, and then...

Whoosh!

Her back hit the soft surface of the airbag, followed by a series of increasingly cushioned rebounds.

Tess was furious. She turned on her side and rolled toward a standard floor mat upon which she could stand. She was about to restart her climb when she heard Bob clapping.

"Bravo! I declare James the winner!"

Tess looked up. Jim Morrison Jr was sitting on top of the wall, his legs dangling in space. He was waving his arms in victory.

"Dominika, second place, Rr'naal, third, and Tess, last," Bob decreed. "The next round is on you, Ms Heiden."

"She cheated!" howled Tess, pointing at the Russian's receptacle. "She pushed me off!"

"She did what had to be done to achieve her goal. On a mission, all means are fair to get the job done."

"Great way of looking at things."

Tess's three teammates came back down one after the other. Rr'naal touched ground first. When it was Dominika's turn, she landed with her knees flexed and then stood up extending her hand toward Tess.

"No hard feelings?"

"Yeah, right!"

Tess caught hold of the offered hand and tried an unorthodox judo move. She wanted to throw her adversary over her shoulder, but she misjudged the strength of the other receptacle. Dominika fell on top of her and crushed her. Tess tried to struggle free, but the Russian pinned her to the soft mat, gripping her by the wrists. Tess was outmatched.

"Feeling calmer yet?" Dominika asked in a low virile voice with a hint of macho swagger.

Tess spat in the receptacle's face.

Dominika was about to hit her, but Bob halted her.

"Stop it, that's enough! I remind you both that you're supposed to be forming a team, not trying to kill one another…"

"She's the one who–"

"Stop this childish nonsense!" It was James who had just spoken. He'd returned to the ground level and was walking toward the two pugilists, wagging his finger at them. "None of that on my team!"

"*Your* team?" Tess yelled. "Hey, just who do you think you are?"

"At least on that point, I agree with her," added Dominika.

She wiped the saliva still spread on the receptacle's face and then she freed Tess, who got to her feet.

"I won the contest," James said, "and Bob has promoted me to team leader. So, from now on, you'll have to obey me, whether you like it or not!"

Both young women gave him the finger.

"*Why all this violence?*" wondered Rr'naal, ignored by everyone.

Bob sighed and looked at his watch.

"OK, I can see that things are starting to click," he muttered ironically. "Get ready to return to your original bodies. Countdown starting now. Ten… nine… eight…"

Tess turned toward Dominika.

"*We'll see if you still have the upper hand once we're back in our real bodies!*"

"Whenever you like, little girl!"

"Two... one..."

There was a blinding flash, accompanied by a sizzling sound.

It was over.

CHAPTER 5

Tess grimaced as soon as she set foot in the Red Light. It was party night in the club, and despite the terrible music (a kind of syncopated industrial rock that made Nine Inch Nails seem like Vivaldi), the dance floor was heaving.

Tess had tried to avoid the whole ordeal, but Bob left her no choice: "You're buying a round of drinks for your teammates, that's an order. It will give you a chance to get better acquainted." Tess had no desire to become better acquainted with a lizard-man or a pretentious Englishman, still less a Russian woman ready to do anything to win. As soon as they emerged from the capsules, Tess and Dominika had immediately attacked one another again, and it had required three members of security to separate the pair. Bob had covered his face with one hand, exasperated.

Tess looked around the big room, eyes squinting to protect her retinas from the bright flashes. The space at the centre was occupied by a big horseshoe-shaped bar. Several extraterrestrial creatures were propped up against the counter, but most of the clientele were humans. Grunts, whistles, and roars of laughter rose from the motley crew. Some of the skins were covered in scales, others with greasy mucus. A reptilian tail poked out of one individual's outfit. Tess noticed a sort of cousin to Rr'naal, except this one looked slightly larger and more massively built. She had trouble imagining her teammates on the dance floor. And she was right. She spotted the trio a few seconds later, tucked away in one of the side alcoves that allowed one to enjoy a drink in quiet.

Tess made her way through the frenzied mob, which seemed more like a hydra with a hundred heads than a group of people partying. The dancers seemed to be either having an irritable fit or lost in ecstatic bliss.

I'm going to punch out the first one who bumps into me!

Tess was not in the mood.

Entering the alcove, she passed through a membrane, a sort of invisible curtain that isolated this pocket of space from the surrounding noise. *That's much better*, she thought. The music was starting to inflict serious damage on her eardrums.

"Good evening. We saved a place for you," said James, pointing at an empty chair.

Tess muttered an unenthusiastic "Evening," and sat down.

"We ordered while we waited for you," James continued.

Tess looked at the cocktails sitting on the table in front of James and Dominika.

"What are those?" she asked.

"They call this an Asylum," replied James, stirring the iridescent contents of his glass. "They've named their cocktails after famous missions, apparently."

"Is it any good?"

"It's... drinkable."

Dominika was lost in contemplation of her cocktail, which looked like a bluish milkshake. The Ganymedian was busy methodically chewing some sort of yellow root. A white juice drooled from his lips. His big honey-coloured reptile eyes blinked several times when he realized Tess was staring at him, with the hint of a disgusted scowl on her face.

"Do you want some?" he asked, holding out the root.

The young woman's stomach churned.

"No, thank you. I'm going to have a drink instead."

"You have to order at the bar," James said.

Tess stood.

"The second round is on me. A promise is a promise. What are you having?"

"The same again," said James. "An Asylum."

"I'll have an Endurance," Dominika muttered.

"I don't imbibe alcohol," Rr'naal informed Tess, with much tongue clicking.

He gestured toward the jar of water placed next to his unappealing yellow root.

Tess drew in a deep breath and plunged back into the orgy of decibels. The air was filled with the chirping beat of the music. The stench of sweat mingled with several different kinds of perfume. It took her well over two minutes to reach the bar through the dense mass of dancers, and she almost had to yell at the top of her lungs to place her order: "An Asylum and… two Endurances!!!"

The cocktail Dominika had been drinking looked less sickly sweet than James's choice.

The barman, an androgynous creature with an oddly elongated neck, signalled that he'd heard her request and started to mix several amber liquids in a shaker.

Tess passed the time by mentally photographing the room. All these people partying together... Which ones were agents? And which were members of the station's administrative staff? She spotted at least a couple of "classmates" she'd previously seen attending lectures. That cat-man over there with the grey fur... And the bearded man who looked like a Viking. Had they already completed their first run? No, probably not. Most likely, they were still undergoing trials, as she was.

"You're Tess Heiden, aren't you?"

The young woman gave a start. The man who had just spoken to her must have almost pressed his mouth to her ear to make himself heard. He was tall, in his forties, badly shaven, with greying temples. Rather handsome, but in a manner that immediately set her on edge. Tess had already rubbed shoulders with creeps like him: club dealers, informants, working for the cops one day, and committing crimes the next... Impossible to pin down. The kind of guy who made you check whether your watch was still on your wrist if you ever risked shaking hands with them.

"Do I know you?" asked Tess.

"No, but I know you..."

"Oh, yeah? So, who are you?"

"An admirer... I've heard a lot about you."

The man was about the same height as Tess, and his eyes were staring directly into hers. He was too close, and too inquisitive. She shook her head.

"Quit screwing with me."

"I'm not."

"If this is your technique for hooking up, I'm warning you it's off to a bad start."

The guy smiled. He was a charmer, no doubt about it. A charmer and completely untrustworthy.

Then, suddenly, his expression became serious.

"You have no idea how important you are, Tess Heiden."

"Me? Important?"

"You think your name just popped out of the computer at random?"

"What do you mean?"

"You're here for a very specific reason. I'll contact you again when the time is right."

The barman set down three cocktails in front of Tess.

"An Asylum and two Endurances. That will be twenty units."

Tess gave him her card.

The stranger continued to stare at her insistently.

"It's amazing how much you look like your mother," he said with an aggressive smile.

Tess frowned, unsure she had heard him right. Was this guy actually talking about her mother?

The man slowly raised his glass, as if signifying an ironic "To your health". Then he retreated, letting himself be swept up by the dancers.

"Hey, wait a minute!" Tess yelled.

This guy had either said too much or not enough.

The crowd closed around the stranger. Tess went after him, a glass held in each hand, and the third pressed against her belly with her right arm. Not very practical. Especially with people jostling her. Again she was forced to progress shoulder to shoulder to make any headway.

"Hey!" she yelled. An over-excited dancer had just spilled part of her Endurance all over her *Star Trek* suit. "Out of my way, asshole!"

If Tess's hands had been free, she would have gladly punched him in the face... but she didn't want to lose any more of liquid.

She scanned the crowd surrounding her and sighed in discouragement. The stranger with the stubbled cheeks had vanished; there was no point in trying to track him down.

My mother? What the hell does my mother have to do with this?

Tess finally returned to the shelter of the private alcove, glad of the respite it offered.

"Here you go," she said as she set down two cocktails in front of her human teammates.

She kept the last glass, the one that had been half-spilled, for herself.

"What happened there?" James enquired, pointing to the stain on the front of her outfit.

"A little accident on my way back here," Tess replied through gritted teeth. She turned to Rr'naal. "Are you sure you don't want anything?"

"The water here is just fine for me," the extraterrestrial assured her.

He had finished eating his root. His scaly skin was semi-transparent in certain places, so that, depending on the lighting, one could catch glimpses of his internal organs, rosy hints of throbbing viscera suggesting digestion at work.

Tess repressed an urge to throw up.

There was an awkward silence. They could hear the beat of the music and the uproar of the dancers, despite being muffled. In the alcove, however, no one uttered a word.

Should I tell them about the guy at the bar?

If they were still in "telepathic" mode, the question would not even arise. She had not achieved sufficient mastery over her thought processes to prevent the other three from reading her mind. But now her teammates were looking at her expectantly, waiting for her to speak first.

"Well, what should we toast?" Tess finally grunted, her elbow in the air.

"To our future missions," offered James.

Dominika joined them in clinking glasses, but with a baleful look in her eye. Neither a word nor a smile on her part. Rr'naal raised his glass of water and attempted a smile, but the resulting rictus was pathetic and even a little frightening.

Tess took a long sip from her drink. It tingled and tasted almost salty, but it was refreshingly cool. Surprising, but not in a bad way.

"Let's play a game," suggested James. "We'll each try to guess the date of birth of the three others."

"Mine won't mean much to you," Rr'naal said.

"How old are you, in Earth years?"

The Ganymedian thought about it, taking his time to work out a conversion that didn't seem simple. He looked like he was about to stick out his serpent tongue to simulate concentration.

"I am two hundred years old, more or less."

"And is that young, where you come from. Or old?" asked Tess.

"Somewhere between the two," answered the extraterrestrial with a double tongue click combined with other mouth noises.

His eyes each had two lids, which, unlike those of humans, closed like theatre curtains. It was very disconcerting.

Tess turned her attention to the Englishman. The other day, Bob had explained that the intervention teams were formed from agents born in periods that were fairly close to one another, on the scale of human history, over spans of no more than two hundred years, the idea being to limit misunderstandings due to cultural shifts. With his small moustache, his hair parted to one side, and his prim manners, James looked distinctly old-fashioned from Tess's point of view. She imagined his portrait being fixed on silver-based film and then printed out in a sepia or black-and-white photo.

"You, I'm guessing you were born at the beginning of the twentieth century... Around 1910, am I wrong?"

"You're making me out to be younger than I actually am. I'm flattered. But go back further."

"1880?"

"Even further."

"1850?"

James nodded and took a sip from his cocktail. When he lowered his glass, his expression was charged with memories.

"I was born in 1852. During my entire terrestrial life, I knew no other reign than that of our dear Victoria."

His reply gave Tess food for thought. The man seated

before here had witnessed locomotion go from horse-drawn carriages to steam engines!

"Did you live in London at the same time as Jack the Ripper?" she asked him. "What was that like?"

"The agency recruited me before that series of murders occurred... And in any case, I left England when I was fairly young, in the 1870s."

"To go where?"

"South Africa."

Tess nodded and directed her analytical gaze toward Dominika, hunting for clues as to her origins. Was her hairdo (cut short, with straw-coloured bangs in front) the result of a recent visit to one of the salons on the space station, or did it date to her previous life?

Dominika examined Tess in return, and her eyes, bright with a challenging gleam, seemed to say: "Well?"

Tess rubbed her nose.

A spy working for the KGB? No... There was something stolid about her, peasant-like and not at all urbane, which did not fit with the refined picture one had of secret agents. She'd grown up on a farm, or else worked in a factory. Her hands were rough and callused. She was solidly built, not the kind of physique one associated with an office employee. Tess imagined that she was brave and hardworking. This woman had fought in a war, if rumour had it right. The short hair might be a confirmation of that hypothesis. On a battlefield, one wouldn't want to run the risk of having long hair that might become entangled in barbed wire or anything like that. It was just a question of figuring out which conflict she had taken part in. During both World Wars, Russian women had been sent to the front and paid a heavy price before the hostilities ceased. Especially under Stalin. Dominika looked about twenty years old, which would place her birthdate around...

"1920?" Tess ventured. "1915?"

"Right between the two: 1917. And you... Let me guess..."

"She was born in 1993," Rr'naal declared calmly but firmly.

"How do you know that?" asked Tess, astonished.

"I read the files for all three of you on my personal computer."

"The ones in our rooms? They only grant access to the station's bogus Intranet!"

"Let's just say I bypassed some security protocols to achieve my purpose, but it wasn't very complicated. I'll show you the method I used."

"You know how to do stuff like that, do you?"

"And why not?"

Tess let out a little giggle, both amused and impressed.

A lizard-man hacker... Now I've seen it all!

"So, you know everything about us?" Dominika asked warily.

"About you two, yes," replied the Ganymedian.

He pointed at the Russian woman and the Englishman with his longest finger, which ended in something that looked more like a claw than a fingernail.

Then his globular eyes shifted back toward Tess.

"With her, it's a little more delicate. Part of her file is encrypted, inaccessible. I don't know why."

Tess twitched slightly. She thought again about the man at the bar and, above all, his enigmatic words: *"You have no idea how important you are"* and *"You think your name just popped out of the computer at random?"*

Dominika thrust her chin out at the young American.

"Do you have something to hide?"

"I… No… I don't think so."

"The part of the file that was encrypted involved your mother," Rr'naal told Tess. "Was this human being somehow special? A major anomaly in any way?"

"Except for being paranoid and making me crisscross the country with NRA fanatics, well no, I think I can safely say she was a perfectly ordinary mom."

Tess tried to answer in a humorous manner, but her nonchalance failed to mask some deep wounds.

The four team members ruminated in silence for a few seconds, before Dominika looked at her companions gravely.

"They are hiding things from us," she declared.

"Who do you mean, 'they'?" muttered James.

"The agency. We don't even know who we're working for, really."

"She's right," Tess nodded, almost reluctantly. "A consortium finances the agency, all right… but who's involved in this consortium? Which companies? What's it like on Earth, in the year 2469? How do we know we're actually on the edge of the Sculptor Galaxy and not… in an entirely different part of the universe?"

"Well, just look out of the porthole," James sighed.

"It is indeed the Sculptor Galaxy," the Ganymedian interjected. "That much I can confirm."

"And what about these Syaans, who we've been told are the big ugly villains," Dominika pitched in. "Who are they, exactly? Have you ever met one?"

"That, too, was part of the encrypted data," Rr'naal admitted.

There was another long silence.

Should I tell them about the man who approached me at the bar? Tess asked herself again. *The man who claimed to know my mother?*

She was still plunged in her thoughts when Dominika spoke up again: "What about Bob? Do you think we can trust him? I have my doubts."

"You have doubts about everyone," James groaned.

"He seems to be on the level to me," Tess said.

Rr'naal cleared his throat.

"I have discovered two or three things about him, on the quantum Web."

"Do tell."

"He was part of the team that invented the tachyonic transfer, in Switzerland."

"The one led by Professor Ronn?"

"That's right. Deirdre Quartes, the current director of the TIME Agency, was another member of this famous group of researchers. These scientists were the core founders of the existing organization. Other names keep cropping up in the records. Notably Laura Quartes, Deirdre's daughter, who died in an accident..."

Dominika was growing impatient. "And what was Bob's role in all this?"

"He was one of the first people to travel in time. A guinea pig. A pioneer. It's even said that he was the first person to travel in a parallel reality."

"I guess he got promoted after that," Tess said drily. She shook her head and finally allowed herself to smile.

"I don't know why, but I can't help liking the dude."

"Even so, I find it bizarre," said James.

"What?"

The Englishman hesitated.

"Taking orders from a *kaffir*."

"A what?"

"A... man of colour."

"You must be kidding!"

"Perhaps it's normal, where you come from, in the year 2000, but I ask you to believe me that in 1880 one didn't find many Blacks in posts of responsibility. All the more so in South Africa, where I spent my youth."

Tess scowled. *'Oh what times! Oh what customs!' as Cicero had put it.*

Dominika coughed in her fist and returned to the subject of the agency: "I suggest that, given the existing situation, we keep our doubts to ourselves. Wait and see what our bosses have in store for us. We'll meet here to review any new developments on a regular basis. OK?"

The others nodded. For the first time, the group seemed to be bonding into a unit.

"They're growing suspicious."

The female voice that floated in the air seemed to be coming from both everywhere and nowhere.

Bob was in his office, sprawled in a comfortable armchair made of synthetic leather. The only light was the soft glow of the computer screen. Bob's eyes were fixed on the image of Tess Heiden and her three teammates. None of them had noticed the tiny surveillance camera embedded in a corner of the alcove.

Bob scratched his chin, wearing a worried expression.

"You allowed the Ganymedian to search the Infosphere?" he finally asked, without looking away from the screen. "I'm surprised at you, Laura..."

"He only gained access to some trivial details. I made sure of that."

Bob nodded.

"It would seem that young Tess likes you," the female voice added.

"The feeling's mutual," Bob conceded. "She's not the type who allows people to step on her toes... And she's as sharp as a tack! When are we going to tell her the truth, about her parents?"

"In due course."

On the screen, the four rookies stood up and made their way toward the club's exit. With a wave of his hand, Bob switched cameras. He now had a high-angle view of a hallway lined with portholes. Bob clenched and unclenched his fist twice, zooming in on the quartet, who parted company after exchanging handshakes.

"I have to leave you," the female voice announced. "There's a crisis meeting with Sand, Giltek and the legate from the SOLEI conglomerate."

"At this hour?"

"Crisis situations don't obey schedules. You know that as well as I do."

"Well, good luck with that. We'll speak again soon..."

Bob remained absorbed in his thoughts for a few long seconds, and then he began to tap frantically on his touchscreen.

The video reversed. Bob played with the different views offered by the cameras installed in the Red Light. He finally halted on the one aimed at the centre of the main room, giving a good view of the bar. Tess was conversing with the badly shaven man in his forties who had come up to her while she was placing her order. With the music and the hubbub from the crowd, it was impossible to hear what they were saying. And their position prevented him from reading their lips.

Bob emitted a dry, joyless chuckle.

"Pete, you old rascal... You just had to go talk to her, huh? But what are you telling her, exactly?"

"Nothing too sensitive, don't worry."

Bob was startled, an event rare enough to be noteworthy. Pete emerged from a pocket of shadow. How had he managed to enter the cabin without being detected? Unless he had the power to walk through walls, it should have been an impossible feat.

"I hate it when you do things like that," Bob grumbled as he stood up. He made a visible effort to contain his irritation. "Do you think she's ready to hear the truth?" he asked after drawing in a deep breath.

"Not yet, but the time will come. It's necessary. Too many things depend on her. I'm preparing the ground."

"Yet we asked you to stay away from her. And when I say 'asked', I mean 'ordered'."

"We can't keep putting this off indefinitely... Time is running short. I talked things over with the professor this afternoon, and all the scenarios converge: whatever we do, the agency as we know it will cease to exist. Tess is our only hope of limiting the damage, you know that as well as I do..."

Pete went over to his host's minibar and took out a bottle of some aged alcohol from Earth. Fancy label. It contained a cinnamon-coloured liquid, whose aroma he sniffed after removing the cork with a loud pop.

"Shall we drink to that?" he proposed, in a tone imbued with dark irony.

"To the end of the agency? You're quite the cynic…"

"That's part of my charm, it would seem!"

CHAPTER 6

Excerpt from Tess Heiden's diary:

The days go by. Then weeks. The tests and exercises continue. Still no temporal jump. We switch bodies but remain aboard this space station. Yesterday, we carried out a trial run known as "the Titanic!" The four of us were placed in a room mounted on actuators. The decor was pure early twentieth century. The woodwork was in the Art Nouveau style (or do I mean Art Deco? I always get the two mixed up). James must have felt at home. Uhh, no, actually, he's even older than that. The previous generation, at the very least! This "Titanic room," it had only one door, massive and made of oak. Very solid. Then they (and when I say "they" I mean Bob, of course) told us we had only ten minutes to locate the key that would open it. The portholes were all sealed with big bolts, so there was no hope of escaping through them. And to make things even more of a challenge, the room started to fill with water. It had a blue-green tint and it was cold. Perhaps not as cold as the North Atlantic on the evening of 14 April 1912, but I wouldn't want to be splashing around in it for hours on end... All of this reminded me of my experience in the sinking Mercedes. Not one of the more pleasant memories from my previous life... I said, "Don't panic. We should divide the room into four, and each of us will search their sector." The others agreed. Everyone except James, that is, who made a face. He didn't like it too much when any of us encroached on his leadership role. "It's me who should be giving the orders," he complained. "I'm the Time Captain for this team." This assertion failed to impress the rest of us. In fact, I would say it even seemed completely ridiculous, coming from the mouth of a boy of ten or eleven with a high-pitched, prepubescent voice. Our so-called leader was having difficulty imposing his authority from within a receptacle wearing short pants. "That's right," I replied. "But we'll deal with the chain of command issue later. In the meantime, take your little pail and little shovel, and go play somewhere else!" Dominika and the Ganymedian were already opening drawers and cupboards before looking under the bed... James started searching as well, grudgingly. I looked through a wardrobe filled with old clothes that smelled of mothballs. Lots of frills and lace... James discovered a safe, hidden behind a painting (classic). Dominika found a drawer filled with sets of keys. Trying them one by one would have taken us an hour, at the very least, and by now the water was up to our thighs. Rr'naal was freaking out. Water seemed to terrify him, or more precisely, it terrified his receptacle, a small man wearing glasses who looked like a timid civil servant. If this guy was aquaphobic, Rr'naal was going to have a hard time keeping control. For my part, I was also wearing the body of an adult male (the same obese man that Rr'naal had tried out during our first transfer). After several trials, I was now used to the change of sex, but at the beginning it was bizarre. Very bizarre. Not simply because of the alterations in body build or vocal pitch. The first time I pissed in a urinal I found it impossible to aim; at least now I understand why guys make such a mess! Anyway, end of trivial digression. The fat man who served as my receptacle during this Titanic trial had been a Jesuit priest, in another life. This guy's faith in God was so dominant, so intense, that it almost made a believer out of a hopeless atheist like me. Almost. During the final stages of this test, I had to struggle with a part of "me" to keep from joining my hands in prayer. Mental arm-wrestling while the room continued to fill up with water. It soon reached the level of our chins, and that was the moment when Rr'naal completely lost command of his receptacle. He waved his arms about, hysterical, screaming that he didn't want to die. We were in a bad situation, really. Even though, deep down inside, I was thinking: They're not going to let these training receptacles die. It costs them a bundle to bring these people into the future. So, they won't allow us to drown them during a stupid training exercise, will they? Except that Bob and co. seemed determined to let the experience play out to the bitter end. Just before the water reached the ceiling, we all took big, final breaths, and there we were, looking at one another with inflated cheeks and wide eyes. Dominika (in the guise of a well-to-do lady wearing delicate silks, embroidery, and the whole nine yards) was frantically trying to open the door, with both hands on the knob. But it was hopeless. The door remained obstinately shut. Rr'naal was the first to crack. He screamed. A string of bubbles escaped from his wide-open mouth. Perhaps we (when I say "we" I mean our receptacles, of course) were going to die, after all. Fade to black, the end, curtains, game over!

But just then, without any warning, a section of wall pivoted, like an entry to a secret passage, and we found ourselves ejected into a hallway along with thousands of gallons of water. We were spitting and coughing. The water ran out through a metallic grate and pretty soon the four of us were all that *remained, washed up pitifully on top of this deck. Rr'naal continued to scream, panic stricken, and we had to slap him several times before his receptacle recovered some degree of self-control.*

A door at the far end of the hallway opened to reveal Bob, hands behind his back, with a smug little smile on his face, as if he had just played an excellent prank.

"That was a setup, and you fell into it headfirst," he said mockingly.

"What do you mean?" I asked.

"You needed to use muscles this time, brute force rather than your brains. There was no key to open that door, but if you had cooperated from the very beginning, you might have been able to batter your way through..."

"That would have been cheating!" protested James, looking more infantile than ever.

"Let that be a lesson to you," Bob simply replied.

It was at moments like these that we all wanted to wipe that sadistic smile off his face, the expression that said, "You had it coming!" But it was also one of those moments that helped the group to bond further... I wouldn't go so far as saying we became BFFs, but as we talked things over and traded confidences, we gradually got to know one another better.

Dominika had not had an easy life from what I gathered. She had grown up near the city of Smolensk. Her father was a railway worker, and her mother had died when she was a child. She had to take care of the household and her younger sister, Olga, almost on her own, since her father worked long hours every day. One evening when she had drunk several Endurances (still her favourite cocktail), she told us about the invasion of Russia by the Germans, in June 1941. I can reconstitute what she told us from memory. It's not word for word, but here's the gist:

"The wheat was ripening. Our troops were retreating everywhere. They left behind lots of tanks. The Germans were advancing rapidly. They were masters of the sky. They bombed the bridges and the stations... Then their foot soldiers came. They occupied everything and imposed their law on us. They did not allow anyone to leave their homes or travel more than a few miles without a special pass. They killed people, hanging them from the trees. There was a whole lane lined with all the young partisans they had executed; sometimes there were two hanging from the same branch. To make an example of them. Everyone in the village went to see and was horrified. My father was working at the railway station. When trains passed through, sometimes there was straw left behind, on the platform. My father would gather it up as fodder for our cow. One day, the Germans arrived by train and decided that my father looked like a Jew, because his beard and hair were black and wavy. They beat him up, kicking and punching him with their feet and fists. They broke his teeth. He had to remain in bed for two weeks and, after that, he was always frightened. But despite that, he went back to work. He had to feed us and he had no choice. But he was very afraid, and so were we. It was a time when death prowled everywhere. Later, other Germans came, and they took my father along with all the other men in our village. They raped many of the women. My sister was too young, but I was not able to escape that. Then they set fire to the houses. They took our only cow and they killed our dog, because it barked at them. I never saw my father again. I entrusted my sister to a family, some neighbours whom I knew well. Kind people. Then I joined a resistance group in the forest.

They taught me how to survive and use a rifle. I killed lots of Germans. My heart was filled with hatred... One day, a man came to see me. He claimed to be appointed by the government. He said he wanted to train intelligence agents... He took me to a special camp, a training camp, where they made me take strange tests. At the beginning, I didn't understand at all what it was about... But you can guess the rest..."

This tale had a sobering effect on us all. My life with my wacky mother and her collection of oddball boyfriends seemed almost like a fairy tale, next to that. As for James, he always refused to talk about his past when we questioned him. Rr'naal told me what he had managed to find out about our British comrade from his personnel file. Apparently, he was from an aristocratic family. Gentry, even lords... He grew up in a manor, with servants and everything. But he suffered from an inferiority complex with respect to his elder brother, the sort who succeeded at everything, top of his class, and so forth... James was the ugly duckling, in comparison. He was expelled from several schools, notably Eton with all its prestige, and he failed the entry exam to the Royal Military Academy of Sandhurst. In a fit of spite, he went off to South Africa and enlisted as a British soldier in the First Boer War. According to his file, he would not have survived the Battle of Majuba Hill, in 1881. The agency recruited him just before that fatal date, saving his life in the process. He had plenty of things to prove, James did. To himself, and to others.

And then there was our favourite lizard-man. Rr'naal. A strange character, that's for sure. He told us a little bit about his world. There were many castes on Ganymede, and apparently, our friend belonged to the lowest caste of all. If I understood correctly, he was Fey'ol, a genetically modified race raised in special incubators and created to carry out hard labour in particularly hostile environments. They weren't considered individuals, but units. These creatures suffered from accelerated ageing and had no choice about their future. Their fate was determined from birth. A Ganymedian version of Brave New World, so to speak! The slaves lived in funnel-shaped cities built on vast arid plateaus. There was an ocean, but it was underground. The Fey'ols worked in mines where seismic quakes were frequent. I don't know what they mined there, exactly. Some kind of gas, I think… Rr'naal formed part of a special program. An artificial intelligence was grafted to the brains of a dozen newborn Fey'ols. Our pal wasn't raised on a battery farm like most members of his caste. He developed a certain talent for anything to do with computers and was assigned to administrative tasks in a mining city, where he was recruited by the agency. The city exploded shortly after his departure for the Sculptor Galaxy. A gigantic gas leak. It was quite a fireworks display, it seems. Rr'naal lost all his "hatchery siblings." I told him the story of Superman, an orphan from the planet Krypton, which fascinated him. "I'll look it up on the Infosphere," he said. Unfortunately, there aren't many vestiges of twentieth century pop culture still around. The Great Upheaval swept most of it away. I frequently recall the words of my recruiter, Rusk, as well as those of Bob: "Few or no attachments." In a way, we're all Clark Kent: people uprooted from the worlds they originated from.

What else can I tell you about the Fey'ols of Ganymede? They worship a single god, N'galooc. Their food is disgusting (roots, larvae, that kind of thing)… And oh yes: they're hermaphrodites. Don't ask me for the details. Rr'naal was about to tell me all about their mode of reproduction before they enter *the incubators, their mating season, and so forth, but I stopped him dead. "Not interested," I said. Just thinking about it made me want to puke.*

Between exercises, I have sessions with Eva, the neuro-shrink assigned to me, a woman who never ever smiles. Compared to her, Bob is a barrel of laughs. She always has a mournful expression on her face when she asks me questions. Maybe she finds her job depressing, I don't know. "What's the hardest part for you, during the integration phase with a receptacle?" she asked me last week. The hardest part? Not changing sex, you get used to that. It can even be amusing, in a way. The other day, I experienced desire in a male body for the first time! Very kinky…

The hardest part, to be frank, is dealing with all the emotional baggage of the receptacle: unresolved griefs, traumas, and phobias… Try crawling through an air duct when your host is claustrophobic, for example. You have the feeling that you're suffocating, of being buried alive. It's horrible. Experiencing racist urges is also pretty shitty, when you're not used to it. Once (I was in the body of a guy of the skinhead persuasion, which should have tipped me off), I was surprised to feel a wave of repulsion whenever I looked at Bob, who I actually like a lot. At moments like that, you want to scrub your brain just like washing your hands. You feel… I don't know… soiled. I hope I never find myself stuck in the body of a receptacle with paedophile tendencies, because I'm not sure I could tolerate that.

My neuro-shrink gave me a guide, actually an app, along the lines of "Everything you ever wanted to know about the psychological consequences of tachyonic transfer but were too afraid to ask." The titles of the different chapters take the form of questions: "How do you simplify the most difficult moral questions?" "How should you manage the physiological needs of your hosts?" Or even: "How can you use telepathy without problems?" There's a special course on that subject, involving some sort of futuristic New Age-yoga-relaxation bullshit sessions. But it's not very complicated, finally. You just need to compartmentalize your thoughts. You associate a certain mental image, or a colour, say green, to "public" thoughts, and another, say red, to thoughts you want to remain private. And that allows you to regulate the different thought flows. Obviously, it's harder when you're stressed and under pressure, like during a mission or an exercise. But with a little training, you should be able to police yourself. I'm the best in my group at that little game, even if I still let some things slip through involuntarily, from time to time. The one who has the most difficulty with it is Rr'naal. I guess his grafted AI complicates things, by creating a kind of mental "threesome." We pick up everything he thinks, poor guy!

In the guide, there's a chapter devoted to possible disorders linked to the prolonged practice of transfers. There's a whole catalogue of neuroses… They range from guilt over letting your host die to the fear of becoming a host yourself, a receptacle possessed by another party. There's also temporal loop syndrome (you have a constant sensation of déjà-vu) and a host of others… Essentially, I may be out of the asylum, but my mental health could experience some turbulence in the weeks to come…

For now, things are OK. I feel fine. Or at least, as fine as possible if I ignore this nagging sense of paranoia. Dominika has succeeded in making me have doubts. I think she's right. The agency is hiding stuff from us… but what, exactly? A very big question.

I haven't seen the old guy who approached me in the Red Light again. I can't stop thinking about what he told me. Why would I be so important? What's so special about me? And most of all, where and how did this guy meet my mother? I'd really like to talk to Bob about all this, but I somehow sense that it would be a mistake.

"Wait and see," as James would say.

CHAPTER 7

It was the final day of training. In principle. They still needed to pass one last test.

Bob summoned the four rookies to a new setup. This time, it wasn't a single room but an entire apartment that had been put together for the exercise. "A handsome surface," as an estate agent's sales pitch might put it. The place must have occupied about 1,600 square feet, with a superb, impeccably polished parquet floor and ceiling mouldings, signs that the operation was supposed to be taking place in an old Terran building.

An elegant apartment, dating from the beginning of the twenty-first century, Tess assessed after a first glance. *White wooden shelves filled with old books, watercolours, a poster for the musical* Cats *under glass. Typical of New York yuppies!*

"Another escape room?" Dominika sighed.

The four of them were sick of hunting for keys.

"Yes, it's an escape room," Bob conceded. "Except that this time, you're not supposed to try to leave, but to get in…"

"Huh?"

"I'll lay out the scenario for you."

Bob led the future agents to the most spacious of the

apartment's three rooms. Knick-knacks from the four corners of the world suggested that the owner had done a lot of travelling. The decor was old-fashioned: a wicker armchair, a tasselled lampshade... It seemed somewhat dated.

"Our services suspect the old man who lives here of being in league with our enemies, the Syaans," the master instructor informed them. "This man, whom we'll call Mr Dunbar, has an artefact in his possession that interests us greatly... A cube about this size." Bob spread his thumb and index finger about five inches wide.

"We'll call it the 'quantum cube' to keep things simple."

"What does it do, this cube?" asked Tess.

"Just find it and bring it to us... But that's not the sole objective of this mission."

"Huh?"

Bob allowed himself a teasing, almost treacherous, smile.

"You've entered Mr Dunbar's apartment at night, and he has mistaken you for burglars."

"But that is what we are, actually," James observed.

"In a manner of speaking. But you're no ordinary thieves... In any case, the old man was frightened so hid in his highly secured refuge."

Bob pointed at the wall facing the windows. It was bare, except for an entry code pad, the only clue that indicated the presence of an adjoining room.

"A 'panic room'?" giggled Tess. "After the *Titanic*? Whoever's making up these tests must be a real film buff."

Bob frowned, but ignored her remark.

"The air recycling system is defective," he continued. "When you entered the apartment, Dunbar, who has been locked away in his armoured compartment for thirty seconds, is already suffocating and on the point of losing consciousness. In five minutes, he'll be in a light coma, in ten minutes, an even deeper one, and then..."

"Death?" Rr'naal guessed.

"That's right. So, you have ten minutes to find the quantum cube *and* extract the owner from his hideaway in order to interrogate him later. We want to know exactly how he came to be in possession of the artefact."

"Do we start interrogating him ourselves?"

"No, that's the Special Security Unit's job. Just rescue grandpa for us... Don't forget that it's night and that you're in a residential building with neighbours. Avoid making a lot of noise while you search the place. Friendly advice. Any questions?"

The four teammates' receptacles looked at one another. Tess resembled a junkie, there was no other way of putting it: thin and skimpily dressed, with rings under her eyes, a corpselike complexion, and nervous tics, one of which consisted of scratching her arms. Tess seethed. She'd managed to quit smoking since she had set foot on the station, and now she found herself in the body of a receptacle addicted to hard drugs.

What were Bob and co. thinking when they recruited a girl like this?

No doubt she had some redeeming qualities, but they must have been well hidden, because her residual memories revealed nothing of the kind. Entire days spent looking for dope, or money to buy dope. Thefts and scams of all kinds. Although they did require a certain ingenuity. Maybe that explained why she'd been selected.

How long had this girl been aboard the orbital station? Tess bet that it had been a recent transfer. Otherwise, she'd be clean by now. It was unlikely that the agency would have continued to supply her dose without batting an eye.

Brought on partly by stress, Tess felt her smoker's reflexes come flooding back to her. The urge to have a cigarette was right there inside her body. It was like a black hole, a vortex in the middle of her chest. And it also circulated in her veins. Tess wanted to bite her nails, something she never did, ordinarily.

Come on, keep cool, breathe, stay focused...

She examined her colleagues' receptacles with a critical eye.

James was in the body of a girl, a Latina who looked like she came straight out of *West Side Story*. Rr'naal was a young white guy, his fingers heavy with gold rings. Dominika was in control of a colossus of a man who resembled the wrestler Hulk Hogan.

"I have a question," said Rr'naal, raising a finger almost timidly.

"Go ahead."

"Ten minutes... Why the countdowns, every time?"

"To put pressure on us, numbnuts!" snapped Tess.

"Yes, but not only that," Bob replied. "The countdown trains you to accomplish your mission in a limited timeframe. Tachyonic transfers are so expensive that we require our teleported agents to respect a tight schedule out in the field."

"How tight? An hour? Ten minutes?"

"It's calculated by the TD on a case-by-case basis, depending on the context, the complexity of the mission, and the distance of the places to be explored…"

"The TD?" asked Dominika.

"The Transfer Directorate. Each insertion must be approved by it. The calculation must be accurate. We always hope that our agents will succeed in making a perfect run, the first time around, but that's rarely the case… Especially with newbies like you!"

Tess groaned. "You know what we newbies say to that?"

"I can guess," Bob said with a smile. "Is everything clear now? Any more questions?"

The four rookies remained silent. Bob made an elegant wrist movement, clicked his clearplast watch, and declared: "In that case, begin!"

The master instructor left the room. Tess opened her mouth. She was on the verge of uttering a series of instructions, but James interrupted her. "No, that's my role, let me remind you. I'm the Time Captain!"

Tess sighed.

James commenced with his instructions: "Rr'naal, you know computers. You search that." He pointed to the PC placed on a table, opposite the bed. Tess, you look in the other two bedrooms. I'll take care of the living room, with the library… Dominika, you will be responsible for the rest of the apartment."

There was no time for discussion or procrastination, that was one lesson they had retained from previous exercises. The group split up. In less than thirty seconds, Rr'naal was already clicking, double-clicking, and opening windows in the PC's virtual office. Tess rushed into the bedroom opposite Dunbar's. It was a guest room, decorated in an impersonal style. There was no wallpaper, but instead a thick blue fabric. Tess opened drawers, found a letter opener, and used it to rip open the fabric. She tugged at the tear which peeled away silkily. Nothing behind it... except the wall. No secret compartments. No suspicious notches.

"Dunbar is a widower," Rr'naal announced in the form of a telepathic message. By now, all four had mastered the mode of non-verbal communication, more or less. *"The other two bedrooms are reserved for his daughter Glenda and his granddaughter Doris. They sleep here whenever they visit New York..."*

"Try their first names on the entry code pad. And their dates of birth..."

"Already have," replied the Ganymedian. *"No result."*

"Nothing in the kitchen..." reported Dominika.

"Tess?" enquired James.

"Nothing in the first of the two bedrooms..."

"We have seven minutes left. Let's hurry up!"

Tess moved into the kid's room. She was expecting to find a décor in eye-popping candy pink. But it was nothing like that. No posters of ponies or ballerinas, but instead, photos of space: the planets of the solar system, the Milky Way... An astronomical telescope was placed on the edge of the window, next to construction sets, unfinished puzzles, brain teasers... Tess pictured little Doris as an intelligent, dreamy child. Shy? Lonely? Self-conscious. A cascade of thuds from the living room distracted her from her thoughts. The racket clearly indicated that James was emptying the contents of the bookcases on the wooden floor.

"What an asshole!" thought Tess. *"Good thing Bob asked us to be discreet!"*

"I heard that," James grumbled.

Tess bit her lower lip. Personal commentary could slip through her self-censoring filter if she wasn't careful. That sort of thing was now rare, but it still happened.

Suddenly, someone knocked on the door.

The four receptacles froze, as if turned to stone.

"See what you did, screwing around like that?" Tess snapped at the Time Captain.

"I'll take a look through the peephole," said James.

Tess did not dare make another move. She waited. Her ragged breathing counted out the seconds. A patch of sweat was making her T-shirt stick to her back, between her shoulder blades. She wrinkled her nostrils as she became aware that her receptacle stank. Her host's hygiene! When it was bad, it was at least as awful as any traumatic memory or sharp pain.

"Damn, it's the police," James said.

"How did they get here so quickly?"

"The old man must have called them before he locked himself in the panic room."

Bom bom-bom! The knocking became more insistent. Adrenaline surged through Tess's bloodstream. She would have given her left arm to take a drag from a cigarette, right then and there! Of course, all of this was staged, just a game… but it was tempting to let herself be carried away by it.

"And if we fail, we'll have to do another semester of training!"

"Out of the question," decreed James. *"We're going to succeed…"*

Tess heard the bolts opening, then the feminine voice of the Time Captain, in the body of the young Latina woman.

"Good evening, sirs…"

A masculine voice answered her, deeper, almost husky: the drawling voice of a macho John Wayne-type.

"Miss… We were patrolling down in the street and we received a call from central advising us of a burglary at this address…"

"There's… there's surely some mistake. My grandfather is in bed. He's been asleep for the last hour, at least…"

"What's going on with all these books on the floor?"

"I… I was doing some reorganizing."

"Funny way of reorganizing. May we come in?"

"That's not really…"

"Move aside!"

That was Dominika.

"Hey!"

"Look out!"

There was a crash. A cry. Then a series of impacts, fists hitting flesh. Bones cracking. Two bodies falling to the floor.

Tess rushed out of the bedroom and dashed down the corridor that seemed endless, as if it were stretching even as she ran, before ending up in the entry hall, out of breath, her chest on fire.

Dominika, in her Hulk Hogan receptacle, had knocked out the two cops.

James exploded: "Bravo! What do we do with the bodies, now?"

"We tie them up," replied the Russian, dragging the first unconscious man into the living room.

Tess pulled the second after them, grabbing him by the armpits. He was heavy. Too heavy for her frail receptacle. Dominika came back to lend her a hand.

"Tie them up with what?" continued James, furious. "Have you found some rope anywhere?"

"No, but I found this," the Russian answered. She pointed to a roll of packing tape.

"We're out of time!" spluttered James.

"Calm down or I'll slap you," Tess ordered without opening her mouth.

"Go ahead, try it!"

Tess clenched her fist. James took up a defensive stance, ready to fight. Rr'naal's voice suddenly interjected itself into the flow of their thoughts.

"I've found the code. It's an anagram combining the two first names of the daughter and granddaughter."

Doris and Glenda. Tess went through the permutations in her head. She'd always been good at Scrabble. She took a guess: *"Sordidangel?"*

"No."

"Dragon slide?"

"No."

"Danger solid?"

"Bingo!"

"Bravo, I'm on my way!" James exulted.

Dominika sat the two cops back-to-back, on the floor, against the rear side of a sofa. She put the finishing touches on her handiwork by gagging both men with thick brown adhesive tape.

"We're going to rescue the old man. OK, but where is the cube?" she asked, not addressing any of the group in particular.

Tess emitted a loud "Holy shit!"

She'd just had a sudden hunch.

"In the kid's room. There were toys, and one of them was... a Rubik's Cube!"

"What are you waiting for? Go get it!" James scolded her.

Tess went back down the corridor as fast as she could run. She was out of breath in five seconds.

"What is it with this crappy body?"

A little old man with arthritis would be in better shape than this junkie that served as her receptacle!

She entered the child's room, grabbed the cube, and...

"Time's up!"

Bob's voice was still echoing over their heads, when the retractable walls of the décor pivoted simultaneously, revealing the artificial nature of the setup...

The master instructor advanced toward Tess, one eye on his watch. "Ten minutes, the time allotted to you has run out."

James and Rr'naal appeared on the threshold of the bedroom. They bore the body of an old man with a moustache whose chin rested upon his chest. Bob asked them: "Have you checked whether he's still breathing?"

James nodded. "He's still alive."

"Good. First part of the mission completed. And the cube?"

Tess tossed the toy toward Bob, who caught it on the fly. Good reflexes.

"Is that it?" asked the young woman.

Bob spun the cube round and round in his hands, until there was one colour on each face. The object then lit up with a green glow.

"Second part of the mission accomplished. Good work."

"So, does that mean... we get our diplomas as spatio-temporal agents?"

"It means that, according to our criteria, you're ready to work for the agency... But before anything else: debriefing."

The four teammates rejoined their original bodies. They followed Bob along a grey, cold corridor.

"Go in," said the master instructor after opening a door located at the very end.

The debriefing room has all the charm of the inside of a refrigerator, thought Tess as she sat down in one of the five chairs placed around a cream-coloured table made of a substance called plastec.

Bare walls. Screens. A corner with a coffee machine. In short, a depressingly administrative design. Bob handed out touchscreen tablets to his protégés.

"It's not forbidden to take notes," he informed them, in the time-honoured manner of tyrannical teachers.

Then he took a seat at the end of the table.

The first screen was split into quadrants, each displaying a different view.

"Each window transmits the mission as it was experienced through your eyes, and your ears," Bob explained. "We recorded everything thanks to the cortical sensors attached to your heads, inside the capsules."

He pointed to another screen, also in a split-screen mode, displaying wide-angle views from above, filmed in black and white, with a time code running along one side.

"Here, you have the feed from the surveillance cameras

hidden in the fake apartment. One in each room."

He typed on an aqualid tablet embedded in the table, and then, index finger pressed to the screen, he turned his finger counterclockwise. All the images then seemed to go backward, rewinding at an accelerating rate, until each time code read: 00:00:00.

"Will teacher be giving out merits and demerits?" asked Tess in a mocking tone.

"The purpose of this session is to highlight areas of your performance that still need to be improved."

Bob's image appeared in each team member's personal window and in the view from the surveillance camera in room one. In the debriefing room, the instructor snapped his finger, and the videos began to play.

"In that case, begin!" commanded the digitally recorded Bob.

The timer started, and the digits progressed in the lower left-hand corner of the frame. The master instructor turned around and left the shot. As he crossed the fake apartment's various rooms, the four subjective cameras juddered around chaotically. Panoramic shots in every direction. James issuing orders. Bob paused the input.

"It was wise of you to split up, but one of you should have remained with Rr'naal. Looking for data on the computer, then having to get up each time to test the different combination on the wall pad cost him precious time. It would have been preferable for him to have a partner. If the search of the other bedrooms and the living room-library was necessary, the entire kitchen-bathroom part could have been skipped. Dominika, you would have been more useful helping your Ganymedian comrade."

The Russian woman simply nodded. She was tight-lipped, as usual. The images began to play again, a kaleidoscope of animated windows. On one of them, Tess tore the wall lining in the second bedroom.

"I recognize your delicate touch there," Bob grumbled.

"With only ten minutes on the clock, there wasn't time for delicacy," the young woman protested.

Three minutes had gone by according to the timer. Tess's subjective camera moved back out into the corridor, and then performed a forward tracking shot before penetrating the child's room. Her subjective viewpoint swept across the décor: the telescope, the posters on the wall, the toys... Another freeze-frame.

"We ask you to find a cube and you don't even react when you see this one?"

Bob zoomed in on the Rubik's Cube placed on a shelf, between a model rocket and a figurine of Buzz Lightyear. Tess did not make any snappy retort, aware that she had screwed up in this case.

Five minutes on the timer. Half of the time allotted for the mission had been used up, with nothing to show for it, so far. That was when the knocking on the door started. The lines with numerals showing the heart rate of the three agents of human origin suddenly spiked. Only Rr'naal appeared to keep his calm, his rate flattening out at forty beats per minute. James was the most freaked out, reaching 125bpm when his personal camera looked through the peephole, capturing the two cops distorted by the fisheye lens.

"You opened up to them too quickly," Bob commented. "You should have let them stew a while longer. Like, 'Wait a minute, I'm naked, I'm putting on a bathrobe,' etc. You need to improvise. As soon as they saw the library had been turned upside down, it was over."

There was a brief exchange between the fake Latina and the fake policemen. Dominika's subjective camera observed the scene from the corridor leading to the entry hall. Her heart rate was spiking again, indicating that she was about to take action. Her forward tracking shot had all the subtlety of a bulldozer. From there on, things went very quickly. The two cops saw a mountain of muscles coming toward them, and then, before they had time to unholster a gun, taser, or baton, Dominika went into berserker mode. A stiff arm to the face, an elbow to the belly, blows to knees, and above all, jackhammer strikes with her fists. Tess knew that the Russian woman trained in martial arts several times a week, in the evenings, but it was the first time she had witnessed a demonstration of Dominika's talents.

"Impressive," she said, after an admiring whistle.

"But reckless," James carped irritably. "She acted without awaiting my orders."

"You know where you can stick your orders. Sometimes, you just need to go with your gut, your instinct."

On the surveillance screen, the two men in uniform fell to the floor with heavy thuds.

"They were actors, weren't they?" asked James. "Extras paid by the agency?"

"Yes, that's right," replied Bob. "Luckily, we have an outstanding medical unit. They'll be back on their feet later today."

"Wouldn't real policemen be more reactive? More difficult to neutralize?"

"Not necessarily. Obviously, it would be better to encounter some old guy close to retirement or a steady family type than some young hothead brimming with fast reflexes... But whoever the person in front of you, the rule is always the same: avoid combat as much as possible. You need to be quick and stealthy. Always favour the 'feline' approach over the 'pit bull'."

"Ah, you see!" cried James, happy that the master instructor supported his view.

Bob continued: "One or more injured parties can disturb a timeline considerably. Think of the aftermath!"

Eight minutes on the counter. Only 120 seconds to complete both parts of the mission. The receptacles' heart rates hadn't slowed down. Even Rr'naal's spiked when he typed in the right password. A series of metallic bolts unlocked from top to bottom. A false section of wall slid open, and a new surveillance camera activated. A man lay on the floor of the panic room, apparently unconscious. The room looked like a jail cell, comprising only a toilet and a bunk more like a sailor's berth than a bed. (*It reminds me of my room at Fatelmeyer's,* Tess thought.) The Ganymedian rushed over to lift up the supposed double agent working for the Syaans. He was soon joined by James. The two of them each took hold of the man by an armpit. Tess raced back to the child's room while Dominika finished binding and gagging her two victims. A closeup of the Rubik's Cube. Tess's hand enters the frame and grabs it. Three, two, one... zero!

Bob froze the image.

"You managed to catch up, toward the end. But it was a close call. On the positive side, you complemented one another and were efficient, each in your own way. You weren't paralyzed for too long when things turned out to be less straightforward than planned. You're resilient and have a sense for improvisation. Sometimes, a little too much." He gave Dominika a disapproving glance. "On the negative side: you still need to work on your coordination. Each of you is playing their own tune. Too many soloists and not enough team spirit."

"That's what I've been saying over and over," griped James.

"And above all, avoid punchups. Our missions are infiltration operations, not wrestling or boxing matches."

"Sometimes, we don't have a choice," Dominika tried to defend herself.

"Sure, but violence should only be used as a final recourse."

Bob clicked on a transfer icon and, immediately, a new file appeared on the tablet of each rookie. Tess opened it and recognized... the names of cocktails: *Endurance, Asylum, Estrella Drive, Lumen Fidei.*

"Debriefings from several missions carried out by your predecessors. I advise you to study them in detail to benefit from all the lessons they provide."

"These are actual missions?" asked Dominika. "Not training runs?"

"Yes. Actual missions."

Rr'naal ran down the code numbers with impressive speed. "There's an episode missing, isn't there?" he noted. "The numbers are sequential, and then there's a gap."

"A confidential mission. You don't have the clearance level required to view that debriefing."

Bob stood up.

"We're going to take you back to your rooms," he said. "Rest up, relax... but don't forget to revise those files, it's important."

"When do we get thrown into the deep end?" asked James impatiently.

"Soon."

"Does that mean 'very soon'? Or 'in two weeks' time'?"

The master instructor smiled.

"Don't worry about that. Time management is our business, after all."

PART THREE

CHAPTER 1

Four subjective cameras (one per temporal agent) explored a macabre decor, which might have served for one of those ghost train rides at a funfair. The place resembled a rustic dining room, and its wooden walls and floor seemed to be covered with a thin layer of frost. And then, of course, there was the body that swung limply, a slipknot squeezed tightly around its neck. It was that of a woman. The cold had preserved it, but it was still awful to behold. The tongue was pink, swollen, grotesque. The eyes bulged from their sockets.

"How horrible!" exclaimed one of the receptacles.

Although the agency's technology was not yet capable of picking up its agents' thoughts, their voices, along with the imagery from their subjective cameras, were recorded and stored on the quantum Web for posterity. A time code was running at the bottom of the images, counting down the time remaining in the run that had started a few minutes earlier, in the boiler room of a ship trapped in the ice.

They're wasting too much time, thought Tess, chewing on her optical stylus.

Lying on her bed, she was watching the film of the *Endurance* mission, which took place in the icy wastes of

Antarctica in 1914. She had already reviewed *Asylum* and *Under the Masks*, two great classics, taking copious notes on her data pad. So far, no team had managed to carry out a perfect first run. Each unsuccessful attempt (due to time running out or the death of all the receptacles) was invariably followed by a reboot, like in *Groundhog Day*. In other words: back to square one!

It must be super-frustrating...

When you started over, you needed to open the right doors again and interrogate the right people, but a little faster each time. Tachyonic transfer was greedy in terms of energy... and therefore money. The consortium might have very deep pockets, sure, but according to Bob that was no reason to dawdle.

Suddenly, a priority message began to blink on the screen:

REPORT IMMEDIATELY TO TRANSFER ROOM 7!

Tess's heart leapt in her chest. She had understood right away what the message meant.

This is it, the great day!

During the week since training finished, Tess had woken up every morning wondering if this would be the day, and she knew her teammates were in the same frame of mind: raring to go.

Tess put on her suit and her shoes, and then immediately left the cabin. Her heart racing, she hurried along a corridor, moving so fast she almost bumped into Dominika at a turning.

"Hey!"

The Russian woman wore an excited smile, and asked: "Does this mean what I think it does?"

"I guess so, yeah!" replied Tess.

The pair of them got into an elevator where they found James and Rr'naal, who looked as keyed up as they were.

"I'm counting on you lot," the Time Captain said. "We work as a unit, right?"

The three others nodded.

The elevator doors opened onto another corridor, which the team took at a run.

They finally reached Transfer Room 7. Today, the place looked like mission control before a rocket launch, but the atmosphere was colder, more clinical: no polystyrene coffee cups scattered all over. Here everything was clean, and nothing was out of place. In common, however, with the launch control rooms of yesteryear was the atmosphere: the electricity in the air. The adrenaline! The technicians confined behind the big glass window were agitated, stressed, and pumped-up, like their NASA counterparts a few centuries earlier. The red light that pulsed non-stop accentuated the feeling of urgency. And yet... two individuals stood out in the midst of the frantic personnel: a beautiful blonde woman of mature years and an old man with a stooped silhouette, and a lively sparkle in his eye. They exchanged commentary in low voices as they observed the goings-on. Both were wearing flowing robes that looked like something you might see on a druid in a history book. The little old man also wore a kind of tall cap, and his long beard twisted its way down to his breast. He leaned on a cane with a silver knob.

Tess was not the only one to notice the two strangers.

"Who are they?" murmured Dominika.

"Deirdre Quartes, the director of the agency, and Professor Ronn," replied Rr'naal. "I've seen their photos in the Infosphere."

Ronn! The man who invented time travel.

"Wow!" Tess exclaimed.

It was like seeing Einstein in the flesh. Or Galileo. Or even a combination of the two.

The two luminaries continued conferring for a few seconds, then the old man's gaze fell on... No, Tess wasn't dreaming. The creator of the tachyonic transfer was looking directly at her with an intent expression! He emanated an undeniable magnetism, the kind of authority that had no need to express itself through shouts or threats. The young woman gulped, feeling exposed. Ronn nodded, and then he and Quartes turned around and moved away, still engaged in an animated discussion.

He looked at me. At me, not my friends, thought Tess, troubled.

Why?

Or was she making this up in her head?

She had the feeling of regressing to when she was a kid, on her first day at school: here she was, already singled out by the principal.

But there was no time to dwell further on the matter: Bob was coming over to his protégés, his features tense and his complexion sallow. Before he even opened his mouth, his expression clearly said, "Things are serious."

"What's going on?" asked James.

"You're leaving immediately for the year 1941, on the 23rd June."

"Where?"

"Here."

Bob pressed on the screen of the tablet that hardly ever left his side. A hologram sprang into view between him and the rookies. The image floated six feet above the ground and slowly spun around, as if attached to a pivoting base.

"A train?" said Tess, surprised.

A military transport, apparently. The cars located at the extremities had antiaircraft guns mounted on them.

"Hitler's train," Bob informed them bluntly.

That came as a shock for the four agents, and particularly for Dominika, who stifled a heartfelt curse.

"Twelve hundred feet long," Bob continued. "And also weighing over twelve hundred tonnes when fully loaded. Two locomotives. Ten cars. A veritable town on wheels with two hundred people aboard, including the best soldiers of the Reich, belonging to Hitler's personal security detail."

Tess gulped again. She had the impression that the temperature had just fallen, and yet she was sweating.

She was about to ask a question when, suddenly, a feminine voice made itself heard. The voice floated, ethereal, in the electrified atmosphere of the control room: "Good morning, I am Laura, responsible for quantum forecasting in the TD. I am the one who evaluates the eco-temporal impact of each transfer. I would like to wish you good luck in person, on your first mission."

Laura? Tess sifted through her internal data like a human search engine. Could this be Laura Quartes, the daughter of the current director of the TIME Agency? A mathematician, she had been part of Professor Ronn's team, back on Earth.

No, impossible…

If Tess's memory wasn't playing tricks on her, Laura Quartes had died in an accident (a drowning) several years after the invention of the tachyonic transfer.

"This mission, what does it consist of?" Dominika enquired warily.

"Hitler's private train left Berlin the day before this intervention and is on its way to his headquarters at Rastenburg in East Prussia, a place better known as the 'Wolf's Lair'. Hitler will supervise an offensive launched against his former Russian allies from this top-secret, ultra-protected hideout. A historian named Emil Kuhn is also aboard this train. We believe that this man is a receptacle controlled by the Syaans. He claims to have discovered a very ancient manuscript containing the plans of a machine capable of travelling through time. You can easily imagine the consequences if a time machine, even a primitive one, were to be exploited by the Nazis..."

Yes, Tess could imagine very well. She'd dreamt about a mission like this. It would be a tall mountain to climb. But right now, she had the impression of facing the Himalayas equipped only with a sweater and some old crampons. Throat constricted, she asked: "Are... are you sure we're ready for this? I mean... Hitler, World War II... that's some heavy stuff for a first mission, isn't it? Don't you have anyone more qualified on call than three humans and one extraterrestrial, all of us complete novices?"

"It was Professor Ronn's decision, and the consortium validated it," Bob replied. "Director Quartes and the professor have examined your files and given their green light. If you're good enough for them, you're good enough for me. Try not to let us down."

"Two of you have lived in the twentieth century, which gives you a significant advantage in the present case," added Laura's disembodied voice. "And in private, Bob was rather eloquent in his praises concerning your group. That's unusual, coming from him."

"Don't exaggerate, it'll go straight to their heads," the master instructor warned. "I just said they showed potential!"

James intervened: "Do we kill the historian? Abduct him?"

"No. Kuhn doesn't matter. It's the manuscript that interests us."

"Where did this manuscript come from? Is it some kind of gambit by the Syaans?"

"We don't know," admitted Laura. "Probably. Maybe–"

"Find it and destroy it," ordered Bob. "Even it means sacrificing the lives of your receptacles… The stakes are too high! By the way, speaking of receptacles…"

He typed on his tablet. The image of the monstrous military train vanished to make way for a gallery of holographic portraits. The six faces rotated, just like the train a few seconds earlier.

Bob supplied the relevant details: "Otto Kluge, fifty-two years old, head steward. Ernst Persicke, forty-one, waiter. Dietrich Krüger, fifty, barber–"

"A barber?" Tess exclaimed.

"Yes, one of the cars has a barber's salon… Let me finish: Ida Fromm, thirty-three years old, communications operator. Anna Barkhausen, twenty-five, chambermaid. Hans Quangel, twenty-eight, soldier… I'll let you choose…"

James pulled a face. "Just one soldier in the whole group?"

"There are only elite troops aboard this train, all of them fanatical warriors, devoted body and soul to their Führer. It would be impossible to have you cohabitate mentally with them. Their residual personality would give you too much trouble. Your mind needs to be free enough to perform at its maximum capacity."

Laura added, "But Quangel is more malleable than the others, given that, for some time now, he has been harbouring doubts about Hitler's regime. He had a cousin, a young mentally handicapped boy, to whom he was extremely attached. Two months ago, he learned that the boy had been sent to a camp to be exterminated."

"Damned butchers!" Dominika spat.

Bob gave her a severe look. "We know that some of you have an aversion to the Nazis. But don't let that affect how you carry out this mission. You are there to accomplish a precise task, a job, just like a plumber or an electrician. And that's all."

"Time-travelling plumbers, great!" grumbled Tess.

Dominika took a step toward the soldier's hologram.

"The only receptacle who's armed, wouldn't you know," grunted Bob. "I'll spell it out to you one more time. You aren't being sent back to 1941 to seek justice, exact revenge, or anything of the sort. Is that clear?"

"Crystal clear," replied the Russian, keeping her expression firmly locked down.

James had advanced toward the head steward with his hard features and stern bearing.

A role he shouldn't find too hard to play, thought Tess snidely.

For her part, Tess chose Ida Fromm, the communications operator. The woman's face appealed to her. And a visit to the train's communications centre might prove useful at some point during their adventure.

Rr'naal hesitated. His globular eyes flitted back and forth, evaluating the three remaining receptacles. He finally settled on Dietrich Krüger, the barber.

"Very well, we're all set," said Bob.

The tension in his voice was palpable. Tess had never seen him so keyed up.

The four novice agents took their places in their respective capsules. Technicians placed cortical sensors on their temples. Small flying robots, cousins to the finned drones that Tess had already encountered on the station, approached each of the capsules.

"Open your eyes wide," said Bob.

Immediately, clamps emerged from the ovoid metal bodies to keep their eyelids open, while a second tool placed contact lenses upon their corneas with formidable precision.

Bob explained, "It's an interface that will always allow you to see a schematic of the location, as well as the mission time remaining, in the lower right-hand corner of your field of vision. Even in your receptacles. Blink your eyelids twice in quick succession, and these windows will disappear. Do the same thing to make them appear again. Any questions?"

"How long do we have for this first mission?" asked James.

"The time remaining will be displayed once the transfer begins."

Laura's voice spoke up one last time, in a solemn tone: "Good luck. We're counting on you."

Bob gave the rookies a wink. "I made a bet that you'd come through with flying colours. So, don't let me down, OK?"

The capsule lids began to lower. Tess tried to control her breathing. Would this new insertion be radically different from those she'd experienced during training runs, when her mind travelled through space, from one body to another, but not through time?

Her mouth was cottony and dry. Her hands, in contrast, were damp from anxiety. This must be what the pioneers of the Apollo space program felt like, waiting for the end of the countdown, sitting in a rocket with its ass full of explosives.

Clack. The lids completed their closure. *Clack clack.* The automatic locking mechanism engaged.

So far, all that was familiar procedure. Nevertheless, Tess felt increasingly scared, a mixture of nerves and raw physical fear. She heard a hiss, and then things grew blurry. The image of Bob, distorted by the clearsteel, began to spin. Tess fell down a dazzling spiral, into a bottomless well…

Only to land brutally, the very next instant, in a new body.

And in new surroundings.

They were in the corridor of a railway car. Tess realised instantly it wasn't the *Orient Express*. There was no ostentatious luxury, handsome wood panelling, or velvet curtains. Everything was sober, austere, functional. She could feel the rocking of the train beneath her feet, along with the familiar sound of this means of transport, a kind of continual *tatakatoom*. The swaying motion forced her to lean against the walls and windows in order not to lose her balance. She was still quite disoriented from the transfer and staggered around like a drunk. On one side of the corridor, the trees of the dense East Prussian forests flew past, their trunks reduced to a succession of lines drawn in charcoal. There were brief blinding flashes when a ray of sunlight filtered through the greenery to reflect off the train's lateral windows. On the opposite side, there was a partition interrupted by four regularly spaced doors.

"So, what do we do now?" asked Rr'naal, in German.

CHAPTER 2

"The past has a light all of its own… and a smell!"

That was Dominika speaking. Or rather, thinking. She looked around her, dumbfounded, with tears in her eyes. Tess had never seen her this emotional.

"The smell of wood polish…"

It was true that after spending several months in an aseptic tin can in space, the memories aroused by this olfactory trigger were disturbing.

"I'm back home again…"

"Home? On a train full of Nazis?" James retorted out loud.

"I meant… back in my own time period."

Tess understood what Dominika must be feeling, but for now she was too busy taking possession of her own receptacle to participate in the conversation. Ida Fromm, the communications operator, was frightened. And then there were all her memories to take on board and digest in a single gulp. Ida Fromm was like many Germans. For years, she had admired Adolf Hitler (he'd saved the country from the economic crisis, giving work and food to the people…), and then there were his first victories – in 1939 and 1940 – swift and spectacular.

But… attacking the Soviet Union? Opening a second, Eastern front? Was this not an act of folly? And the rumours about extermination camps? Was there any truth to them? Yes, the regime had always been very hard toward the Jews, but if the camps were real, it would be… monstrous.

Tess massaged her temples. Transfers were not just taxing mentally. The process of physical and sensorial adaptation was also complicated. Fromm suffered from migraine headaches. Tess had the feeling that a drill was boring into her brain, and the throbbing pain was accompanied by bouts of nausea. She looked at her reflection in one of the corridor windows. A flattened nose. Short wavy hair. Everything matched the hologram she'd seen in Transfer Room 7. Tess touched her new face, exploring its features and contours, fascinated. Then a particularly sharp jab of pain made her grimace.

Her discomfort had not escaped the notice of Rr'naal, who asked her, "Are you OK?"

"Headache."

"Shit!" James suddenly said.

"What?"

"We don't have much time… only twenty-seven minutes!"

Oh yeah, the countdown. Tess blinked twice. The numbers displayed themselves, down and to the right, decreasing with relentless regularity. The schematic of the train appeared in the opposite corner of her field of vision. Tess imagined the train seen from outside, clinging to its tracks: a stubborn beast with a lowered snout charging across the countryside.

"We're close to the end of the train," the Time Captain

observed. "Car 8. The cabins are reserved for the service personnel. I doubt we'll find anything interesting around here."

Tess examined the schematic quickly. There were two more cars behind them: car 9, also known as the "command car," where her receptacle worked in the communications centre. At the very end of the train, in car 10, there was an assault team, armed to the teeth, as well as several 20mm guns mounted on swivel carriages.

A door opened at the forward end of the car. An SS officer came down the corridor toward them. He was tall, with a face like a knife blade and bleary grey eyes sunk deep in their sockets. He wore a fur-trimmed coat and his hat, decorated with a death's head and the Nazi eagle, sat low over his forehead, the visor level with his eyebrows. The four temporal agents saluted him with a snappy *"Heil!"* to which he responded in a distracted, almost careless manner, his mind obviously elsewhere. The foursome moved to one side to let him pass. But suddenly noticing the presence of Tess/Ida, he halted and asked her, "Why aren't you at your post, *Fräulein*?"

"I… I don't feel very well."

"Your migraines again?"

"Yes, that's right. My pills are in my cabin. I'll be back right way, *mein Herr*."

The officer nodded and headed off towards the command car.

James, keeping his eye on the end of the car, waited until the Nazi had disappeared, and then turned to his teammates. "All right. We need to find the cabin belonging to this historian, Kuhn, and search it…"

"Car 5," said Rr'naal, after consulting the schematic. "That's the one reserved for guests."

"Search it?" Dominika queried, addressing James. "Do you even know how to pick a lock?"

"No need," retorted the Englishman. "As head steward on this train, I have... these!" He showed them a hefty bunch of keys attached to his belt, before continuing: "Rr'naal, Dominika, you come with me. Tess, I believe they're expecting you in car 9. I'm afraid that if you don't show up soon, it will arouse suspicion."

Tess nodded, and even that slight movement provoked a series of sharp pangs within her skull.

Damn migraine!

"We'll remain in telepathic contact," James ordered.

Only twenty-four minutes remained before the end of the mission. The group split up.

Tess tottered toward the rear of the car. A jolt from the train threw her to one side. She banged her shoulder and swore. Did Ida Fromm suffer from a faulty sense of balance, or was this a side effect due to a rougher tachyonic transfer than usual? Tess would have liked to ask Bob about it. Each jolt sent mechanical shudders down the length of the car.

"We're in car 7," announced James. *"Another car reserved for the service staff. Nothing to report..."*

Tess reached the passageway between cars 8 and 9. It was guarded by two armed soldiers who apparently knew the operator well, because they smiled at her.

"So, those headaches of yours?"

"I... I'll be fine..."

Tess entered the next-to-last car. In front of her, there

was a small room where three officers were bent over an army map, moving pieces around like war gamers.

"All they need are some dice!"

"What?" the three other agents exclaimed simultaneously, and Tess realized that she'd accidentally leaked this last thought.

"No, nothing…"

Tess recognized the officer she had encountered in the corridor. He raised his head and asked her, "Are you fit for work?"

"Yes, I believe so."

Then he went back to examining the map. The discussion with the other two officers was animated, not to say heated. It concerned troop movements on the newly opened Russian front. Tess told herself that if each token placed on the map represented a regiment, or even a division, these officers were playing with the lives of thousands of men. The mere thought made her feel dizzy.

The room opened on another corridor, with windows on the right and a partition to the left. She passed in front of a first compartment in which teleprinters chattered. Bands full of figures spewed out in a jerky fashion and coiled up on the floor. From time to time, operators tore off strips covered with cryptic data after giving them a brief glance. Tess thought she recognized an Enigma machine, one of those famous coding devices that were the pride and joy of the German intelligence until a certain Alan Turing discovered their secret.

One of the technicians looked over his shoulder and stared at Tess. She ventured a timid smile. Not receiving any response from the man, she decided to continue onward.

"We've just passed through car 6," James announced. *"Incredible! They have bathrooms, and a sauna! We're now entering car 5, the one for guests... And you?"*

"I'm in the command car. Everything is going OK, at least I think so..."

She reached the next small compartment, still on the left: Tess immediately recognized the communications centre, even though she had never seen it before. One of the benefits of tachyonic possession. A small brown-haired woman was plugging and unplugging cables linked to a switchboard. She wore a set of headphones over her ears. Her face lit up when she saw her colleague arrive.

"Ah, so you've come to relieve me? It's about time..."

She stood and handed the headset to Tess.

"I'm taking my break."

"I... All right... fine."

"You look dreadful. Don't tell me your migraines are tormenting you again, are they?"

Tess nodded. Once the small brunette left the compartment, she sat on the stool left vacant. It wasn't very comfortable.

"How can people work like this for hours on end?"

"What?"

Tess bit her tongue. She'd been thinking again on the "shared channel." With this damn headache, she was really having more trouble than usual controlling her thought flow.

She looked at the switchboard in front of her. The jack plugs and outlets, the cables... Would she be able to manage? She could feel her stress mounting. She started to sweat, and she could picture the graph of her heart rate going through the roof. She tried to access Ida's memories to draw upon the operator's professional reflexes and know-how, but the migraine prevented her attempts to concentrate. This receptacle had definitely been a bad choice!

"That's it... We're in Kuhn's cabin!" James declared triumphantly. *"Ah... shit!"*

"What?"

"There's a safe." That was Dominika who made the last remark.

"Rr'naal, can you deal with this?"

No response.

Then there was something like a hiss of static on the mental link...

"What's going on?" asked Tess.

Her sweat suddenly turned cold. She stood up and removed the headset she had just put on.

"We've been discovered!" Rr'naal exclaimed, and his thought conveyed a sense of panic.

"Shit, shit, shit..."

Tess remained frozen in place, unable to make up her mind. What should she do? Stay here? Move? Try to help her companions?

Nineteen minutes left...

She left the compartment, her heart beating like mad. It accelerated further when she heard the first gunshots.

"Damn!"

The noise came from the middle of the train...

"Caught in the act–" Rr'naal had time to think, just before Tess suddenly lost contact with him, as if the channel had been cut off.

Tess understood instantly what that meant: her friend's receptacle had been killed.

"James? Dominika?"

There was no answer, and the sound of shots was still coming from four cars ahead of her.

"Too many of them!" James cried.

Tess headed back up the corridor. Heads with frightened faces popped out of the teleprinter compartment before quickly ducking back inside.

She reached the small meeting room. The two guards had left their posts, no doubt summoned to the middle of the train as reinforcements, and only one officer remained. Standing at the side of the table, he was folding up the map.

When he spotted Tess, he shouted, "Go back! Return to your post!"

Seeing that the young woman was not moving, he advanced toward her, giving her a rough shove.

Not a good idea.

Old reflexes came into play. Old demons. Tess-goes-berserk was on the loose, today!

She swung her forearm at the Nazi's throat. The man's Adam's apple was hard beneath the edge of her hand, but she struck it with all her might and he collapsed with a strangled gargle. Tess bent over and removed the Mauser pistol from the holster on her victim's belt.

"Achtung!"

The barked order came from behind her. A squad of soldiers had arrived at a trot, machine guns hanging from their straps. The first of these elite commandos observed that the young woman was armed, and then he saw the boots of the officer stretched out on the floor.

"Terrorist!"

He raised his weapon. Tess dropped him with a bullet to the chest. The shot cracked loudly in the confined space of the train car. Tess's ears were ringing and her hand trembled. She smelled the peppery odour of gunpowder, stinging her nostrils. Her migraine had become the least of her worries.

The Nazis progressed in single file, the narrow corridor hampering them. Tess wounded a second soldier in the belly. She was about to dive to one side when the third member of the squad opened fire...

And hit her.

The bullets were like bolts of fire, burning hammer blows...

She just had time to think: *So, this is what dying feels like?*

And then she was projected into a white, luminous universe. Ethereal. She was floating, weightless.

Her three teammates were also there. She couldn't see them, but she sensed their presence.

"Ah, bravo!" thundered Bob's voice, like some mocking spirit. *"All four of you dead in under ten minutes... You've just broken a record, for worst performance ever on a first run! When I said, 'flying colours', I didn't mean spilling blood everywhere! Just where did you think you were? At the shooting gallery? With a giant teddy bear for every Nazi you mowed down?"*

"They surprised us. We didn't have time to–"

Bob interrupted James: *"I couldn't care less about your excuses and justifications. Next time, post someone as a lookout in the corridor. You're going to start over. And do me the favour of getting things right this time. No more screw-ups!"*

"Wait!" cried Tess. *"I... I want to change receptacles!"*

"*What?*"

"*The migraines, they're unbearable...*"

Bob sighed. "*We'll see what we can do. Which one do you want?*"

"*The... the waiter!*"

Silence in the ether. Tess's soul floated, disembodied, drifting in unpredictable quantum currents. Then, suddenly, she felt herself being sucked up. She slid along an interminable cosmic slide, passed through the eye of a tachyonic needle, and found herself in the body of–

CHAPTER 3

Ernst Persicke, forty-one years old.

Tess left the cabin and found herself back in the train corridor with her friends. She looked at them like a patient emerging from a coma and discovering her loved ones at her bedside. Ida Fromm was there, too. The communications operator wended her way through the group, making apologies: "Excuse me... excuse me... I'm needed in car 9."

Tess watched her go, rubbing her temple. She knew exactly what the young woman was enduring at this precise instant: a sharp pain that electrified her scalp. Real torture...

But there was no headache in the skull of good old Ernst Persicke. On the other hand, he had a raging toothache. A cavity, maybe?

You should really visit the dentist, Ernst...

And then there was the sensation (always the same, whenever one entered a male receptacle) of carrying around some excess baggage between one's legs.

Now the man's memories came to her all at once. A jumble of flashing images, sounds, and odours... She tried to sort them out... Ernst was both happy and afraid of being here. Happy because serving aboard the Führer's train represented a real feather in his cap. It was a prestigious post and handsomely paid. Ernst ate well every day, from the finest produce available, a considerable perk during wartime rationing. The problem, because of course there was a problem, was that Herr Persicke was homosexual, and frightened to death that his secret would be discovered; he dreaded to think how difficult, and how short, his life might become if he were found out.

James snapped his fingers beneath Ernst's nose.

"Hey! Are you with us?"

Tess blinked twice. The train schematic displayed itself. She was in the corridor of car 8, as during the first run. The timer's figures had resumed their infernal dance in the lower right-hand corner: twenty-seven minutes until the end of the mission. No time to waste!

"This time, we all go to car 5 together," said James.

There was a collective nodding of heads.

They were just about to set off when the officer in the fur-trimmed coat, the one with the bleary eyes, made his appearance at the other end of the corridor. They made the formal salute and stood aside to let the Nazi pass.

As soon as he disappeared, James ordered, "Let's go!"

Car 7 was the twin of car 8. It had the same austere corridor, with the doors to the cabins on one side and windows on the other. Filtering through the passing trees, sunlight projected a lacy mosaic upon the partition to the right. The train sped on… Just like the figures of the timer: twenty-five minutes left.

The next car was different. Glancing to the right, Tess discovered a small but fully functional barbershop. A man in a white smock was cutting the hair of an officer seated before a mirror, looking stiff with his jaws clenched. He was wearing an impeccably pressed uniform, not a single crease out of place. The barber addressed a knowing look at Rr'naal, who answered him with a smile, and Tess remembered that the Ganymedian had adopted the role of a barber.

Through the half-opened door of the next compartment, Tess caught a glimpse of a changing room with wooden panelling. She mentally consulted her schematic. It was the antechamber to the sauna. There were items of feminine clothing hanging from hooks on the wall. A blue-green skirt, stockings, and a cap, along with civilian garments. Laughter could be heard; people were chatting and joking on the other side of the partition.

The small group passed by other smaller, individual changing rooms. They opened on to shower cabins. The temporal agents picked up the pace and reached the passageway linking cars 6 and 5.

"This is where things get complicated," James announced.

"Who surprised you, the last time?" asked Tess.

"A chambermaid. Dominika, you take care of her. Tess, you stand lookout in the corridor."

The corridor of the guest car opened before them. The historian's cabin lay behind the second door. James brought out his bunch of keys. This time, he knew right away which one to use. That saved them two minutes. Tess checked the timer. Twenty-three minutes... No, twenty-two...

James and Rr'naal entered the cabin.

Left together outside, Tess and Dominika exchanged worried looks.

"Stay right here, don't move," murmured the Russian woman to her teammate.

Then she turned her back and went to meet the chambermaid who had just appeared at the other end of the car. Tess recognized her as the last potential receptacle, still unused.

"What's the name of this girl again?"

"Anna Barkhausen," Dominika replied.

"Don't tell me you're going to–"

"Shut up!"

Tess swallowed hard. Her heart was racing again, synchronizing with the frantic, syncopated sound of the train wheels. From a distance, she observed a brief verbal exchange between the chambermaid and Dominika. The supposed Wehrmacht soldier dragged the chambermaid into a side cabin. There was a muffled cry, followed by a dull thud...

Dominika emerged from the cabin, softly closing the door behind her.

"How are things going out there?" James asked.

"Everything's fine," replied Dominika.

She returned to where Tess was standing.

"What did you do to her?" Tess asked with a tight throat.

She searched for a trace of Dominika behind the sinister mask of this man she did not know, this soldier with the face of a boxer. It was rather frightening. She probed his gaze, looking for a familiar spark.

"Knocked her out," the Russian answered coldly. "I hid her body behind a trunk, in the baggage room."

Tess nodded, slightly reassured. But only slightly. Ten thousand grains of sand could still find a way of infiltrating this operation and cause its fragile mechanisms to seize up.

Are we going to get any further, this time around? Tess wondered.

She was thinking on her "private channel" so no one answered her. She watched the rear of the car while Dominika looked toward the front. The repetitive noise of the jolting train punctuated their vigil with its cold hammering.

Tess ran her tongue over a rear tooth, the one that ached. People who were born with good teeth did not how lucky they were!

Dominika was growing impatient. *"Good grief, what are you two doing in there?"*

"We're working on the safe," replied James. *"But we're having trouble…"*

"We've tried several numerical combinations, including Kuhn's date of birth…"

"How do you know that?"

"We found his identity card, on his nightstand…"

"So, we're stuck…"

"We're still searching the cabin!"

Tess shook her head. *"Maybe the code is a combination of numbers that have been given to him,"* she suggested.

"Would he have those numbers somewhere on his person? On a piece of paper?" James asked.

"He might, if he doesn't know the combination by heart…"

"Then we need to find out where he is, right now!"

Tess felt a watch on her wrist. She looked at it. It was 1:30 pm, local time.

"Kuhn is probably having lunch… Is there a restaurant car?"

"There's a dining room in Hitler's private car," James replied.

Hitler's private car… Nothing less! Probably the most closely guarded place in Europe, at the point in time when this mission was taking place.

"I'm a waiter," Tess sighed. *"With a little luck, I should be able to gain access."*

"And what are you counting on doing once you're in there?" James snarled. *"Rummage through the historian's pockets between courses?"*

"Why not?"

"It won't work… Are you a pickpocket? A conjuror?"

"Do you have a better idea?"

Silence from the Englishman.

"I'm coming with you," said Dominika, sounding determined.

Tess did not need to read the Russian woman's thoughts to guess what she had in mind: to kill the monster indirectly responsible for the death of her father and her own rape, the evil man who had plunged the world into a chaos of fire and blood.

"You can't do that, as you very well know," Tess replied, in a strangely gentle tone of voice. She touched Dominika's arm in sympathy. The Russian woman was boiling, subjected to violent warring emotions. "The consequences of such an act would be incalculable."

There was a moment of fragile communion. Dominika inhaled deeply and regained control of herself. Her eyes shone with tears, but she nodded her head. She had understood.

"You stay here to cover for the guys. OK?" Tess said.

"OK…"

"Tess, what are you doing?" James asked.

"I'm on my way," she replied.

She turned around and headed toward the front of the train. Hitler was in car 3. Before she could gain admittance, she had to pass through the car housing the kitchen.

Tess felt frightened. The Führer's car, who would have believed it! The expression "entering the lion's den" had never seemed so appropriate.

Thirteen minutes left.

She was in the kitchen car. A masculine universe. Not a single woman among the staff. Men in aprons greeted Tess.

"Ernst, where have you been, for crying out loud?" shouted the head chef, a big formidable-looking man with a moustache.

"Intestinal problems," apologized the waiter.

She quickly inspected her surroundings, scanning the entire place in a glance as she had trained herself to do. There was a big table made of stainless steel, used for peeling and chopping vegetables. There was a stove with numerous burners. Some enormous refrigerators. A vat full of boiling oil, smelling of grease. The air was humid and smoky. Utensils clattered. Men came and went, brushing against one another, barking orders. Suddenly, their ballet came to a complete halt. They stood completely still, like a band of kids playing "red light, green light." Even the smoke was frozen in mid-air, as if someone had hit "pause" in the middle of a video.

However, Tess could still move, breathe, and speak: "What the hell–?"

One of the cooks, a slender young man with fine features, turned to her and said, "I've created a stasis bubble."

The other cooks had not moved a muscle. Tess, still in

a state of shock, struggled to regain her wits. She finally managed to say, "Huh?"

"It was the only way to speak to you again without raising the agency's suspicions."

"Again?"

"We've already met. At the Red Light."

This was not the same man. The one in the Red Light was in his forties and...

"We don't have much time. The bubble dissipates in less than a minute."

"I don't understand."

"Our entire conversation will not last more than a quarter of a second on the neural recording of your run. It will be impossible to detect during a replay, at least at normal speed, and I doubt our friends in the SSU examine each mission image by image."

"What do you want from me exactly?"

"Have you discovered why you were recruited?"

"I... No, I..."

"Then go visit the archives room and take a look at mission number NT-19-92. Can you remember that?"

"I... I guess so... But why–?"

"You don't need to know more for now. You still have a mission to complete."

"This man... this historian..."

"Kuhn?"

"Yes... Is he a Syaan?"

"No."

"Then who does he work for?"

"For creatures that are much more dangerous than the Syaans, take my word for it."

"Huh?"

"We're out of time. Sorry."

The man spun around and regained his post. Immediately, the "film" started up again. The smoke rose once again toward the ceiling. The cooks yelled at one another. One of them presented two heaping plates of food to the waiter hosting Tess. She was still reeling from her brief conversation with the man who kept his back turned to her, busy chopping carrots. Her distress had not escaped the notice of her comrades who were voicing their concern on the shared channel:

"What's wrong?"

"Why are you thinking about the archives room, all of a sudden?"

Tess pulled herself together:

"No, nothing, everything's fine. I just… got… distracted!"

"Now is not the time," James scolded her.

"I know!"

"Well, get a grip on yourself!"

"Yes, papa!"

She directed her attention to the plates she held in her hands. In the first one, there were scrambled eggs with salad; in the second, boiled meat in a sauce.

"Hurry up!" urged the man who had given them to her. "You know he doesn't like to wait."

It didn't require a psychic to guess who "he" was…

Tess slowly nodded her head. She seemed to remember reading somewhere that Hitler had opted for a vegetarian diet toward the end of his life. No doubt the salad was for him. She was sweating and afraid it would be noticed.

A man in uniform plucked some of the salad with a fork.

The Führer's personal taster, thought Tess, impressed.

The taster slowly chewed his mouthful, eyes closed, concentrating. All eyes in the kitchen were fixed upon him. At the end of ten seconds, he swallowed and said, "It's good, you can proceed."

Another waiter received two more steaming plates. They had the same boiled meat, but with fried vegetables this time. Tess stood aside to let her colleague pass. She did not want to be the first to enter the private car of one of the most hated men of all time.

"Come on, come on, let's hurry things up!" shouted the head chef.

"Where are you now?" enquired James on the shared mental channel.

"I'm about to enter car 3…"

Tess's stomach was tied in knots and her sweat had turned cold. She hesitated, fear causing her to lose her nerve.

But no, she was trapped in this situation. *You've made your bed, now you must lie in it.* Wasn't that how the proverb went? She had to see things through to the end.

Of course, there were guards at the entrance to the Führer's car, two colossal members of the RSD (the Reich's security service) standing in front of the double doors like Vikings from ancient times who had been dressed up in brand-new uniforms and polished boots, ready for a parade.

Tess felt herself liquifying. The guards inspected the dishes, sniffing them, and then with a nod of the head they allowed the waiters to penetrate the inner sanctum.

Here we go…

Preceded by the other waiter, Tess entered car 3. Upon doing so, the young woman felt almost disappointed. The interior of the car looked like some middle-class apartment, decorated without any taste. The only painting visible was a still life by a painter from the Dutch School, which to an untrained eye seemed quite ordinary.

Four people were seated at the table in the dining section. Two high-ranking officers, a civilian and… him.

The Big Man. The devil in person. The boss at the end of the level.

"Adolf frigging Hitler!"

CHAPTER 4

What one noticed first about Hitler were his intense blue eyes and his extremely penetrating gaze. He listened in silence as his officers expounded their views. Apparently, whatever the two men had to say did not interest him much. The torrent of words washed over him without any effect. He seemed lost in his thoughts. After a while, he turned to the magnificent German shepherd lying on the carpet behind him.

"Blondi!"

The dog leapt up and approached its master in a docile manner. Hitler caressed its muzzle.

The first waiter had set down his dishes in front of the two generals. Then it was Tess's turn. By this point, her heart had gone into turbo mode.

Don't screw up, she admonished herself.

The Führer interrupted his dining partners by asking the civilian, a scrawny man with a bald head, "Have you tried out the services of our bathing car, *Herr* Kuhn?"

"Not yet, *mein Führer*."

"Eleven thousand litres of water on demand. A bathroom in marble, showers, a barber shop, a sauna…"

Tess could not believe her ears. The Wehrmacht was about to make its biggest gamble yet in Russia, and its supreme commander was sitting here boasting to his guest about the train's bathing facilities!

"I believe my assistant is testing the sauna as we speak," Kuhn declared with a smile.

"Did you hear that?" Tess transmitted to the rest of the team. *"He has an assistant!"*

"Good," commented Hitler. "Very good."

Tess placed the first plate (the one with scrambled eggs and salad) in front of the Führer and noticed in passing that the Nazi leader's left arm was trembling slightly. He looked at his meal without any sign of an appetite. The eyes that had seemed so lively a moment earlier now seemed lost and melancholy, almost inert. His arm grew still, but now his eyelids were twitching.

Hitler said nothing and did nothing (indeed, he seemed apathetic and even downcast), yet a truly malignant aura seemed to emanate from him. Tess felt a series of concentric, almost palpable, waves wash over her. It was like standing next to a powerful transmitter.

Tess looked at the Nazi leader's silverware, and more particularly his knife. She could seize hold of it and stab the monster in the throat. By doing so, she would immediately sign her receptacle's death warrant, but how many hundreds of thousands of lives would be spared? How many millions?

Five minutes ago, she had been warning off Dominika; now the same temptation grew within her, like an evil yeast, so strong that it impregnated all her thoughts.

"Do it," urged Dominika. *"A thousand times, do it!"*

"Out of the question," James intervened. *"We can't interfere with events that way."*

"The probabilities," babbled Rr'naal. *"A rupture of the continuum…"*

The dog Blondi seemed to sense something amiss because he turned his muzzle toward this rather slow waiter and began to growl quietly.

Tess's heartbeat accelerated, and she felt her blood pulsing in her throat, her temples, her ears, everywhere. She could no longer hear anything else. She looked at Hitler. Hitler turned his head and looked at her, as if suddenly remembering her presence.

Tess had seldom gone to church. It was not one of her mother's customs. Once, just once, one of Mom's boyfriends (a fundamentalist convinced the Apocalypse was imminent) had dragged them both to Sunday service. Tess recalled the sermon, delivered from a pulpit by a preacher who seemed inspired, even intoxicated, by his own windy speech. At one point, he'd quoted a passage from Ecclesiastes, something like: "The fates of both men and beasts are the same. As one dies, so dies the other."

At this precise point in space and time, the quotation seemed entirely appropriate. We all die in the end, but in the case of the beast named Hitler, better now rather than later.

Tess could do it. She was going to do it.

But then she backed down, defeated by the pair of blue eyes that had become piercing once again.

"Danke," said the Führer, very coldly but politely.

There was relief on the shared channel, except from Dominika, who railed at Tess, *"Coward!"*

"The mission," Tess repeated mentally. *"We need to complete the damn mission…"*

Tess turned her attention to delivering the plate to the historian, and–

"Oh, I'm so sorry!"

With a movement of her elbow she had tipped over Kuhn's glass. A red wine from France. A fine vintage, of course.

"Clumsy oaf!" yelped one of the officers.

The dog growled, more and more nervous. Tess continued to apologize profusely.

"Truly sorry... There was a jolt and–"

"It's nothing," grumbled Kuhn, mopping at his stained jacket with a white napkin that quickly turned red.

The Führer remained impassive, his inquisitive eyes moving from the historian to the waiter.

"What are you up to?" asked James.

"I'm improvising."

There were only five minutes left on the timer.

Five short minutes...

"I can make the stain disappear," Tess proposed to the historian. "Some salt, some hot water..."

"Hot?" snorted one of the two generals.

"It's gone all the way through," mumbled Kuhn, rolling up his jacket sleeve to examine the state of his shirt.

"Come with me to the lavatory, *mein Herr*, I beg of you. It will only take a moment. I am so sorry."

The historian stood up and addressed his hosts, "Gentlemen, if you'll excuse me."

"As you will," sighed Hitler.

He started to eat. He seemed to have already lost all interest in the incident, returning to his inner world, a vile continent that he was endlessly exploring.

Tess consulted the train schematic. There was a lavatory just beyond the dining room, at the beginning of a new corridor. She picked up a saltshaker and asked Kuhn to follow her.

Tess opened the door to the lavatory. The Führer's private facilities. The place was spotless, from floor to ceiling, and smelled of ammonia.

"Take off your jacket, *mein Herr*, if you please."

Kuhn came inside with her. Tess/Ernst closed the door... and promptly pressed the historian up against the white tiled wall, her hand on his throat.

"Hey! What do you think you're doing?"

"The combination!"

"What?"

"The combination to the safe! The manuscript is inside, isn't it?"

Tess tightened her grip on the man's windpipe.

"Three minutes!"

"Speak. Right now!"

She slapped him.

"Speak or you're a dead man."

"Are you mad? Do you think you're going to get away with this?"

A second slap, harder than the first. The historian's cheek turned bright red.

"My assistant... She's the one with the combination..."

"The assistant! The changing room for the sauna!" Tess screamed in her head.

"Understood," said James.

"Two minutes left, we won't have time," Rr'naal moaned.

"We have to try. I'll go," offered Dominika.

Tess imagined the Russian woman dashing toward the rear of the train, in the body of a German soldier.

Suddenly, there was knocking at the lavatory door.

"What's going on in there?"

The dull thuds against the varnished wood became more insistent.

"Nothing. Everything's fine in here," replied Tess in an unsteady voice.

"He's a madman, he's taken me hostage!" screamed Kuhn, panicked.

"Open up!"

"They've cornered me now, goddammit! Dominika?"

"I'm in the changing room... I can see the assistant's jacket..."

One minute left.

The lock burst apart and the lavatory door flew open. Tess shoved Kuhn toward the first soldier who tried to enter. There were shouts and milling about in the corridor behind.

Thirty seconds.

"I can't find it," said Dominika in a lifeless voice. *"There's nothing in her pockets..."*

"Are you sure?"

"Yes, I mean no, I..."

Tess stopped listening. She threw a punch at the chin of a second guard, missed, and...

The gunshot pierced her eardrums, just as the bullet penetrated her gut. She dropped to her knees. Two men threw themselves on top of her, showering her with blows.

"Who sent you? Are you going to talk, you bastard?"

"Tess? Tess, are you there?"

More punching and kicking.

"Who do you work for? The British?"

Three. Two. One.

Game over.

Back in limbo. The white universe, quantum paradise for time travellers...

Bob's voice sounded even more furious this time than during their first passage through this ethereal, limitless space.

"I asked you to proceed cautiously and you end up creating chaos in the Führer's personal car?"

"The historian was there," Tess said, attempting to defend herself.

"Don't go anywhere near Hitler. Period. Make him sneeze and the fate of the world could be completely transformed... In which case, we erase the entire mission and you'll have to start over from zero, even if the manuscript has been destroyed. The reboot of a sequence involving a figure as important as the Führer consumes an incredible amount of energy. So, forget any Lee Harvey Oswald-style fantasies you may have!"

Tess's mind was split between guilt and worry. Bob hadn't mentioned anything about what transpired in the kitchen. Had her brief exchange with her "Deep Throat" from the future really gone undetected? She placed her thoughts under a double lock. Or at least she tried.

"You still spent too much time gabbing! You should have searched the sauna changing room, the first time you passed in front of it!" the master instructor continued.

"According to Dominika, the assistant's pockets were empty!" protested James.

"*I'm not so sure of that,*" said the Russian woman. "*I really didn't have time to–*"

"*Then go back and finish the job, once and for all! We can't keep sending you to that damn train, again and again!*"

CHAPTER 5

They returned to the corridor in car 8.

Twenty-seven minutes on the timer...

Here we go again, thought Tess, with an inner sigh.

"OK, once more unto the breach!" said James.

Huddled together in the middle of the corridor, the four agents (Ida Fromm had already left for the adjoining car) looked a little too much like a group of conspirators.

They started to walk, in single file, swaying from the inevitable jolts. When they arrived at the junction between cars 7 and 8, they crossed paths with the officer in the fur-trimmed coat and stood aside to let him pass.

"*Heil, Hitler!*"

"*Heil...*"

Now they were in the corridor of car 7, where the cabins were reserved for the service personnel. Nothing was amiss. The train advanced relentlessly, the locomotives seeming to pant as the cars trailing behind jounced along the rails.

The next stage in their journey was the bathing car, the Führer's pride and joy. Rr'naal said a quick hello to the barber as he passed in front of his salon. The officer having his hair cut was too absorbed, like Narcissus, by his own image in the mirror to glance out at the corridor.

Twenty-three minutes remaining.

"Continue toward car 5," James said to his troops. "I'll join you there."

The fake steward slipped into the sauna changing room and took up where Dominika had left off, searching the assistant's clothing.

Tess, Rr'naal, and the Russian entered the guest car.

"Nothing," announced James over the mental channel. *"The combination to the safe must be in the assistant's cabin... I'm on my way!"*

Tess and her companions halted. Logically, Kuhn's assistant should have a cabin located near her boss's. But where, exactly? There were two individual rooms to either side of the one occupied by the historian. Which one should they inspect first?

"The chambermaid will be appearing soon," thought Tess.

"I'll take care of her," replied Dominika.

The Russian went to the front of the car, where she almost bumped into the maid. The servant was carrying a basket full of clean laundry. There was a brief discussion. As during the previous run, Dominika pulled the chambermaid into the baggage room.

James arrived while this was going on.

"Well?"

"We're waiting for you to open the doors," said Tess. "We're not sure which one it is."

They opted for the closest. The bed was made. There were no personal effects lying around (bedside book or other). Evidently, no one currently occupied this cabin.

Twenty minutes.

Dominika emerged from the baggage room and walked

back toward her friends. The next cabin was Kuhn's, which they'd already searched. James opened the third door thanks to one of the keys that jingled noisily on his belt. There was an embroidered handkerchief on the bedside table. Tess searched the drawers. She discovered a passport under the name of Hildegarde Bauer... and a piece of paper on which a series of figures were jotted down:

"6302 6302!"

The group left the cabin in a rush.

"Dominika, you remain in the corridor and cover us," James ordered.

He opened the door to the historian's cabin. Only eighteen minutes remained until the end of the run. Tess searched the bedside table while Rr'naal twiddled the numbered dials on the safe.

"I've already looked in there," said James, indicating the drawers Tess was pulling out one by one. "There's nothing of interest in there."

She found a copy of *Mein Kampf* signed by the Führer in person: "For Emil, with all my consideration. Adolf Hitler."

"How nice," said Tess.

She leafed through the book. Some photos fell out of it. Erotic snapshots; no, actually pornographic. A plump woman in a camisole spread her legs on a bed covered with a duvet. Tess grinned. "Is that the assistant?" she whistled. "Bauer?"

"So it would seem," replied James. "Apparently, *Fräulein* Hildegarde does not limit herself to assisting *Herr Professor* Kuhn in his theoretical research. Her duties include practical work."

The Englishman bore a pinched expression, bordering

disgust, and for an instant Tess could almost recognize his true face behind that of the receptacle.

"I'm in!" exclaimed Rr'naal.

The safe opened with a final click. The three agents bent down to see the contents.

There was a notebook bound in old leather. Its pages were yellowed and wrinkled.

"That's it!" said James, euphoric.

He took the small book and opened it to the first page, the paper making a crackling noise. It was handwritten, in ink. There were very few blots or crossing-outs. The letters were slender and sloped evenly. Elegant-looking.

"That's Latin, isn't it?" asked Tess.

"It would appear so."

He turned the pages. There were diagrams, calculations, drawings. Plans for a bizarre machine in the form of a tetrahedron.

"That's what we're looking for," James confirmed.

"It reminds me of Leonardo da Vinci's notebooks," observed Tess, a little dreamily.

When she was younger, she had read a biography of the great Italian genius, and she'd been fascinated.

Fifteen minutes!

"We have a quarter of an hour to destroy this thing," said Rr'naal. "Should we throw it out the window?"

"That won't be enough," replied James. "The Germans might stop the train and send back a patrol alongside the railway until they find it."

"What if we tear out the pages and throw them away?"

"That sounds better."

Tess hurried over to the window, just behind the bedside

table. She pulled on the horizontal bar, and grimaced...

"It won't open!"

James himself tried and was equally unsuccessful.

"It's stuck... or been blocked deliberately, I don't know. But it certainly doesn't help matters for us."

"Who has a lighter?" asked Tess. "The paper will burn!"

There was no answer from the two others. Just the rhythmic racket of the train.

"None of us are smokers?"

Rr'naal looked at his yellowed fingers and sniffed them.

"I'm a smoker, but I left my lighter back in my cabin. I'd have to go back to car 8."

"There's no time for that," James groaned.

"*I'm a smoker,*" Dominika announced from the corridor. "*And I have my lighter on me. But–*"

"*But what?*" the Englishman asked impatiently.

"*Shit!*"

The adrenaline level of the trio inside the cabin suddenly spiked.

"*What's happening out there?*" Tess demanded to know. "*Dominika, answer us!*"

"*Hildegarde... Her hair is wet... She's coming back from the sauna. She's in the corridor, in front of me...*"

"Goddammit!" swore Tess, her stomach knotting in fear.

She put her ear to the door of the cabin. She heard the assistant conversing with the fake German soldier. The exchange grew heated. Dominika was explaining to Hildegarde that the cabins were being inspected as a security measure, a routine precaution. The story sounded plausible, after all. Aboard the Führer's train, impromptu searches must be a frequent occurrence. But the assistant seemed outraged. She got up on her high horse, threatening to complain to the leader of the Third Reich in person.

"I'm not going to be able to delay this bloody woman for long!" Dominika warned.

Tess consulted the timer: twelve minutes left.

There was no question of failing this time!

"We can't afford to mess around," Tess said. *"Give her a headbutt!"*

"Huh?"

"And then put her with the chambermaid!"

"That baggage room will be crowded."

"Shut up and move!"

"But–" James started to protest.

Boom! Too late. There was a cry, or rather a yelp, and then…

Tess opened the door. Dominika was holding Hildegarde, completely limp, in her arms.

"I did what you told me," said the Russian.

"Good," nodded Tess. "Bravo!"

James seized Tess by the collar.

"I'm in charge here! No one should take any initiatives without referring to me first!"

"Dude, we don't have time for this!"

Rr'naal placed what was intended to be a soothing hand on the Time Captain's shoulder.

"We are running out of time," he confirmed.

James took in a deep breath and then, with a motion of his head at Dominika, he ordered, "Go on. Put her in the baggage room…"

Dominika nodded, took out a lighter from her pocket and tossed it to Tess.

"Thank you."

Then the Russian unholstered her Mauser automatic pistol and held it out, butt first, to her three comrades.

"I hate weapons," said Rr'naal, raising his hands.

"You might need it," Dominika said in a sombre tone.

James nodded and finally took the pistol. Dominika kept her machine gun.

"Good luck…"

The Russian dragged the dead weight of the unconscious Hildegarde to the other end of the corridor while the rest of the group headed in the opposite direction, toward the rear of the car. Tess entered the lavatory compartment with the precious notebook and the lighter. Rr'naal and James remained outside, near the passageway between cars 5 and 6.

Only nine minutes left.

The lavatory door lacked a big solid bolt. Tess turned down the simple latch, opened the notebook, tore out a page at random, and crumpled it into a ball. She flicked on the lighter. The fire had trouble starting… It definitely seemed as though everything was conspiring to prevent them from completing their mission…

Damn it, it's just paper!

Finally, the crumpled page was set alight. A miracle!

Tess started again with a second page, and then she tore out more in twos and threes. She tossed the burnt, blackened pages into the toilet and flushed. A blueish liquid stinking of disinfectant immediately filled the bottom of the bowl.

Suddenly, she heard gunfire!

It was coming from the far end of the guest car.

Tess, James, and Rr'naal all launched the same call simultaneously: *"Dominika?"*

"A patrol caught me in the baggage room!"

"I'm coming," said James.

"No, don't bother... There's no point–"

A withering burst of shots cut off the Russian in mid-sentence, leaving little doubt as to her fate.

"Damn, this can't be true, it's a nightmare," hissed Tess.

She had the impression that she'd already lived out this scene. With good reason. She began tearing out pages faster. How many were left to burn? Twenty? Thirty? Too many... Far too many. Her heart was a trapped prisoner pounding against her rib cage. Her clothing was soaked in sweat.

"Shit, shit, shit!"

There were still six minutes and thirty-two seconds left in the run.

The thump of boots approached, superimposed on the noise of the train. The security patrol was coming down the corridor on the double. James waited for them without budging. A voice cried out in German, "You, out of the way! Now!"

It was answered by the dry bark of the Mauser.

"Aaaargh!"

"Watch out, he has a gun!"

"Traitor!"

The noise of the shootout reached Tess in the form of a muted popping. Sporadic bursts from a sinister fireworks display. The Mauser answered the patrol's fire, shot for shot. It sounded like Morse code. Tess did not know how many bullets there were in the pistol's clip, but one thing for sure was that James would not be able to hold off his opponents for long.

Only five minutes left!

Tess started tearing pages out the notebook by the half-dozen and threw them into the toilet without bothering to set them on fire. The blue liquid used to flush transformed the bottom of the bowl into a thick pulp.

There was another burst of gunfire, followed by a cry of pain. Rr'naal had been hit.

A second group of soldiers had surprised James and the Ganymedian from behind, coming through the passageway from car 6.

"We didn't see them coming!" cried the Englishman with a note of panic.

He knew that he was almost out of time.

"Tess, how much longer?"

"I'm almost done!"

Tess tried the toilet flush again. It wasn't working anymore. No doubt it had been used too often in the past few minutes.

Three minutes and fifty seconds.

Only two pages filled with sketches and abstruse formulas remained. Tess rolled them into a ball, put them in her mouth, and started to chew. They tasted bad, bitter and dusty. She tried to swallow them, but they wouldn't go down.

She heard James, or rather his receptacle, who was screaming, wounded, perhaps fatally. Then the entire universe disappeared, fading into a blinding white light.

The countdown wasn't even finished...

"Mission accomplished!" announced Bob's omnipresent voice.

PART FOUR

CHAPTER 1

The return was not easy: the agents suffered from nausea and vertigo when they emerged from their capsules... Apparently, the side effects of tachyonic transfer were worse when time travel was combined with space travel.

They barely had time to take a shower before they had to face Bob's wrath in the austere debriefing room.

"Does the expression 'bull in a china shop' mean anything to you?"

James pleaded the team's cause. After all, it was "his" team, his responsibility. "We were successful, in the end!"

"But at what cost? A mission isn't a way for you to let off some personal steam! You committed real carnage on that train. Luckily, the damage to the timeline turned out to be minor, but just imagine if one of the soldiers you shot dead had been the grandfather of a future German chancellor or some other important figure!"

Once the official debriefing was over, however, the master instructor had nuanced his verdict with some grudging compliments. The mission had been delicate. Complex. Its success (even after three attempts) had demonstrated that the group did in fact have some effective skills.

Laura, the mysterious AI who had manifested herself just before the first run, returned at the end of the session to congratulate the rookies. This time, she appeared in the form of a holographic face, that of a young, smiling woman in her thirties with long straight hair and regular features.

"Emil Kuhn tried to redraw the plans of his time machine from memory, but was unable to do so," she declared. "From that point of view, your mission was a complete success. We have no qualms about sending your team out on another mission, very soon."

That evening, in her cabin, Tess reviewed the tumultuous events that had marked their baptism of fire.

She stared at the white clearplast ceiling, her eyes wide open. In her head, she replayed the film of the second run, the sequence when that strange parenthesis had opened. Who exactly was this man who insisted on throwing her off balance with his strange revelations? Did his stasis bubble really work? Tess supposed that it did. If not, she would have been cowering right now in one of the Special Security Unit's interrogation cells. The attributes of the SSU, a kind of internal affairs department for temporal agents, were not well defined. Its members had violet clearance, meaning they could circulate anywhere on the station. They had their own uniform and their own hierarchy (their chief, Commander Sand, had all the personal warmth of a snowdrift). Rr'naal, who had done some research, claimed they were independent of the agency's direction and accountable only to the consortium. The SSU seemed a lot like the KGB or the

Gestapo... Such a high level of secrecy couldn't be a good sign, could it?

Tess sat up in her berth and ordered a coffee vocally. According to James and Dominika, coffee in the future was terrible. To be honest, Tess couldn't taste much difference from the American coffee of her own period. She got up to collect the steaming cup in the dark kitchenette. She took a first sip and then went to sit at her desk, next to the bed. She turned on the computer (by vocal command again) placed on the plastec surface. She ran a search on the Infosphere. Rr'naal had given her a few tips on how to penetrate beyond the restricted local network. All she had to do was type in a code and – boom! – the twenty-fourth century Infosphere opened up for her, infinite and teeming with data...

What had happened to the receptacles used during the "Hitler's Train" mission (soon to be an item on the cocktails menu at the Red Light)?

A few seconds went by... Tess finished her coffee in a couple of sips... Several sites devoted to history were displayed. Tess consulted one of them, detailing the various assassination attempts against the Führer. The incident on 23 June 1941 was listed. But there was no mention of an old manuscript or a historian named Emil Kuhn. The alleged assassination attempt was only sketchily described. Four members of the staff aboard the train had plotted to kill the Nazi leader but had failed to come near him. The receptacles of Rr'naal and Dominika (the barber and the soldier) had died during the shootout, but those occupied by James and Tess had apparently been captured alive. Tortured for more than a week, they had not given up the names of the plot's masterminds (and for good reason!). According to the website's summary, the poor wretches had pleaded temporary insanity; they said they had no recollection of their seditious acts. They were sentenced to death and guillotined, just like the members of the White Rose, a dissident cell composed of young students at the University of Munich.

Tess's heart squeezed painfully. She thought again about Ernst Persicke, who had been so terrified of his sexuality being discovered.

The poor man... He didn't deserve to die like that...

The receptacles were mere pawns, as Bob had repeated several times, and Tess suspected that the temporal agents themselves weren't worth much more in the eyes of the agency... Indeed, one only needed to see what became of the recruits who refused to carry out missions: they were now receptacles reserved for training novices, puppets condemned to remain prisoners aboard the station.

Tess launched another search, this one concerning Laura Quartes. Could she find out anything more, surfing on the quantum Web? Were the AI and Deirdre Quartes's daughter one and the same person?

An image appeared. The team of scientists who invented tachyonic transfer, posing for posterity: Professor Ronn, the ingenious physicist, wearing a white lab coat and sporting a Sigmund Freud-style goatee, not as long as the one he had now... Deirdre Quartes, the blonde woman Tess had glimpsed with Ronn, just before the mission earlier that day; and next to her, her daughter Laura, twenty years old...

The spitting image of the hologram!

Tess zoomed in on the photo, blowing it up to maximum. The pixels became as big as ping-pong balls, but there was no room for doubt: Laura Quartes was the AI responsible for... what was it again? Quantum forecasting? Yeah, something like. In any case, she certainly looked identical: the same fine features, the same long black hair, as straight as could be.

Tess typed in a query, mumbling each syllable of the keywords: "Lau-ra Quar-tes... Bio-gra-phy..."

A brief note came up on the screen.

Young Laura had been a brilliant mathematician (PhD from the University of Meyrin in 2452). And she had indeed been part of the Tachyon Insertion project along with her mother and Professor Ronn, during the initial research that had been carried out in Switzerland. She had died in 2458, drowned in a lake at a nature reserve, on Earth.

How did one go from being a body in a morgue to head of quantum forecasting?

One more mystery...

Tess went back a few virtual pages and halted on the group photo. A link was indicated: "The pioneers of temporal exploration." This led to another page, with another photo. Tess's heart skipped a beat. She recognized Bob in the snapshot. Bob in his twenties... with hair – an Afro, no less! He stood close to another young man with the physique of a street brawler, also in his twenties.

Tess's throat tightened in shock.

She also recognized this person: it was the same man who had approached her in the Red Light (and hence, logically, on the Führer's train).

He was much younger, obviously, but it was definitely him.

She read the caption beneath the photo: "Robert Calavicci and Pete F. Razovski, the first two men to travel in time."

Tess chewed the inside of her cheek.

Pete Razovski... Pete Razovski...

She typed in a new search. Tess's brain tried to connect the dots, waiting for a coherent picture to emerge.

Razovski's official biography... Not much to go on. A career in the military. Back when the experiments on time travel started, he was responsible for security at the Meyrin laboratory. One thing lead to another: he grew close with the scientists working at the site, to the point that he became one of their regular "temporal guinea pigs." Apparently, he was good friends with Bob and Laura. Supposedly he had gone into retirement a few years previously. His biographical note didn't say where...

Lots of shadowy areas. And few answers. Tess was navigating in the dark.

And then there was this nebulous business of mission NT-19-92, in the archives room.

What does that have to do with me?

She recalled the words of the fake German cook, during the second run: "Have you discovered why you were recruited?"

Tess exhaled a long stream of air. She thought she'd been selected for her intelligence and ability to solve problems...

Now she needed to make sure of that.

The days passed and training sessions continued. These were extremely varied: fencing, horseback riding (on a sort of robotic steed), simulated piloting of all kinds of vehicles... Even though the acquired knowledge of their receptacles was supposed to get them out of any trouble in the course of a mission, it was useful to be able to count on one's own skills.

Tess was looking for the slightest opportunity that would allow her to speak confidentially to her teammates. But how could they be sure that the climbing wall, the Red Light, or the changing rooms weren't full of microphones and cameras? It was imperative that what she had to say remained secret. The young woman bided her time, waiting for the right opening. Private moments were rare. The agents were almost always in earshot of Bob or another instructor.

The opportunity she had anxiously been seeking came ten days later, when Tess's team was urgently summoned, early in the morning.

"You're returning to the twentieth century," Bob announced loudly, as soon as the foursome set foot in the transfer room.

They only had five receptacles to choose from, this time. All men. Fishermen.

"A temporal anomaly has been detected off the coast of Newfoundland, on 13 October 1993," Bob informed them.

The year I was born, thought Tess.

Laura's voice took over: "You are going to become part of the crew of a trawler that is fishing in the Grand Banks, a zone particularly rich in fish and exploited intensively by the boats in this region."

"An anomaly? What kind of anomaly?" asked Dominika.

"We're not really sure. But one thing is certain: it's radiating quantum energy."

A map of the Great Banks appeared in the middle of the room. To the north lay the island of Newfoundland. To the west was the peninsula of Nova Scotia. To the east they saw the Flemish Cap, a zone of shallow waters, dreaded by sailors due to its frequent storms. A half-dozen luminous dots were scattered across the map.

"The anomaly appears and disappears at random, but it always remains within this zone," Laura continued.

"Sounds like the 'Bermuda Triangle', this thing of yours," commented Tess.

Bob gave her a puzzled look.

"It's an old Earth legend," the young woman explained. "Boats that disappeared in a kind of... cursed zone. Planes too. A supposedly supernatural phenomenon."

"There's nothing supernatural about the present case," Bob told her. "I'm betting it's a type B vortex."

"And what exactly is a type B vortex?"

The master instructor shrugged, and simply said, "It's bigger than a type A vortex."

Tess chuckled wryly. "Right... And once we're facing this type B thing, what do we do?"

"You will suture the rift. Exceptionally, we're transferring some special equipment with you to help you in this mission. It's sort of a... temporal soldering iron. It's very simple to use, don't worry about that... The device is about this size." Bob extended his arms as wide as he could.

"We've hidden it in the boat's hold, with the fishing gear," Laura informed them. "Once the rift has been sutured, get rid of the device. We don't want twentieth century Terrans getting their hands on this technology."

"All right, no more dawdling, let's move!" Bob interrupted, in his usual brusque manner.

Tess chose the portrait of the fisherman that floated in front of her. It didn't matter to her which one she picked. They all seemed the same: rough-looking men with weather-beaten faces, stubbled cheeks, and woollen caps on their heads. James headed toward the vessel's captain (of course), a handsome man in his forties, with regular features and small eyes, almost narrowed to slits. Dominika and Rr'naal chose two young men with unkempt hair. They resembled one another closely. And for good reason: they were brothers.

"Ah, one last thing," Bob added. "We're changing captains for this mission. Tess, you're in charge."

James reacted immediately, as if he'd received a slap in the face. "What? But why?"

Tess did not say anything, but she was as surprised as the Englishman.

"We've analysed the data from your last mission and decided accordingly," the disembodied voice of Laura explained.

"Why weren't we informed before now?" seethed James.

"We are your superiors," Bob scolded him. "We don't have to justify our choices to you. You've served in the army; you should understand that better than anyone."

James shut up, but he was clearly finding it hard to absorb the affront to his dignity. Tess felt awkward. A ball of nerves grew in the pit of her stomach.

"I don't know if I–" she started to say.

"End of discussion!" Bob proclaimed impatiently. "Now, let's go!"

The four agents entered their respective capsules. James had time to give Tess a look full of reproach, to which she answered in thought, *"Hey, calm down! This had nothing to do with me,"* even though she knew they would have to wait until they woke in their new bodies before they could make use of telepathy.

The temporal agents settled themselves as comfortably as they could in the space allotted to them. The whole procedure, including the sensors and the safety, had by now become routine.

Clang! The capsules' heavy clearsteel lids lowered into place.

Tess looked at Bob. He was speaking... into thin air. No doubt he was addressing Laura.

A hissing filled the capsule. The air was cold and smelled of ozone.

Tess closed her eyes, held her breath, and began a countdown in her head...

She still hadn't reached zero when–

CHAPTER 2

Her eyes opened to a completely different view.

The ocean, as far as the eye could see.

The sky was clear, but in the distance a bank of fog crept over the water like a shroud. There were no big waves, just a gentle rocking motion.

Good, Tess said to herself. Given their profession, it was safe to assume that their receptacles were resistant to seasickness, but she would not have wanted to carry out this mission in heavy seas.

The young woman (or rather the burly fisherman) found herself at the rear of a forty-five-foot boat.

"It's called the stern, isn't it?" Tess thought.

"That's right," James said mockingly on the shared channel. *"It looks like you know all about navigation!"*

Tess scowled at him. The Englishman was at his proper post, like any good captain, with his hands gripping the helm, standing before the wheelhouse. Dominika and Rr'naal, the two brothers with unruly hair bleached by the sun and the salt, worked in silence, busy attaching bait (small octopi and mackerel) to the hooks on a big fishing net. Their job looked about as exciting as working on a factory assembly line. It was long (four hours straight without a break, according to receptacles' residual memories), repetitive, and dangerous. One moment of distraction and you could slice open your hand with a hook. To make matters worse, the net was moving: a giant drum turned by a motor let it slowly unwind into the ocean, forcing the "baitmen" to keep pace. Tess was in charge of this drum, judging by her position on the deck. A fifth fisherman was posted by a pulley that guided the net over the bulwark before it descended into the cold waters of the North Atlantic.

"*Oh shit, I wasn't expecting an extra man to be on board,*" Tess muttered into her three-day beard.

Laura's voice resounded over the shared channel. "*I know what you're thinking: a boat with only four crew members would have been more practical for you... But* Little Nellie *(that's the name of your trawler) is the closest vessel to the zone that interests us in this timeframe. We'll let you deal with the... problem.*"

"*Gee, thanks!*" Tess replied sarcastically.

She observed the "fifth musketeer" out of the corner of her eye. He was a slender boy with wiry muscles, vigorously chewing gum as he checked the net's floaters and hooks. He looked like he was bored stiff. How could he possibly suspect that his four companions were no longer masters of their own thoughts and deeds?

Tess let her receptacle's memories invade her, without seeking to resist or evade them. His name was Mark Harper. He was forty-three years old. He was divorced and involved in a dispute with his ex-wife over alimony. Evidently, his work as a fisherman had wrecked his marriage. He saw his son Tommy from time to time. Not often enough, according to him. He missed his kid, and the kid missed him. This feeling was like a hot poker, searing Mark's heart. Tess tried to think of something else. From a physical point of view, the receptacle was in good shape. No illnesses. His last serious injury had occurred several years ago (a hammerhead shark accidently captured by the net had bitten him in the thigh, and he'd been evacuated to the nearest coast by helicopter); it had long since healed. Mark liked food and beer, as witnessed by the bulge above his belt.

Tess blinked twice. The map of the Great Banks superimposed itself upon her vision, along with the inevitable stress-inducing timer, which had started running down in the lower right-hand corner.

Forty-five minutes…

That was longer than for Hitler's Train… except that the zone to be explored was vast (tens of miles in every direction), and the temporal agents had no idea where the "anomaly" might appear next…

"What do we do, cap'n?" James muttered mentally, still not reconciled to his eviction as the group's leader.

"Before anything else, I need to speak to you. I have to ask all three of you something," Tess announced.

She told herself that it was now or never. The two brothers baiting the hooks gave her a brief startled look before resuming their task. All one would see, reviewing the mission later, was a crew of fishermen concentrating on the job at hand.

Tess did not quite know how to begin…

"A man contacted me…"

"A man?"

"What man?"

"What are you talking about?"

Tess told them everything. The first encounter at the bar of the Red Light, the stasis bubble in the Führer's train, the enigmatic references to her mother, the file on the "mystery mission" hidden in the archives room… It was a lot to take in. Too much for some members of the group.

"Did it ever occur to you that this guy might be a Syaan agent?" James challenged her. *"That he was manipulating you?"*

Tess had suspected beforehand that the Englishman would be the hardest of the three to convince.

"Yes, of course I thought of that," she replied. *"But who's manipulating whom, in the end? Do you trust the agency completely? Do you really believe the bosses of the consortium are a bunch of white knights, philanthropists only concerned for humanity's well-being?"*

"There aren't thirty-six different ways of making sure," Dominika declared. *"At the very least, we should take a look at this famous archives room… Unless Rr'naal can gain access using his personal computer."*

"Not possible," replied the Ganymedian. *"I've tried. It's ultra-secure, with all sorts of protective systems."*

"Would you be willing to help me?" Tess asked her friends.

Friends? Yes. Tess suddenly realized that she hadn't felt this close to other people in ages. Dominika was a stand-up person. If the Russian gave you her word, you could count on her. Rr'naal made her laugh. The Ganymedian had a naïve side, with his disarming kindness. But, at the same time, he was really smart. She even liked James, despite his priggishness. Everything they had gone through had brought them closer together. How could it be otherwise?

They'd sweated blood in the training rooms, braved the dangers of space and time, and taken on Adolf Hitler's elite troops. The least one could say is that it had been one hell of a bonding experience.

"I can't speak for the others, but I'm OK with this," Dominika said. *"I've never put much trust in our employers, you know that…"*

Rr'naal (or actually his blond-headed receptacle) nodded his head.

"You can count on me!"

James let out a sort of mental sigh.

"All right, all right. Since everyone else seems willing…"

"Don't feel obliged," Tess told him. *"You can stay out of this!"*

"In any case, I'm already complicit because I know your intentions. So, if I don't turn you in, I might as well take part in your endeavour."

Tess was touched.

"Thank you. Thank you all," she thought, with tears in her eyes.

She had to get a grip on herself. It would seem bizarre, especially to the man stationed at the pulley, if this big fellow hosting her suddenly started sobbing on the deck of the fishing boat.

"By the way, what are we going to do with the fifth guy over there?" Tess asked.

"Each thing in its own time," James advised. *"First, we need to find that damned rift, or vortex, or what have you! In which direction should I set our course?"*

There was silence on the shared channel.

"Yes, I'm speaking to you, Tess," James said. *"You're the boss now, aren't you? So do your job!"*

Dominika glared at the man at the helm. *"Hey, pipe down! Tess didn't ask to be Time Captain. It's not her who decides these things–"*

"Yes, all right, but the result is the same," James interrupted her. *"We need directives, and in the meantime, we're going nowhere!"*

Tess ran her tongue over her chapped lips. She concentrated.

"Shut up. All of you. And let me think…"

She ignored the scenery and focused all her attention instead on the map of the Great Banks. She examined the six places where the anomaly had appeared, along with their respective time codes.

"What if the appearances aren't random and chaotic but follow a cycle?" she suggested.

"I don't see any apparent pattern in there," Dominika muttered. *"Two hours between the first and second appearances, a half-hour between the second and the third, six hours between the third and the fourth, et cetera. The only constant is that the appearances are shorter and shorter, apparently…"*

"Shorter and shorter, for sure, but also more and more intense," James observed. *"Look at the level of disturbance on the tachyonic counter during the last anomaly; it's gone through the roof!"*

Rr'naal cleared his throat, and all the receptacles turned toward him.

"Perhaps there is a logic to it," he said excitedly. *"If we compare the frequency of appearances with their spatial coordinates."*

"Huh?" replied his three teammates.

"Take latitude as the horizontal coordinate, and longitude the vertical, and then–"

"Got it!" Tess exclaimed mentally. *"Rr'naal, you're a genius!"*

"You're the one who had the idea of the cycle," said the extraterrestrial modestly.

"Yes, well, when you've finished complimenting one another..." James sighed. *"Rr'naal, can you calculate that for us?"*

James' old habits as team leader were clearly dying hard.

"Yes, no problem," the Ganymedian replied.

The blond fisherman who served as his receptacle halted in the middle of his work. His pale blue eyes were fixed on the horizon and, during this time, the net continued to unwind slowly and relentlessly into the ocean.

"Hey!" yelled the young man by the pulley. "What are you doing?"

He addressed Rr'naal, but the Ganymedian, deep in his highly complex calculations, ignored him.

"Damn it, are you deaf or what? You think you're getting paid to daydream?"

The fisherman jumped from the bulwark onto the deck, furious. He walked toward his distracted colleague, who did not react. Dominika, on the other hand, had risen from her stool to interpose herself between the two men.

"Calm down," she said.

"Oh you, taking your brother's side, as always," the other man railed.

Dominika butted him in the head. The fisherman fell heavily on the antiskid surface of the deck, in the middle of the fishing tackle.

"I recognize your delicate, subtle methods there," commented James, looking down from his post above the scene.

They could all speak out loud now.

"Well, at least this one won't be causing us any more trouble for a while," the Russian replied without a hint of remorse.

"Take him down to the hold, the cargo bay, whatever, and tie him up," ordered Tess.

She consulted the timer. There was only a half-hour left before the end of the run.

Dominika tried to lift the unconscious fisherman. "He's too heavy. I'm going to need some help."

Tess lent her a hand. Their receptacles managed to carry the body below, to the fish hold. A mountain of ice occupied most of the space. Pieces of swordfish (their heads and tails had been cut off) rested on crushed blocks. There must have been a tonne of it. Dominika found a thick rope, which she used to swiftly truss up her victim. She'd obviously done this sort of thing before.

The two agents returned to the deck, just in time to witness the triumph of Rr'naal, who stood like Archimedes in his bathtub. "I've found it!"

The three others were all ears.

"According to my calculations, the next anomaly should appear right between its first and second manifestations..."

"How long from now?" asked Tess.

"I'd say twenty minutes..."

"And how long will it last?"

"Five minutes, no more."

Tess looked up at James.

"Is that doable, would you say?"

"If I push the engine to full, maybe... According to the controls here, this tub can do ten or twelve knots..."

"Then let's not waste any time. Full speed ahead!"

James confidently took control at the helm, happy to have learned how to pilot a similar boat in the simulator just a week before. He could of course have leaned on the experience of his receptacle, but it felt somehow more assuring to rely on his own knowledge and skill.

A noise rose from the innards of *Little Nellie* as the diesel engine started up. The boat began to move. James set course toward the northeast.

"We should get rid of the net," said Rr'naal. "Otherwise it will only slow us down."

Tess and Dominika nodded. Searching through the chests stowed against the bulwark, they found a pair of machetes. The cutting blades hacked the thick hemp cords. After one last blow, the net fell away behind the trawler, held up by its yellow floaters. The temporal agents felt a slight twinge, a feeling of guilt that was no doubt prompted by their hosts: they had just sacrificed thousands of dollars' worth of bait and equipment! Birds began to circle above this unexpected bounty. The gulls dove down and came back up with bits of food in their beaks. They expressed their joy with raucous cries.

Tess glanced at the time: they still had twenty minutes before the next reboot.

And what if they carried out a perfect run, with no errors on their first try?

The fact remained that, freed from its heavy net, the trawler picked up speed; at least one knot, perhaps two. They heard the crash of the water, cleaved by the boat's prow before sliding along the flanks of the vessel. James maintained a heading of north-northeast. His eyes stared out at the horizon. There was something fascinating about observing the sea. The reflections of the sunlight formed constantly changing patterns. The fog bank had disappeared. The sky was a bright, almost electric blue. In some places on the water's surface, one could make out drifting patches of algae, turned yellow by the burning sun.

Little Nellie was making good progress, but so was the mission time. They all prayed that Rr'naal's calculations were accurate.

"Fifteen minutes," thought Tess, her mouth gone dry.

She needed to stay busy. Waiting was unbearable.

Suddenly, she thought of the device the agency had transferred with them, in the trawler's hold. At least it should be there, according to the plan. She entered the wheelhouse and descended the stairway leading to the hold. The fisherman who sat bound with his back to the mountain of crushed ice had woken. The smell of fish made Tess gag.

"What the hell is going on?" the poor guy yelled. "Why did John knock me out? He goes nuts and it's me who's tied up down here?"

"Sorry, no time to chat," said Tess.

But the other man wasn't going to let matters lie.

"Hey, we've always gotten along, you and I, haven't we? Untie me… Come on! I don't have anything against you…"

Tess did not reply. She searched among the netting, the equipment chests, and the barrels.

"Goddammit, what is the matter with all of you today?" the banged-up fisherman asked angrily.

Tess lifted one last lid. Her face lit up when she saw a sort of case made of silvery metal. Its surface was studded with dials, knobs, and buttons. A flexible tube with a ringed sheath hung from one side.

"That must surely be the device!"

Ignoring the prisoner's calls, alternating between insults and pleas, Tess lost no time in returning upstairs.

"Hey! Where are you going? Come back!"

Tess closed the hatch in the floor. The fisherman's plaintive voice was no more than a murmur lost in the racket coming from the engine room. When she came out on the deck, the cold air relieved her burning cheeks.

"You're just in time!" James shouted.

He pointed at something on the horizon. Tess looked out in the direction indicated by his arm and finger.

The young woman managed to stifle an obscenity before it reached her lips.

The phenomenon looked like an unlikely cross between a tornado and an aurora. The central column spun slowly, majestically, and energy seemed to crackle at the heart of the strange funnel.

"What is that thing?" muttered Dominika uneasily.

Rr'naal remained silent, as if overcome by some superstitious dread.

All four teammates stared at the anomaly, paralyzed.

"How far away are we?" asked Tess, her stomach in knots.

"I don't know," James replied. "I'd say a mile and a half, at most."

Still ten minutes on the counter. It was doable.

Dominika spotted the case that Tess had brought back from the hold. "Is that… their temporal soldering iron?"

"Yeah, I guess so."

"Do you know how to use it?"

"I haven't a clue."

Out there, in the distance, the anomaly was a festival of multicoloured reflections, but little by little the auroral ribbons were broken up by the whirling winds. The light, on the other hand, intensified, accompanied by an increase in the crackling energy. Then there came another sound. A kind of whistling that drilled into the eardrums of everyone aboard the trawler.

"Shit!" Tess swore. "You need to accelerate, James, as much as you can!"

"The engines are already working flat out!" groaned the Englishman, pushing the throttle lever as far as it would go.

Tess grabbed the flexible part of the device she'd found down in the hold. It looked like the tube of a vacuum cleaner. Instinctively, she aimed it at the temporal disturbance. Rr'naal was kneeling beside her. He examined the dials, knobs, and indicator lights, before pressing a button. No result. Dominika approached.

"What is this thing, exactly?" she asked. "That nozzle at the end, does it suck things in?"

"I'd say it projects something, more likely," replied the Ganymedian.

"Projects what?"

"Tachyons, judging by the measuring instruments. It's a tachyonic cannon."

"Huh?" Tess said, almost choking in surprise.

She spun toward Rr'naal, who retreated with a short hop, his hands raised.

"Hey! Don't point that thing at me, will you?"

"Oops, sorry."

Tess redirected the nozzle back toward the disturbance, which looked more and more like a tornado of light. The whistling had become even louder. Its intensity was becoming unbearable.

The agents were now forced to yell in order to be heard by their teammates.

"Bob talked about 'suturing the rift', didn't he?"

"Yes," replied Rr'naal, who was back down on his knees in front of the case.

Images started to become visible within the vortex. Exotic scenery from unknown planets. Moors lit by multiple suns. Forests with luxuriant, colourful vegetation. Strange landscapes the agents had never seen before – but perhaps they would someday. And then in the middle of this procession of images, they caught a glimpse of a building of terrestrial origin. A palace.

"Anyone know what that is?" cried Dominika.

"I think it's Versailles," replied James.

The whistling now felt like a needle piercing the ears of the fishermen.

"I think I've got it!" Rr'naal yelled.

He pressed another button. Tess felt the flexible tube swell with energy. It quivered, animated by a life of its own, and she had to tighten her grip on it with both hands to keep control. Solidly planted with her legs well apart, her feet held in place by the antiskid surface of the deck, she pointed the nozzle in the direction of the anomaly. The whistling transformed itself into a kind of roar from a wounded beast. The air undulated like one of those mirages that fool travellers lost in the desert. Vibrations ran through the tube and spread to Tess's body with a power of a jackhammer. The high-pitched sound had ceased to torture her eardrums, and she could hear her teeth chattering in a frenetic manner.

The vortex twisted, convulsed, and was racked by spasms. It looked like a reptile seeking to escape from a tormenter who had trapped it beneath the heel of their boot. The light grew dimmer. The atmosphere turned violet, mauve, red... And suddenly, the anomaly was gone.

The sky became blue again, with an untroubled purity.

It was as if the disturbance had never existed.

Tess was standing in the middle of the deck, panting for breath, and yet she hadn't moved an inch during the past few minutes. Rr'naal shut off the device. He stood up, his mouth half-open. Dominika and James removed their hands from their ears. The only sounds were the lapping of the waves against the trawler's hull and the cries of the seagulls in the distance.

"We succeeded, it would seem," said James.

Tess smiled. There were thirty seconds left on the timer.

"The perfect run," Dominika crowed. "We did it!"

Rr'naal pointed to the tachyonic cannon.

"We still have one task to complete."

Tess nodded. As she recalled, the orders from Bob and Laura left no room for ambiguity.

"Understood," she said, just before she heaved the heavy case overboard.

The gadget from the future disappeared with a huge splash. The four companions exchanged looks filled with a mutual respect. They smiled at one another. Tess nodded her head.

"Mission accomplished," she announced, her chest swelling with pride.

There was a blinding flash and then–

CHAPTER 3

"To us."

"Yes, to us!"

The glasses rose before they clinked together. This evening, the cocktails kept coming.

Tess and her companions had met at the Red Light to celebrate their victory. They had established a new record. Their perfect run was now inscribed in letters of gold in the agency's annals.

"Hell, I thought we'd never pull it off," said Tess as she set down her glass.

She'd drunk too much and she knew it, but it was so good to chill out. She felt light-headed, euphoric, like a kid who'd just won a medal in a sporting event.

"You guys really rocked," she continued. "And the girls too." She looked over at Dominika. "Not forgetting…" she turned toward Rr'naal, "the aliens!"

She burst out laughing. The others had never seen her like this. She raised an arm to hail a waiter. "Hey, innkeeper, we'll have another round!"

James looked at the waiter, wagging his finger negatively.

"Thank you, but we're fine here," he said.

"Huh? But why?" protested Tess.

"You've had enough," Dominika grumbled.

Tess turned to the Ganymedian. Always a good sport, Rr'naal usually gave her his unreserved support.

"They're right," the extraterrestrial said in an apologetic tone.

"No, but just listen to yourselves! What a bunch of party poopers!"

She pointed at James before turning toward the two others. "Coming from him, I'm not surprised... But from you two?"

Dominika stood up. Her hand closed on Tess's arm. Her grip was gentle but firm. "Come on, I'll walk you back to your cabin."

"But... I want to have fun tonight!"

"We'll have some fun another time..."

"Damn, as buzzkills go, you guys really take the cake!"

"We need to get up early tomorrow," Rr'naal pleaded. "Just because we succeeded in doing a no-fault run today doesn't mean the agency is going to allow us a holiday any time soon."

Tess hiccupped and looked like she was about to throw up, but instead said in disgust, "Just look at you three! Like you're attending a funeral. We aced it today!"

"And now we have a reputation to maintain," said James. "Go on, Dominika, take her back to her room... In any case, we'll be leaving soon too."

He tapped his index finger against his almost empty glass.

"I can manage on my own!" Tess bellowed.

She knocked into the table as she suddenly stood up. The glasses teetered without tipping over, but Tess was staggering dangerously. Dominika caught her before she fell to one side.

"Whoa!" she said. "Easy there!"

Tess freed herself from the other woman's grasp. "I'll make it, damn it. I'm OK…"

She headed off in the direction of the exit. Dominika immediately went after her. As every night, the dance floor was crowded and the music deafening. The club's customers parted before Tess, who advanced with her head down and fists clenched, looking ornery. From time to time, one of the dancers gave her a congratulatory thumbs up. Others applauded as she passed or patted her on the shoulder. News of the "perfect run" had made the rounds of the station in a few hours, and the members of Tess's team now enjoyed the status of local heroes. Missions successfully completed on the very first try were rare; they could be counted on the fingers of two (human) hands…

Dominika was not far behind her friend. She also received signs of admiration, to which she responded with an almost embarrassed smile, as Tess continued to barge through the crowd, her jaws clenched. She picked up the pace in the hope of shaking off her teammate, but the Russian hung on her tail.

"Leave me alone!" Tess yelled over the music. "I don't need a nanny. I told you I could look after myself!"

"I'm not so sure of that…"

The two women emerged from the club. Dominika followed Tess to a bank of elevators. They got into the first cabin available. Dominika pressed the touchscreen. They both lived on the twelfth level. There was complete silence except for the quiet vibrato of the elevator. Then, suddenly, the Russian pressed halt.

"Wha–?" said Tess, surprised.

Her shock went up a notch when her colleague pressed her up against the wall and placed her lips against Tess's. For a moment, Tess couldn't believe this was really happening. She felt Dominika's tongue slipping between her teeth and turning around in her mouth. Tess's head was turning too. She was on the point of letting herself be carried away by this mad waltz, but–

"No!" With a sudden start, she pushed her friend away. "What's gotten into you? Are you mad?"

Dominika was short of breath. She had trouble meeting Tess's gaze and looked down. "Sorry... It's... I... It's just that I've been wanting to do that for a long time."

Tess was stunned. She didn't know what to think. Especially since, as surprising as it had been, the kiss had not been unpleasant. Far from it.

God, what's happening to me? Tess thought.

The world around her was humming and it wasn't coming from the elevator, which was still not moving. The beating of her heart made her veins quiver. She had never been especially attracted to girls. At least consciously. But being kissed... Arms embracing you... Holding someone tight... It was good to feel free of constraints and to be available. How long had it been since that had happened? She searched her memories and had a flashback. She saw herself with her last boyfriend. Homeless like her, a rather good-looking kid. His difficult life had not yet damaged him much, physically speaking. His hygiene left something to be desired, and their couplings were hurried, fleeting, and frankly, rarely satisfactory. But it had been better than nothing.

Dominika looked pale.

"Excuse me," she mumbled. "It won't happen again."

She was about to release the elevator, when Tess intercepted her hand halfway to the touchscreen.

What am I doing?

Tess recalled reading an article in a women's magazine claiming that "ninety percent of people are bisexual, but most of them prefer to ignore the fact." She remembered snorting derisively, sure of her choices, her tastes, her orientation.

But now...

Her heart was pounding furiously. Her body seemed to be boiling, just like her brain. The atmosphere within the elevator cabin was saturated with pheromones.

She sensed she was doing something stupid. She knew it for sure.

But it did not stop her from kissing Dominika squarely on the mouth.

The next morning, waking was difficult (to say the least), due to Tess's hangover.

She had a headache, of course, which throbbed painfully in her temples. It reminded her of the atrocious migraines suffered by Tess's first receptacle, on Hitler's train. Plus the disagreeable sensation that her palate was covered by a doormat.

But that wasn't all.

Tess looked at the woman still asleep beside her in the bed.

The *woman*!

When she had opened her eyes, she couldn't remember anything, or at least not very much: the Red Light, the cocktails, the beginning of an argument with her friends...

But after that, there was a fog, a black hole, or rather a "whiteout," like when the minds of agents found themselves together in the ether, between two runs, accompanied by Bob's voice, often raised in anger...

Then her memory started to return in bits and pieces, entwined like the two bodies making love. The images hammered at the doors of her skull, synchronized with the jabs of her headache.

Goddammit...

Her thoughts fanned her pain like the bellows of a forge.

She looked around the room. Items of feminine clothing were scattered on the floor made of plastec, or solido, or some other damn material of the future. A metallic skirt, T-shirts, panties too... The way in which these clothes had been discarded clearly indicated the urgency, the fever that had devoured their owners.

Tess dredged up the courage to turn back to Dominika, and her gaze landed like a caress upon the sleeping body, half-hidden by the sheet.

They had made love for a good part of the night.

And it had been good!

So why had this liberating sensation now been replaced by a growing awkwardness, not to say shame?

Dominika opened an eye.

'Hi..."

"Hi."

The Russian woman sat up, venturing a timid smile. She

touched her finger to her temple while pointing her chin toward Tess. "Head hurts, huh?"

"Yeah. Pretty bad…"

A silence fell, betraying the women's unease.

"Are you having regrets?" asked Dominika.

"What?"

"About last night…"

"Oh, that? No, it's just…"

Tess left her sentence dangling. She felt idiotic. And embarrassed. And upset.

"'That?'" repeated Dominika in a wounded tone.

Visibly, "that" was of some importance to her.

Tess stood up, gathered her clothes, and started to get dressed in an attempt to regain a sense of dignity.

"I'm afraid that this will complicate everything," she said. "You know their stupid regulations, don't you?" The agency did not forbid relationships between teammates, but it frowned upon them heavily. "Mixing work and… and other stuff. I don't know if it's a good idea."

"Yes, of course," nodded Dominika.

Her timid smile upon waking had faded to the point of vanishing completely. She was obviously feeling the blow. It was troubling to see this woman who was ordinarily so strong suddenly become so vulnerable. She was as white as the sheet that partially covered her.

"I'm going to leave now," said Dominika, rising from the bed to collect her own clothes. "In any case, we have training this morning, right?"

"Yeah."

The words were hurried, the gestures clumsy. The two women avoided brushing against one another, much less any actual touching. Tess was angry at herself for being so cold and hard. She felt contemptible and hated herself.

"We'll keep this to ourselves, right?" she asked.

"Yes, of course. No problem."

It was what one said in such circumstances, between consenting adults, acknowledging mistakes and accepting the consequences without complaint.

Except that Dominika, the big woman, the proud Russian, the former sniper, and nemesis of the Nazis, was standing there with eyes glistening a little too brightly.

She left the room without saying another word. Tess's heart felt squeezed by her feeling of guilt. But right now, she wanted only one thing: the burning spray of a steaming shower.

And an aspirin for her headache.

CHAPTER 4

Two weeks had passed since the "incident." Tess and Dominika hadn't spoken about it again. There were occasional furtive glances between them. There were also silences and awkward moments, but it hadn't affected their work. Routine had reasserted itself. Apparently, their teammates hadn't noted any change.

Training continued, day after day, as they awaited their next mission.

Today, fencing was on the schedule. But not just any kind of fencing. They would no longer be fighting with buttoned foils. This time they would be using more serious, heavy-duty weapons: two-handed swords, and maces. And they would be wearing full armour.

Some kinds of "physical" training took place using receptacles, allowing the agents to become accustomed to moving with a body that was not their own. Tess and her friends made use of a climbing lesson, then a rowing session, to agree in secret on the main outline of their operation to gain access to the archives room. Communicating by telepathy was the only means of avoiding the risk of being spied upon by the agency. In theory, everything had been planned in advance, but it was going to be tight. As during an official mission, there was a time limit. "I've inserted a Trojan horse into the central computer, but the security systems won't be neutralized for long," the Ganymedian had informed them with what passed for a contrite smile, as the group donned breastplates, knee protectors, and chain mail in the changing room.

Good old Rr'naal, Tess said to herself. *Kindness and devotion in the guise of a lizard-man. It's just like him to be so modest. He's practically apologizing…*

Tess continued thinking about the operation without taking her eyes off Dominika from behind the slits in her helmet. The Russian was wearing body armour along with a plumed helmet and gauntlets. The full kit of the perfect medieval knight.

The training room was as big as a gymnasium, but it was occupied only by the four of them and their instructor. The clash of metal against metal resounded with every blow struck. And Dominika at least certainly didn't seem to be holding back. She, or rather "he" (since her receptacle was a man in his fifties) was swinging a heavy sword with all his might. Tess had taken over the body of a rather athletic woman of thirty-two who was strong and tough, but even she had trouble countering her friend's assaults.

"Hey! Take it down a notch!"

The grip of the sword in Tess's hand was vibrating from the violence of the blows received. She retreated and parried as best she could. It seemed like Dominika had a grudge to settle.

"Tess, you're not concentrating," called out the fencing instructor, a big fellow who was biting into an apple as he watched the combat out of the corner of his eye.

Thirty feet away, James and Rr'naal were also engaged in a duel worthy of a medieval tourney or an epic poem. Rr'naal was hosted by a very large human, while the Englishman found himself in the body of a slender, frail-looking humanoid. It was a role reversal of sorts. James's receptacle was an Allaï, a member of an extraterrestrial race that looked like the Greys so often described by twentieth century UFO nuts. He would not have seemed out of place in an episode of *The X-Files*. Luckily for him, his agility and speed allowed him to evade most of the attacks launched by Rr'naal, slowed as much by his girth as the weight of his armour, and retaliate with a swift slash of the blade clasped in his clawed hands.

Tess grew tired, and she did not like that. She needed to keep her strength for what came next.

"Hey, easy there," she said to Dominika.

"This has to look real, doesn't it?" the Russian replied.

"Yeah, except that if we're injured before the start of the operation, Rr'naal's hack will have been for nothing!"

Dominika was hurting, and her pain could be sensed in her thoughts. It wasn't a physical thing. Just sadness from having been rejected. A sadness tinged with resentment. Tess had plenty of things she wanted to say (that she was sorry, that she hadn't wanted to make Dominika suffer...) but using the shared channel for that kind of intimate conversation was out of the question. Tess was convinced that the sensual interlude the other evening had been a mistake. Even if she thought about it often, with a twinge in her heart...

Dominika thrust with her sword, aiming at the mask of her opponent. Tess parried. In a corner of her mind, she tried to calculate how long she was going to have to hold on. The false alarm should be imminent if Rr'naal was right (and the Ganymedian was not one to make idle boasts). But Dominika was hacking away energetically.

The instructor addressed himself to Tess, "Approach your opponent! They'll have a harder time at close quarters… Reduce the distance between you… Like a boxer seeking a clinch…"

Easier said than done! Every time Tess tried to get close, she was met by a flurry of attacks. Her hair was soaking wet and sweat stung her eyes. She shook her head in order to see better. It didn't do much good. Her right hand was burning from the force of repeated blows. In contrast, Dominika seemed relentless.

Suddenly, an alarm sounded.

"Damn, what the hell is that?" groaned the instructor.

"The fire alarm," James answered, still eager to be first in class.

"Is it a drill?" asked Rr'naal.

"If it is, nobody informed me," the instructor sighed.

He headed off to the changing room, accompanied by the four agents still in possession of their receptacles. Tess raised her mask to look directly at Rr'naal.

"Bravo, my friend!"

"We have a twenty-minute window," the Ganymedian warned, precise as always.

"We'll never make it…" James fretted.

"You should have spoken up sooner," Tess rebuked him.

"I did, right from the start!"

"What's the procedure?" Dominika asked out loud.

"Everyone assembles in a designated secure room," the

trainer muttered. "There's one on each level of the station."

They had barely taken three steps in the changing room when Tess knocked out her superior with a two-fisted blow delivered to the base of the skull.

"Sorry," she said, sounding sincere.

Within their group, they called that the "Dominika method."

Tess couldn't stop herself from glancing toward the surveillance camera lodged in the corner of the ceiling.

"Are you sure they've been blinded?" she asked Rr'naal.

"Yes, as I've already told you: all of the station's security systems will be down for the next twenty minutes."

"Nineteen," James corrected.

Tess removed her helmet, liberating a cascade of brown hair. Her receptacle was named Lara Rastelli. She was an Italian who had been recruited during the 1970s. The so-called "Years of Lead," when political terrorism had reached a height in Europe. Lara was a member of the Red Brigades in Italy. She had killed two men, a judge and a prison guard. She'd believed in the better future promised by Communism the same way other people believed in heaven.

The four companions got rid of their cumbersome armour, tossing it to the floor. A jumble of plates, chainmail, gauntlets, and knee protectors soon piled up with a clatter like that of a busy kitchen. Stripped down to their basic training outfit, a sort of ninja costume made of something like Lycra, the agents stepped out into the corridor which was already thronged with employees and technicians. There were no signs of panic, but on a space station a fire alarm was not treated lightly, drill or not. Disciplined, the personnel all proceeded in the same direction, toward the designated assembly room. Only Tess and her friends moved against the flow, picking up bits of conversation as they passed.

"It's the second time in less than a month!"

"Did you back up your data?"

"And I was hoping to catch up on my work..."

A woman accosted the four "ninjas." "You're going the wrong way!"

"We absolutely need to get something from B-23," Tess lied.

She had picked a room number at random. The woman shrugged her shoulders, as if to say: *"Have it your way..."*

The foursome turned left, entering a deserted passageway as the alarm's siren continued to moan. Thirty seconds later, they were in front of the elevators.

Phew, we're lucky we didn't run into a security agent! Tess thought.

The tough men and women working for the SSU would have been much harder to fool than office employees.

The elevator doors opened without any problem. But the cabins wouldn't go up or down. During an alert, they were blocked in place. James the Allaï climbed on Dominika's shoulders and unscrewed a trapdoor in the ceiling of the cabin, with the help of the tough claws at the end of his fingers. All four backed away before the plaque hit the floor. Now they needed to climb up onto the roof of the elevator. Rr'naal was the one who had the most difficulty here. He huffed and puffed, but with the help of the three others, he finally managed to hoist himself up, cursing.

"The archives room is two levels above us," Tess said.

The voice of her receptacle (softer and more musical than her own) echoed against the walls of the elevator shaft. The shaft looked like a chimney flue, dark and straight-lined, with cables and greasy pipes running up and down. Luckily, there was also a metal ladder on one of the walls. Small lights were spaced along it, glowing islands amid the shadows.

Tess gripped the rungs of the ladder and was the first to start climbing. There was no time to lose. She was followed by James, Dominika, and lastly Rr'naal, still handicapped by the corpulence of his receptacle.

She passed by a first set of elevator doors, then a second. With her sleeve, Tess rubbed away the accumulated dirt from a plaque rivetted to the metal wall, which read: LEVEL 31. It was the floor they were looking for. She climbed another three feet, and then tore away the mesh panel giving access to an air duct. The panel whirled downward before bouncing off the roof of the elevator cabin immobilized thirty feet below.

Tess examined the dark air duct cautiously. It was narrow. She wondered if Dominika, much less Rr'naal, would be able to slip through it.

They'd have to find a way.

She entered headfirst, followed by her shoulders, and finally found herself crawling along inside, with pushes of her hips and the help of her knees and elbows. The top of her skull grazed the ceiling overhead. Her deep regular breathing sounded like that of a diver using a snorkel. She also heard her friends crawling behind her, in single file.

"How's it going, Rr'naal?" the young woman asked.

"I'm doing my best…"

The Ganymedian was trying to be reassuring, only his thoughts betrayed his fear. Tess imagined the receptacle of her friend becoming stuck in the air duct, unable to advance or retreat. He had about as much leeway as a man about to be shot out of a cannon.

At least he's the last in line, so he won't block the others, she thought, careful not to broadcast this uncharitable thought over the shared channel.

A second later, she berated herself for being so cold and calculating. The agency's "utilitarian" philosophy might be rubbing off on her.

Any loss is acceptable as long as it allows the mission's objectives to be accomplished, right?

She tried not to think too hard about it. Leave the ethical debates until later. For now, they needed to keep moving forward.

The only sources of light came from beneath the grates that punctuated the tunnel every thirty feet or so. They lit up the agents with a chequered pattern whenever they passed over one.

Crawling like this was tiring. Tess's face (or rather that of her receptacle) was covered with sour sweat, as it had been when she was fighting in armour.

When she reached a crossing, she questioned her teammates. *"Which way do we go?"*

"To the right," replied Rr'naal. *"Then to the left at the next intersection…"*

"We have barely ten minutes remaining," James announced.

Tess picked up the pace, even though her elbows and

knees were hurting. Her arms and legs moved like pistons, while her panting seemed to fill the echoing space of the air duct.

She reached another grate. The one they were seeking, if the Ganymedian's calculations were correct.

Tess looked down, her eyes needing two or three seconds to adjust to the luminosity. She could make out the floor of the archives room through the fine mesh. Along with a swivel chair. Empty.

"Rr'naal, are you sure the technicians evacuated this room?"
"If they followed procedure, yes!"
"OK..."

In any case, they had to take the risk. There was no other choice.

Tess advanced to allow James access to the grate. Once again, he used the claws of his receptacle as screwdrivers. Once the grate was removed, he slipped down into the opening. Tess followed. She landed gracefully, twelve feet below. The arrivals of Dominika, and above all, Rr'naal, were much clumsier.

"Aaaargh!" the Ganymedian complained. The others helped him up, but as soon as he tried to put weight on his left foot, he screamed. "I think I twisted my ankle!"

"Just what we need," sighed James.

"Sorry to be such a burden..."

Tess took the extraterrestrial's receptacle by the shoulders and looked him straight in the eyes.

"You're anything but a burden, my friend. Without you, we wouldn't even be here. And besides, we still need your skills... Will you be all right?"

Rr'naal nodded stoically, like a brave little soldier, even

if his eyes were moist from tears of pain. His friends sat him down as delicately as possible on the nearest chair. He grimaced and let out a moan, followed by a tongue click that sounded a little more like his natural self. Then he started to tap away at the touchscreen installed in front of him.

"Seven minutes," James said.

"That doesn't leave us time to return two floors below," Dominika observed in a fatalistic tone. "Which means we're going to get caught, one way or another."

"I know," Tess replied, looking grim. "Can you keep security away from us, long enough for Rr'naal to find the right dossier?"

Dominika and James nodded and headed toward the exit: a single door located at the far side of the room. The room itself was circular in shape, without any portholes or windows looking out at space. All the light was furnished by overhead neons, the bluish glow of the screens, and the small indicator lights on the consoles.

The armoured door opened and closed with a hiss. Dominika and James had taken up position in the corridor outside. Her throat constricted by anxiety, Tess turned to the injured Ganymedian.

"How are you progressing?"

Rr'naal pressed on a blinking icon. A mosaic of windows opened up before his eyes. "Their menu is a complete mess," he commented laconically. "A Gaawin wouldn't be able to find its chicks in this."

Tess frowned… and decided not to ask for further explanation.

At least concentrating on the search seemed to help her

friend to momentarily forget about his sore ankle.

The chubby fingers of the human receptacle slipped from one icon to another. Some windows disappeared; others changed their configuration. It was like watching a virtuoso pianist play a particularly difficult piece.

"How much time do we have left?"

"Three minutes."

James was right, Tess thought bitterly. *We'll never make it!*

At that very moment, the icon for mission NT-19-92, the "mystery mission," finally unlocked...

"What the hell is this?" asked Tess, feeling suddenly short of breath.

Startling images filled the screen.

CHAPTER 5

The date on the recording indicated 1992. Logical.

It showed a street, at the entrance to a small town. It looked like a typically American town, but the scene was nothing like one of Edward Hopper's peaceful paintings, or *Twin Peaks*. Tess had the impression she was viewing reportage from a country at war, or a disaster zone. Bodies were strewn all over the potholed pavement. A police car lay upside down. There were dismembered limbs and blood scattered everywhere. But that wasn't the most horrible thing. Gaunt creatures in a more or less advanced state of decomposition were wandering with their arms dangling in the air, uttering awful groans. When a police officer tried to extract himself from the overturned vehicle, the creatures threw themselves upon him like a pack of famished hyenas. The man screamed and struggled, but it did him no good. He disappeared beneath the writhing mass of his assailants.

Rr'naal made a disgusted sound. "Have you ever seen anything like this?" he asked Tess.

"Never. Except for *Night of the Living Dead*…"

"Living dead?"

"You know, like, zombies…"

The cortical recording was divided into several chapters. Tess decided to skip some by selecting an icon in the viewing menu.

"We're about to run out of time," James informed them.

"Thanks, I'm aware of that," Tess replied.

"Did you find out anything?" asked Dominika.

"I don't know... I don't understand any of this."

Another chapter, a new sequence: A small cabin, in a forest of oak and pine trees. One could almost smell the resin. The cabin was probably a refuge for hikers. Nothing interesting, apparently. Tess fast-forwarded.

At that precise instant, the alarm siren suddenly fell silent. The alert was over.

Instinctively, Rr'naal raised his head to look at the surveillance cameras installed in the ceiling. The blinking red light beneath each lens indicated they were once again activated.

"We're in trouble now," he said.

Tess started to panic. She pressed icons on the navigation menu at random. Scenes and images went by at a stroboscopic rate: streets, a building that looked like a city hall, the hallways of a high school, then more streets, and the interior of a hotel... There were zombies in every scene, at every corner, it seemed. Men and women had sought shelter in a small church, protected by double doors made of massive oak. A multitude of lit candles helped create an atmosphere of pious reverence. The faces of those present were exhausted, haggard, desperate. They comforted one another the best they could. There were no hysterics, but plenty of quiet weeping. One of the four subjective cameras approached a wounded man, tall with brown hair, in his forties. He seemed to be mumbling a monologue interspersed with sobs and snivelling. Tess returned to normal speed.

"We didn't want things to turn out like this. How could we have guessed?"

What is he talking about?

The confession continued, but it was incomprehensible.

"Tess, we don't have time," Rr'naal said.

She nodded in agreement.

Another change of chapter. Was this a military camp? A base? One could make out barracks, a mesh fence, dead bodies dressed in olive green combat fatigues... Multiplied by four, the chaotic views in split screen made her feel dizzy.

From time to time, zombies entered the frame, and Rr'naal gave a start each time he saw one. One could almost smell the odour of rotting flesh whenever the creatures opened their mouths in a close-up.

"How horrible," the extraterrestrial muttered between clenched teeth.

The heads of the living dead exploded, projecting bits of brain all around. The movements of the subjective cameras, shifting at high speed, made it very difficult to follow the action. The agents were running and fighting for their lives. They seemed to be under attack from all sides.

"There's someone with them," Tess said.

"Huh?" the Ganymedian responded.

"They're taking someone with them!"

Tess paused the recording. A young woman indeed accompanied the agency's personnel. A redhead, whose long hair bounced in time with her frantic flight. Tess's heart contracted, and a clammy sweat ran down her spine.

"No, it's not true..."

"What?" asked Dominika, sounding worried.

"What's going on?" James chimed in.

Tess did not answer them. She zoomed in on the image and put a hand over her mouth, which was wide open, just like her eyes.

"Holy shit..."

The young redheaded woman was her mother, Marcy Culligham.

She must have been seventeen or eighteen years old at the time...

"1992... Yes, that matches!"

"That matches what, for God's sake?" James asked impatiently.

"Not now! Let me concentrate..."

Marcy seemed to be in bad shape. She was as skinny as a stray cat, with scrapes over every square inch of visible skin, an almost corpselike complexion, and big dark rings under her eyes... But it was really her, her mother!

Tess was gasping, astounded.

A tragic truth was emerging...

Scraps of memory were starting to return to her. Snippets of conversations, often overheard by accident... stories that Marcy used to tell – not the pretty kind you tell kids at night, to help them sleep, no... stories of government experiments, mutants, mad scientists. Stories about monsters. Tess has always assumed they were the product of her dear mother's tortured flakiness, but here, suddenly, all her certainties were crumbling. As if a rift the size of the

Grand Canyon had suddenly opened beneath her feet!

"Can you tell me what is going on?" asked Rr'naal, a little frightened by the expression on his friend's face.

Tess resumed watching the recording. The zombies were swarming from every direction. It was a stampede. Shouts. Grunts. Shots rang out like barks, more or less hoarse depending on the calibres being used, but the result was the same every time: the cranium of the target was blown to smithereens. The indicators went into the red with each spike in the sound level. The agents were good shooters, but their devastating barrage of lead could not hold back the flood of monsters. There were too many of them. When one opponent was pushed back, hit at point-blank range, another immediately took its place.

Suddenly, the sound of a rotor could be heard. A small black dot appeared in the sky. It was a helicopter.

"Saved," said the voice of one of the commandos.

But a flurry of arms disarmed the man who had just spoken. Another camera focused on him, and Tess saw he was a muscular dude with a small moustache. This burly guy had placed himself in front of her mother to protect her. A zombie was clinging to him. Another had ripped his carotid artery with its teeth. A third opened up his belly and proceeded to disembowel him while he was still alive. There were screams.

"Oh, no!" Tess moaned.

She fast-forwarded.

"*We have a problem,*" James announced.

"*A big problem,*" added Dominika.

"*What?*" asked Rr'naal.

"*There are people starting to come back... Technicians...*"

"Delay them," Tess ordered.

She wanted to see the end of the recording, at whatever cost.

The helicopter landed. A door slid open. The chopper was full of soldiers with guns, sitting on cases of ammunition. The rangers were wearing bulletproof vests, as well as helmets equipped with goggles. The racket from the rotor covered the yelling and the gunfire. The blades beat the air with the speed of a centrifuge and stirred up a dust storm.

"I don't believe it!"

Tess's heart leapt again inside her chest. She had recognized one of the men in the chopper. His hair was messy, and he had a three-day beard.

Pete Razovski!

He was wearing dark glasses, but it was definitely him.

"It's him," she murmured in a toneless voice. "The guy at the bar. In the Red Light... The one who claimed to know my mother."

And here was evidence of that. Tess watched as Razovski reached out with his hand to Marcy.

"Come on, girl, don't be afraid." Then, looking at the cameras, he said, "Looks like you guys have had a close call, huh?"

"Tess, damn it, we're in trouble out here!" James warned. *"There are security agents coming, along with the technicians!"*

"Deal with it!"

There were thumps and shouts. It sounded like Dominika, or rather her receptacle. Tess could hear the altercation taking place outside the door, but she couldn't tear her eyes away from the video monitor. On the screen, a soldier sitting next to Pete Razovski had just shot a bunch of zombies with a well-aimed burst from his automatic weapon.

"One minute!" yelled the pilot.

Another soldier took a device as big as an antique video game cartridge from a pocket of his fatigues.

"Give me your hand, Marcy," said Razovski.

"What is that?" Tess's mother asked.

"A DNA scanner."

A light started blinking. Green. The words DNA MATCH were displayed on the gadget's screen.

"It's the right girl!"

There was the sound of blows at the door of the archives room, unless it was that of Tess's heart, beating furiously. The universe around her melted into a great white light... She knew what that meant: GAME OVER. And then–

She awoke in her capsule.

Tess felt breathless, with her head full of images and the smell of ozone in her nostrils. She saw Bob, on the other side of the glass, his expression inscrutable. There was confusion around the master instructor: technicians running in every direction. Tess understood the reason for this agitation when she caught sight of a squad of guards from the SSU come trotting into the room, weapons ready in their arms. At their head was a man with hard, angular features, wearing a dark toga. The famous Commander Sand. Bob turned to the members of the security service and raised his arm in an appeasing manner. Tess couldn't hear what he was saying until the lid of her capsule unlocked and started to rise.

"I repeat, everything is under control here," Bob was saying, very calmly. "You can call off your hounds, commander."

Tess got out of the capsule. Her three friends followed suit. They looked a little dazed. Regaining a grip on reality was a delicate phase, even when you had numerous transfers under your belt. There was always a moment of disorientation. This time was even more disturbing than usual as Tess was still trying to absorb the shock of what she had learned during her visit to the archives room.

She looked around her: the technicians had retreated behind their wall of glass, as far as possible from the armed guards. Bob provided a buffer between the two groups. Beside him floated the holographic face of Laura Quartes. Commander Sand had turned his eagle profile toward the four temporal agents, still tottering on their feet.

"These persons knocked out one of their instructors and entered a non-authorized sector after hacking our surveillance system!"

He pointed an accusing index finger encased in a black glove at Tess and her friends.

Tess was about to reply, but Bob signalled to her to remain silent with a peremptory gesture.

Laura's voice then resounded in the room: "Our agents were acting with my assent and that of Mr Calavicci."

Bob nodded his head, hands tucked behind his back.

"What do you mean?" asked Sand impatiently.

"The neutralization of the security systems, the infiltration, all that was an integral part of their training. Look at it as sort of a final test."

"Why didn't you inform my service of this... this... exercise?" asked the security chief, his mouth twisted in an angry scowl.

Laura decided to play diplomat. "I realize, commander, that the procedure was somewhat... cavalier."

"That's the least one could say," Sand said reprovingly.

"But the exercise needed to be as similar as possible to real conditions to be meaningful," Bob explained. "If your service had known about it before, how would we be able to judge the effectiveness of our agents?"

Sand digested this information. And the affront to his department. He did not blink, and his expression remained icy. The only visible sign of his annoyance was a slight tightening of the jaw.

"Even so, you should have informed me. I'm going to refer this matter to the other members of the consortium. You may have to appear before the disciplinary board, Calavicci."

"I'm aware of that possibility. And I'm ready to assume responsibility for this whole affair."

There was a moment of silence, marred only by the hum of the machines.

"In future, try to avoid taking this kind of initiative," Sand concluded. "It could be misinterpreted." He turned toward the hologram of Laura. "And that applies to both of you."

Laura smiled faintly.

"Duly noted, commander, and we fully understand your... irritation. It won't happen again."

The security chief nodded, snapped his fingers, and the armed guards immediately evacuated the room with a well-orchestrated concert of boots.

Tess had contained herself during the previous three minutes, but she felt ready to explode. She wanted answers to her questions, right then and there.

"Debriefing, now!" Bob barked, cutting short any attempt at a discussion.

CHAPTER 6

The four agents were seated in the austere-looking room where Bob usually critiqued their missions. He took his customary place at the head of the table and ordered the lights to be dimmed. Lit simply by the pale glow coming from the platform of the holographic projector, his face looked like it was made of stone. Graphite or obsidian. Laura floated like a mirage above the console normally reserved for viewing neural recordings.

"Can we speak freely?" asked Bob, addressing the hologram.

"Yes. Our conversation will remain… confidential."

"What about the surveillance cameras?"

"I've taken care of them."

A robot placed cups of steaming coffee before the four humans, and one of a cold viscous liquid in front of the Ganymedian. Without saying a word, Bob pensively stirred his drink with a spoon. He was the only person to add sugar. The silence started to weigh heavily on the foursome.

Tess couldn't sit still any longer. She threw her cup against a wall, where it shattered into multiple pieces.

"What the hell is going here?!"

"Stop that," Bob growled.

"Go screw yourself! It's you who needs to stop! Stop taking me for an idiot, for one thing!"

"We owe you some explanations, it's true," conceded Laura.

"'Some'? More like a huge packet of explanations!"

Rr'naal intervened at this point like a quiet student timidly lifting a finger to attract their teacher's attention.

"Those images… That mission with the… what did you call them? 'Living dead'? What were they?"

"Living dead?" coughed James. He almost spat out his coffee.

Dominika was gaping. She gave Tess a questioning look before asking, "What did you actually see, in the recording?"

"A town… in 1992. It was invaded by zombies."

Dominika frowned. A Russian woman from the 1940s was no doubt unfamiliar with the concept of zombies. The same applied to an Englishman from the nineteenth century, as a matter of fact.

Seeing the bewildered look on her friends' faces, Tess explained, "It involves… dead people's bodies that come back to life to devour the living… The only way to kill them for good is to blow their brains out, if you believe the films and books…"

"It was horrible," Rr'naal confirmed. "Dreadful."

"The town was called Rhineland," Laura revealed. "Located in Wisconsin, near a laboratory–"

"Let me guess," Tess hissed venomously. "Experiments gone wrong? Hubris, sorcerer's apprentices, mad scientists, all that?"

"Something of that nature, yes."

"And my mother? Was she one of the guinea pigs?"

"She was infected, yes. But she was given an antidote before the mutation reached an irreversible stage."

James spread his hands, still looking dumbfounded. "Wait, wait... Tess's mother?"

"What does she have to do with all this?" added Dominika, just as stupefied.

Bob stood up and started to pace, saying, "Four agents were sent back to 1992 to extract Marcy Culligham. It was a high-risk mission. None of the receptacles were expected to survive, which caused some waves, some heated debates within the agency."

"The receptacles all died?" enquired Rr'naal.

"Yes. But Marcy was saved. That was all that mattered to us."

"And Pete Razovski?" asked Tess. "I saw him in the chopper, during the evacuation..."

"Well, I guess you can probably brag about being the only person in the world to have seen their parents meet for the first time."

Bob had an ironic grin on his face, but his words had a deadly serious ring.

All eyes now turned toward Tess. She'd stood up and was shaking her head, as if physically denying the facts could erase them, reduce them to nothing. She'd had too many shocking revelations in too short a time. She simply couldn't believe it. It was all too much to take in at once!

"Did I hear you correctly? He's my father?"

"You heard me loud and clear."

Tess had the impression that reality was receding from her, at the other end of a long black tube, as if she was looking at things from within a tunnel. She'd started to sweat. If this wasn't a panic attack, it sure felt like one.

Bob tried his standard joke, "You're not going to puke, are you?"

"You've already used that one on me."

The atmosphere in the room remained tense. Tess was like a vial of nitroglycerin that needed to be handled with infinite precaution.

She stopped pacing and stood there clenching and unclenching her fists. "I don't understand any of this. Why him? Why Marcy?"

"One thing at a time," Bob admonished her.

"Pete has the ability to travel through time without being hosted by a receptacle," explained Laura, in a more conciliatory tone. "He works for the Syaans."

"He is a Syaan," Bob corrected her.

Reality was becoming harder and harder to decipher. Tess tried to register all the information she was receiving, arrange it in a coherent manner, but it was a little like trying to insert a round peg into a square hole. She was too upset to speak, and it was finally Dominika who broke the silence: "Since the beginning of our training, you've been going on and on about the Syaans being the bad guys, our deadly enemies!"

"We ourselves believed that official version for a long time," Bob sighed.

"That was before we understood that the real situation was far more complex than that," Laura added. "Your father helped us see things more clearly. Without him, we'd still be in the dark."

Tess fell back into her chair. "Damn, I think I'm going to need an aspirin."

"It's not so complicated, really," Laura said. "But another faction exists, a group that makes the Syaans look like a bunch of choirboys."

"Does this group have a name?" asked Rr'naal.

"If it does, we don't know it," Bob claimed.

"What's their goal? Their objective?"

"There again, things aren't clear...It seems that they've been at war with the Syaans since the beginning of time... And they don't care what happens to us poor humans." Bob glanced at the Ganymedian. "I guess the same applies to extraterrestrial races like yours."

Dominika banged her fist on the table in exasperation. "So why continue to feed us the 'anti-Syaan' line?"

Bob's expression hardened, as did his tone. "Because we're practically certain that the agency has been infiltrated, including its highest decision-making bodies."

"Big changes are about to happen," Laura explained. "Big upheavals."

"We think these mysterious creatures, the real 'bad guys', if you will, are going to launch an all-out attack on our base here," Bob continued. "The station's spatiotemporal coordinates are supposed to be a deeply guarded secret, but our adversaries are nonetheless close to locating us, according to my old friend Pete..."

My father! thought Tess, and felt her heart being wrung like a wet rag. She still had trouble believing it. She chewed at her nails. Her whirling thoughts were making her dizzy.

And to think I believed he was hitting on me, the first time I saw him, in the club!

She emerged from apparent lethargy to ask, "So, Razovski, Pete… He's actually a double agent?"

"Or even triple," Bob muttered.

"And you trust him?"

"He's my friend," replied the master instructor with a shrug of his shoulders.

James asked another question: "Do you have any idea how the traitors, if there are traitors, are communicating the station's coordinates to their accomplices?"

"The most likely hypothesis is that they're using quantum cubes," Laura answered. "These cubes form spontaneously during each mission. They are a physical consequence of the transfer, like a trace or a vestige."

"If someone managed to gather all the cubes of all the missions carried out by the agency, these quantum recordings could, by crossreferencing, allow them to triangulate our exact position in space and time," Bob said. He looked directly at Tess and, before continuing, smiled at her. "Luckily, your father found a way to ensure that at least one of these cubes was equipped with a tamper-proof security system."

"Oh yeah? And what is this super-system?"

"You."

Tess was flabbergasted. In the space of a second, her mind went blank, as if it had suffered from an internal short-circuit. She'd believed that she had become blasé by now, vaccinated by all the repeated shocks she'd received. She'd thought that, henceforth, nothing would ever surprise her again. But she was wrong.

Bob continued speaking, "After the experiments carried out on her, your mother presented a certain number of very rare genetic characteristics. Characteristics that we needed. The cube was encoded in such a manner that only a descendant of Marcy Culligham and Pete Razovski could approach it. A little like the sword Excalibur in the Arthurian legends, you see? Only one person in the entire universe is capable of removing the sword from the stone."

"And in your story, Arthur is me?"

"Indeed."

"And the sword is this cube?"

"That's right."

Tess shook her head, before sighing in resignation. "I must be dreaming."

Laura resumed explaining: "If, as we fear, the information contained in all the other cubes generated by our preceding missions has now been hacked by our adversaries, you can imagine how critical this last quantum artefact is for our survival."

"Recovering it will be the objective of your next run," Bob announced. "However, be careful, it's imperative that this mission remains a secret…"

"Are you quite sure that the agency is harbouring a nest of spies?" James asked.

"We're not sure of anything, but as long as we're in doubt, you will be given a fake objective, a cover story. Once you're out in the field, you will carry out the true mission: bringing us the cube!"

Tess would have liked to put a lid on her anger, but it was proving impossible. For the second time in less than ten minutes, she erupted, "So, you're cool with the idea of playing with people's lives? Programming them before they're even born, as if… as if they're some kind of genetic software? Does this stuff amuse you? Is it fun?"

"It doesn't amuse us at all," replied Bob, very seriously. "We aren't in a position to choose the weapons we use. Our opponents are always one step ahead of us. We've had to adapt to that."

"And when, exactly, did you intend on telling me about my father, my mother, and all this other stuff?"

"We wanted to prepare you gradually," Laura answered her. "But your initiatives and those of your father have forced us to reveal everything all at once. I'm truly sorry about this. I'm aware that the things we've just told you aren't easy to take in."

"Oh no, it's all good, just peachy! My mother was a lab rat. My father has so many allegiances that nobody knows who he's really working for. You're counting on me to save the universe. Perfect. I'll buy it. Anything else? Are you sure? Hitler's not my uncle, is he? No? You're all finished? Because otherwise, go ahead, knock yourselves out: it's my round and I'm paying!"

By this point, Tess's cheek was suffering from a nervous twitch.

"Pete was instructed not to get in touch with you under any pretext," Bob sighed. "But I'm getting the feeling that, in your family, you have a very peculiar manner of interpreting orders, don't you?"

Tess, breathing heavily, did not reply. What good would it do? Her eyes were like burning coals. Her closed fists remained glued to the table.

Bob turned to the young woman's teammates. "Bravo for hacking the surveillance systems and that little expedition through the air ducts."

"It was nicely done," Laura added.

"Although doomed to fail," Bob decreed. "Your timing was too tight. Luckily, Laura and I were here to cover for you. An escapade like that could have landed you in jail or condemned you to serving as training receptacles for the rest of your days."

"And this new mission?" asked James. "The one with this famous cube? When will it happen?"

"Soon. We can't tell you anything more for now."

"As usual," said Tess sourly.

"As usual," Bob confirmed. Then he sighed, "All right, that's all, unless you have other questions."

"You're kidding, right?" Tess snorted. "I still have wheelbarrows full of questions!"

"And I have a report to write... Somebody has to clean up your messes, right?"

The four agents stayed silent.

Bob ended the session: "We'll meet again soon. Dismissed!"

CHAPTER 7

The following days passed by in an atmosphere of dreary unreality. Tess had the impression that she was flying blind, lost in a fog that trailed her wherever she went on the station. She no longer knew what to believe or what to think, so she exhausted herself with exercise. She ran, boxed, and swam (there was a great pool on level 24) until she fell into a stupor. Anything rather than let her doubts and her anger overwhelm her. Usually, no matter what activity she was engaged in, there was an SSU guard keeping an eye on her. She knew that her comrades were being given the same treatment. Since the incident in the archives room, the security service had tightened things up.

And when there aren't guards, there are screens, Tess thought, glancing towards the cold eye of a camera.

She was in the middle of putting away her clothes in the changing room of the boxing hall when she saw Dominika.

"Ah, you're here too?" the Russian commented, sounding a little bothered.

"I'm afraid so," Tess retorted.

She had every intention of taking out her frustrations on a punching bag for a good quarter of an hour. It was tiring when you went at it hard. But if Dominika was looking for another fight, like the last time they trained with swords, why not? Tess felt like she was willing to go a few rounds.

Maybe the old "me" hasn't been completely anesthetized, after all...

"I wanted to speak with you," Dominika said.

"Well, go ahead then." Tess closed her locker, the small door banging with a metallic slap.

"I would like to help you," the Russian continued. "What can I do?"

Tess spread her arms.

"Do? There's nothing to do! I've been exploited down to my very core... like my mother before me! And nothing will fix that, except maybe going back in time and dissuading Marcy Culligham from sleeping with that bastard, Razovski!"

"In that case, you wouldn't exist..."

"So what? Would the universe really be any worse off than it is?"

"I'd be worse off..." There was complete silence in the changing room, as two throats knotted up. It lasted a heartbeat, and then Dominika continued, "You heard Bob... He, Laura and also this Razovski... they're all counting on you."

Tess burst out in aggressive laughter. "Ah, the role of the Chosen One... The 'Excalibur Cube' and all that? What a load of crap! Yeah, so here's what I'm going to do: get into a capsule, go back to 1992, and prevent my father and mother from hooking up!"

Her anger had been replaced by tears. It was like a dam giving way, or a tidal wave. Tess collapsed on the floor.

Dominika crouched, took her friend in her arms, and held her tight, caressing her hair. Their breathing was deep and synchronized.

"I'm sick of all this bullshit," Tess hiccupped between sobs, and then continued to snivel.

Dominika dried Tess's tears, delicately wiping them with her thumb.

"I'm here," she said, disarming in her simplicity.

She blotted the remaining tears with kisses, then her lips descended slowly toward Tess's. The movement was natural, like a river flowing into the sea.

Tess let herself go with it. It was intense and it felt wonderful. The breathing of the two women accelerated and they fell together onto a bench. They kissed and caressed one another, clumsy with impatience, until Tess suddenly grabbed Dominika's shoulders.

"Wait..."

"What? You don't want this?"

"Yes, I do... but... the cameras. We'd be better off in my room."

They made love and it was good. Like the first time. Better, even, because this time they were fully conscious of their actions and not fumbling around half-drunk.

Tess allowed herself a smile. She felt relaxed, pleasantly exhausted.

Dominika dozed, lying on her side with her back turned toward Tess, who caressed her slowly. The two women's bodies fit closely together. All their tension was spent. The pads of Tess' fingertips passed over a crease of flesh, an indented scar between the Russian's chest and abdomen. Tess paused. Dominika felt it and stiffened.

"An old wound?" asked Tess.

"Five centuries old," Dominika replied.

She rolled over to face Tess.

"Does it disgust you?"

"No, not at all… A bullet?"

"Yes, from the battle of Stalingrad…"

Tess leaned on one elbow. Her curiosity was aroused.

"You were at Stalingrad?"

"It's not a very happy memory, I can assure you."

"I can easily believe it."

Tess sensed some reluctance from Dominika, but she persisted. "You don't want to talk about it?"

She shrugged. "It was a long time ago, now…"

Tess kissed her friend. Did the term "friend" still apply, when they'd spent the last hour in bed together?

Their lips separated. They looked at one another, their eyes probing, their hands a soothing balm on each other's skin.

"What was it like?" asked Tess.

"Hard…"

"Because of the cold?"

"Yes, the cold, the bombardments, the hunger, dysentery… Our only consolation was to tell ourselves it was at least as hard for the enemy facing us…"

Dominika paused. She hesitated about whether to continue. She gave Tess a questioning look, as if to say: *"Do you really want to hear the rest? It could ruin this beautiful moment…"*

Tess held her gaze, nodding reassuringly. You didn't need

telepathy to read someone else's thoughts, or to respond to them.

So, Dominika began to tell her story: "It was Ludmila Pavlitchenko who trained me. The best sniper in the Red Army. She had returned from a tour of the United States. She'd been welcomed there like a star. The Americans had given her a handsome rifle, a Winchester... I had the basic army issue: a manual repeating Moser-Nagant with a PE 4 scope..." She smiled. "Am I being too technical?"

Tess shook her head. "Go on."

"My rifle was my best friend, my faithful companion. We slept with our weapons, protected them from the cold, looked after them. Our lives depended on them..." She thought for a second. "But no, that's not exactly right... My best friend was a kid named Vassily. Before the war, he was an apprentice shoemaker... Since the beginning of the Nazi offensive, he did the best he could. He survived. He was an orphan. There were hundreds of kids like him, street kids... We used them as lookouts and spies... They came and went between our lines and those of the enemy. They brought back bits of intelligence, when they weren't shot somewhere along the way. They reminded me of Gavroche, in that French novel, *Les Misérables*. Have you read it?"

"No... but I've seen the musical."

"The musical?"

"It was adapted for the theatre, on Broadway..."

Dominika gave a bittersweet laugh. "Ha! You Americans have a knack for transforming everything into a show... War, politics... Anyway, I had taken Vassily under my wing. He would give me useful information: 'Such and such German unit is bivouacked in such and such neighbourhood,' 'Watch out, there's a mortar hidden behind the low wall around the Barmaley Fountain,' that kind of thing... He was a great kid and I liked him a lot. Always filthy, covered with lice (we used to catch lice between our fingernails before flinging them into the oil-burning stove to watch them sizzle), but always smiling. He only had one defect: he was an alcoholic. At the age of twelve. Hooked on vodka. I imagine that it was his way of getting through the hell all around us..."

Dominika inhaled a long gulp of air which she exhaled just as slowly, and Tess sensed in a confused way that the tale was about to become grimmer. She steadied herself, anxiously waiting for her friend to continue, which she finally did:

"One day, Vassily came looking for me in the passage where I slept, along with rest of my unit. We lived underground, like rats. With the rats. It was during the winter of 1943 and it was very cold. Some of my comrades had gotten hold of a frozen horse, as stiff as a wax statue. When Vassily woke me, they were busy hacking up the animal with axes. They were throwing the pieces into a big pot that was boiling on a fire. 'There will be meat in our soup this evening,' someone said. I was hungry. Everyone was hungry. Vassily told me, 'There's a German sniper, a major... Are you interested?' I nodded my head. An enemy sniper, that was the best sort of target you could find for your trophy wall. Much better than a common foot soldier or a radio operator. A sniper was almost worth the same as a colonel. 'Then come with me,' said my young friend.

"I grabbed my rifle and I followed him. Outside, it had snowed but we could still make out obstacles on the ground underneath. Walking in a street strewn with debris covered up by snow was one of the worst things we faced. You could trip on a broken brick or anything. You slipped, your feet got caught in cracks, you were always risking a twisted ankle. There was nothing more treacherous. 'Where is he, this major of yours?' I asked. And the kid told me, 'At the refinery…' That didn't make me happy. The refinery was at the other end of the city, or rather the field of ruins that the city had become. Stalingrad no longer looked like its former self… It was all just rubble and debris… We were going to have to hug walls, what remained of them, for miles. The façades were ripped apart, for the most part. We had a cross-section view of a ravaged city. There was something indecent about this spectacle, like seeing a skirt being hiked up by force. The intimacy of living rooms with their ageing wallpaper, kitchens, bedrooms: all of it was revealed to the light of day. People had laughed, celebrated birthdays, wept, dreamed, and made love in those apartments. Now there were bathtubs and plumbing hanging out into thin air. It was pathetic. Pitiful… Like the groups of prisoners we came across, every five hundred feet or so. They were guarded by our soldiers who smoked and laughed while the proud soldiers of the Reich looked like beaten dogs. They had yellow complexions and thick beards. They were waiting to die, their fists thrust in their pockets. Their boots had been taken from them and they wore rags filled with straw or newspaper tied around their feet. There were almost joyful little snowflakes whirling in the air.

"We arrived at the train station with its warehouses and abandoned sidings. A thin white film was sprinkled over the rails and the crossties. The powdery snow muffled the sound of footsteps. Then, suddenly, I heard a shot, followed by a sound I knew well, the noise of a rifle bolt. I had been taken completely by surprise. I didn't feel the pain right away. I stopped moving when I felt the warm blood running down my belly and along my thighs. I put my hand to my wound, feeling afraid, with my heart thumping like mad. My fingers were all red and sticky. I looked at Vassily without understanding. He was standing still, right in front of me. His expression was unreadable. He was waiting. Then my legs gave way. I felt myself going, leaving my body behind... but it was nothing like tachyonic transfer. It was a much... lighter feeling. I fell to the ground. 'Sorry,' said my young friend, my small comrade.

"I was breathing heavily, lying on my side. A pair of well-polished boots entered my field of vision. German boots. I looked up... I saw a soldier. He was a major. At least Vassily hadn't been lying about that. He had a rifle slung over his shoulder. I thought it was a Mauser 98K, but I'm not sure of that. The scope looked strange to me, bigger than the classic model. I saw there were notches on the rifle's butt. No doubt his body count. An elegant officer, a handsome man, closely shaven. Soon, I would become a notch too, just another notch in the polished wood. That's what my life would amount to, in the end: a scar on a lethal weapon. And perhaps when he pressed the butt against his cheek, this man would feel my presence slightly, like a breath or a vague memory. The German gave a bottle of vodka to my friend. 'As we agreed,' he said. And then he mussed the kid's hair. He ruffled his

hair, like a father satisfied with his offspring. He gathered my
rifle and examined it with the eye of a connoisseur. 'This is
a good weapon,' he said. 'Well looked after. I congratulate
you, madam.' Was he speaking to me? It seemed surreal.
There was no trace of cruelty in his voice. It was simply a
compliment addressed by one professional to another. Except
he wasn't a real pro. A real sniper always goes for a head shot.
Either his weapon was poorly aligned, or he'd been distracted
when he pulled the trigger. And a real sniper never shoots
when it's completely quiet. They wait for an explosion or
another shot to cover the sound of their own fire. I imagine
that this officer was practicing shooting as a kind of sport, to
stave off boredom. A dilettante. He had an unquestionably
aristocratic air about him. Old Prussian nobility? I wouldn't
have been able to say. I didn't know enough about German
accents to notice the difference.

"The major took out a cigarette from a silver case. He
offered one to Vassily. He offered one to me as well. 'Would
you like one, madam?' I shook my head. I didn't have the
strength to speak. The German lit his cigarette, along with
that of the kid, who asked, 'Are you going to finish her
off?' The officer blew out some smoke mixed with a small
cloud of condensation. 'The cold will take care of that,'
he said. 'Every bullet counts.' Vassily looked upset. 'Won't
she suffer?' 'No, don't worry,' the officer said. 'The cold
will numb her, and she'll go gently…' They moved off as
they spoke, like two old acquaintances. I saw them walk
away, from behind, becoming smaller and smaller until
they disappeared. My eyes closed. I didn't feel sad or angry.
Strangely, all of this just seemed to be part of the normal
way of things."

Tess's mouth was dry, and her eyes were damp.

"How did you survive?"

"A Russian patrol picked me up a short time later. A miracle. I woke up in the underground tunnels. The bullet hadn't hit any of my vital organs: a second miracle... And the wound hadn't become infected. It looks like someone, up there, was watching over me..."

Tess nodded. She was moved by this tale. No, more than moved, she was shaken to the core.

"You were lucky," she said. "Very lucky."

"Yeah, but since that day, I swore to myself that I would never trust anyone again."

Dominika's voice had grown hoarse. She looked away.

"So, does that mean you don't trust me?" asked Tess, with a lump in her throat.

"With you, it's different."

The two women kissed passionately.

CHAPTER 8

The long-awaited summons came two days later.

The mission. *The* mission.

Transfer Room 12. They arrived there at a jog. It was urgent, as always. No time to waste. Corridors, elevators... Tess's heart was pounding, and her pulse accelerated even more when she caught sight of Dominika, along with her two other teammates, waiting very quietly in the middle of an operations centre that was clearly already on a battle footing.

The knot in her belly and the butterflies in her chest were signs that did not lie. Tess had deep feelings for Dominika, and it was futile trying to deny it. It was an exhilarating change, but also a somewhat frightening one. The simple fact of breathing, of existing, seemed more intense. Everything became sharper: sounds, and colours... It was as if life, before she had fallen in love, had been like a badly adjusted television set.

Suddenly, a series of holograms appeared. The silhouettes formed a bluish hedge between the agents and their capsules. Tess and her companions approached their future avatars, as if attracted by a powerful magnet. At first sight, these characters seemed to have come straight out of some Roman epic like *Gladiator* or *Spartacus*. The soldiers wore sandals, as well as a tunic protected by segmented armour... But the similarities with legionnaires ended there. Their shields did not have the same shape as those Tess knew from films. They looked like a figure eight covered with cowhide, something you'd expect to see held by a Zulu warrior. The helmets resembled those of Ancient Greek Spartans, with a nose protector in front, while the ostrich plumes that decorated their crests looked Egyptian. It was a curious mix. A nobleman wearing a toga; a gaunt peasant woman, possibly a slave; and a beautiful woman, resembling a courtesan in her revealing outfit and flashy jewellery, completed the cast.

Both Bob and Laura's hologram were also present in the room, of course. The master instructor had been engaged in discussion with a pair of worried-looking SSU guards, but now he turned around.

"Welcome, all of you! I hope you're in top form for this!"

Tess pointed to the receptacles. "Where are we going this time?"

"A legendary kingdom," Bob replied.

"Can you be a little more precise?"

"An island that has vanished... You can't guess?"

Laura ended the suspense, blurting out, "Atlantis!"

"Are you joking?" asked James.

"Not at all," said Bob. "Remember Plato's description: an island bigger than Libya, home to a refined civilization, very much ahead of its times... an island located in the Atlantic Ocean, beyond the Pillars of Hercules..."

"Pillars?" asked Dominika.

"The Strait of Gibraltar, if you prefer," Laura clarified. "Plato wrote in his works *Timaeus* and *Critias* that Atlantis suffered a tragic end: a cataclysm which made the destruction of Pompeii seem like a minor prank... So, in theory, your actions there should not have any impact on history."

"In theory," Bob muttered.

Laura's tone became more solemn: "Nevertheless, as the head of quantum forecasting, I urge you to demonstrate restraint and good judgment in making your decisions."

"In short, don't screw up," concluded Bob.

"That's what I was trying to say," agreed the hologram, sounding a little put out.

Tess gestured for a time-out.

"Wait, wait. I'm having trouble following... What will we be doing, once we're in Atlantis?"

"The mission is delicate. This geographical zone has always been particularly sensitive, from a quantum point of view," Laura replied.

"Meaning?"

"Cosmic currents, disturbances of tachyon flows, and so forth... Atlantis was the scene of one of the very first missions carried out by the agency, but at the time, the flourishing civilization you are about to discover had not yet been born. There were only a few scattered fishing communities on the island. Simple rustic people who worshipped a monstrous creature like a sort of living god. Our agents had to confront this... this thing..."

"A 'monstrous creature'?" exclaimed Tess. "Are you saying... I don't know... that a dinosaur might have escaped the extinction of the rest of its species?"

Dominika rolled her eyes. "Atlantis? A dinosaur? This is completely mad!"

"No, not really a dinosaur," replied Laura, ignoring the Russian's outburst. "Picture instead something more like..." she thought intently, "a kind of kraken..."

"And what is that, exactly?"

James adopted a look of concentration and recited:

"Below the thunders of the upper deep,
Far, far beneath in the abysmal sea,
His ancient, dreamless, uninvaded sleep
The Kraken sleepeth: faintest sunlights flee
About his shadowy sides; above him swell
Huge sponges of millennial growth and height."

Silence greeted this performance by the Englishman, who explained in toneless voice, "It's a poem by Tennyson. I learned it by heart, when I was a boy..."

For her part, Tess was reminded more of the Great Old Ones of Lovecraft, as she asked, "All right, your agents confronted the kraken... And who won?"

"Our team," Laura replied. "Vanquished, the creature left, exiled to the icy reaches of Antarctica..."

Rr'naal intervened: "That reminds me of another mission–"

"Precisely. The 'Endurance' expedition..."

The Ganymedian scratched his neck before venturing a question: "If the monster was neutralized and banished to Antarctica in ancient times, why is the agency returning there now? Where is the problem?"

"It seems this charming creature has found a way to

escape from its prison, which risks disrupting the timeline as we know it," Bob explained.

"And how does it plan on escaping?"

"It has entered into telepathic contact with a very popular high priest within the Atlantean population," Laura said. "The priest is telling anyone who will listen that the banished god is speaking to him in his dreams... He's intending to allow the monster to return by means of an invocation. His spell isn't quite ready yet, but soon it will be. You must neutralize this visionary at all cost before he carries out this plan."

OK, thought Tess. *So much for the official mission...*

She had not forgotten that the real goal of this expedition was the recovery of a quantum cube, the last piece in the puzzle that would permit the agency's enemies to locate the orbital station.

"Any more questions?" asked Bob.

Tess would have liked to know if the story about the high priest was completely fake or if he represented a real menace. In that case, it would mean they had two missions to carry out for the price of one. With a tight deadline, as usual.

Well, yeah. Otherwise, where would be the fun?

Obviously, it was impossible to ask that question in front of the technicians and the handful of SSU guards who were hanging around the transfer room, hands behind their back, as if to say: *"Act like we're not even here."*

"So, I'll let you choose your receptacles," said the master instructor.

Rr'naal advanced toward one of the soldiers. No doubt he'd had enough of being a "burden," as he put it, every time they went on a mission. Then again, it had to be said that the Atlantean warriors really did look impressive. Tess also picked a soldier, drawn particularly by the *gladius*-style short sword tucked into the leather sheath on his hip. James opted, appropriately enough, for the aristocrat. According to the data sheet, he was supposed to be a member of the capital's ruling council. Unusually, Dominika chose a woman. Before she selected the woman with the attributes of a courtesan, she nevertheless made sure that this receptacle possessed a weapon. The dagger hidden in the folds of her robe might turn out to be useful if they got into a fight. She knew that Bob and Laura favoured discretion and non-violence, but… better safe than sorry.

The four companions entered their respective capsules. As she moved forward, Tess met Bob's gaze, his eyes conveying a silent, urgent message. "We're counting on you," they seemed to be saying.

As usual, at the start of a mission, the agents did not have a clear idea of what awaited them. What did this mythical island look like? What kind of opposition would they run into, once they were on site? How much time would the agency grant them? All these questions filled their minds as the transparent lids of their capsules slowly lowered into place.

And already, the countdown had started.

CHAPTER 9

Facing the group was the marketplace of a big city built on a seashore. The square was filled with people calling out to one another, joking together, and haggling over prices in an animated dialect. The agents were instantly able to comprehend all the nuances, thanks to the residual memories of their hosts. The trees bordering the market square looked like classic palm trees, but they were very tall. Their supple leaves swayed gently in the wind. The breeze carried the scent of spicy food.

"It looks like a city in ancient Greece," commented Tess.

Indeed, the columns supporting the pediments of the opulent residences were vaguely similar to the ones she had seen as a child in old Technicolor films. One of her mother's boyfriends had been a big fan of sword-and-sandal epics: *The Giant of Marathon*, *The Colossus of Rhodes*, *Helen of Troy*... Tess had watched them all one summer. Then the boyfriend had disappeared (along with Marcy's savings). The next one preferred action films with Steven Seagal. They were less colourful.

Enough reminiscing, girl, concentrate!

Tess continued to examine the scene before her. There were more modest dwellings mixed in with the handsome ones. These rudimentary constructions, consisting of a single floor, seemed to be made out of terracotta, or even wattle and daub. Like their houses, the clothing of the population resembled those of antiquity: sandals, coloured tunics, loincloths...

She moved her neck, her arms, and her legs, like an athlete limbering up before a sporting event. Her receptacle was in good physical condition. She felt no specific pains or any signs of major psychic trauma. This soldier was a rough, instinctive individual, who lived exclusively in the present moment. He spent his pay on drink, hung out in brothels, and played a gambling game that resembled jacks. A real spendthrift. He paid for a good time and he was no doubt right about doing so. The life expectancy of those performing the hard profession of soldiering was generally short. There was always a revolt to be squashed, a rival city to fight...

"May I be damned by N'galooc!" swore Rr'naal.

The three other teammates turned toward the Ganymedian. His warrior receptacle was staring at something located in the distance, up in the air, a sort of...

"Is that a wave?" Tess gulped.

For a distance of three hundred feet, the horizon was blocked by veritable liquid wall, a motionless tsunami, standing there as if in a state of suspension.

"What is that thing?" James asked in a faint voice.

"I've never seen anything like it," murmured Dominika, looking astonished.

Tess made a face.

"Plato never mentioned that... Or else I missed an episode!"

Immobile, the giant wave formed a long dash between the sky and the sea. It had emerald green reflections running through it and it shone in the sunshine. A plume of white foam rose from its summit. It looked like an immense hand; the hand of an aquatic creature ready to pounce upon the island at any moment. And yet, the inhabitants of the city did not seem impressed at all by this Sword of Damocles hanging over them. They went about their business, paying no heed to the threat.

The temporal agents were still marvelling over this phenomenon when an unpleasant sound of static snapped them out of their fascination. There was crackling, and then Laura's voice exploded in their heads. In a simultaneous reflex, all four of them raised hands to protect their ears.

"Crrrr... CAN YOU HEAR ME?"

"Yes, not so loud," replied James, scowling.

"Crrrr... Is that better? Critttchhh..."

"Yes, better."

"What is it, that big wave thing?" Tess asked.

"Crr... Don't worry about that for now. There's no time to explain... Crrrittchh... I can arrange to jam communications with the station, but not indefinitely... Crritchh...blame it on... tachyonic disturbance...no recording... Crrr... should have your hands free during an entire run, but not more... technicians are already trying to restore the connection..."

Tess blinked twice. A map of the island appeared in transparent overlay before her eyes. The timer indicated one hour and eight minutes!

"How generous!" she thought ironically. *"We've never been allowed this much time before."*

"You'll need all of it," replied Laura. *"You must complete the mission successfully the first time around. The real mission, I mean...Bring back the... Crrr... cube..."*

"And what about the high priest?"

"Don't worry about him!"

Dominika asked, *"Where is the cube?"*

"Crrr... Our agent on site will tell you that!"

"An agent on site?"

"Crrr... temple... Crrr."

There was a salvo of crackling sounds, and then the communication suddenly went dead.

Tess gave her comrades a questioning look.

"Did you hear the same thing I did?"

"Yeah," said Dominika pensively. *"An agent... a temple..."*

The four teammates turned away from the giant wave and scrutinized the large marketplace, looking for a clue. They didn't see anything, apart from the colourful crowd that thronged the stalls, the shops, and the animal pens containing creatures that looked a lot like llamas. There was still no sign of panic. It was apparently a market day like any other. A tsunami as big as a mountain loomed over the city, but nobody seemed to care.

Tess examined the map. The island had no particular shape; its coasts were very indented. Behind the group, there was the port, which nested in a vast natural cove. Except for the marketplace, the streets seemed narrow and winding. A veritable labyrinth. The city was surrounded by walls except at one spot, where a great stairway led to a temple placed at the top of a rocky promontory. This steep hill looked out directly at the giant wave. Tess blinked twice to make the map and timer disappear. She looked at the monumental structure that stood at the end of the stairway. With its numerous statues and ornamental profusion, this building overlooking the rest of the city did indeed resemble a religious edifice.

Rr'naal had reached the same conclusion.

"That must be the temple," he said, pointing to the mysterious building.

The steps leading up there looked like they had been carved from the rocky hillside.

"Let's go," said James, who still found it difficult to abandon the habit of leadership.

He started walking. The others followed. Tess did not want to get into an argument now about their respective prerogatives. It wasn't the time or the place.

The group passed in front of grills on which little octopi were sizzling. A snake charmer played an instrument that looked and sounded like a bagpipe. He blew into tubes that swelled a bag made of hide, and a nasal sound emerged from nozzles. Before him writhed a bunch of frilled reptiles. A beggar in homespun cloth, with a hood concealing his face, held out an imploring gloved hand. Was he disfigured by some hideous disease? Some sort of leprosy, or plague?

"Spare some change, ladies and gents?"

Tess frowned. The expression sounded bizarrely modern...

"We're in a hurry," said Dominika, hoping to discourage this unwelcome stranger.

"I can believe that."

Tess knew that voice. She slowed down. The beggar seized the chance to grab hold of her arm. Her companions immediately reached for their weapons.

"Stay calm, youngsters," said the man.

Pete Razovski slowly lifted the tip of his hood so that the agents could see his features, those of an adventurer with the hint of a cocky grin.

"I'm here to help you."

Tess freed her arm brusquely. She backed up a step and her eyes blazed. She felt the blind mechanism of anger being triggered inside her. "Cool," she said aggressively. "What should I call you? Dad? Daddy?"

The roguish smile disappeared.

"Oh, I see... You've discovered the truth..."

"Isn't that what you wanted?"

"It is, but–"

"I would have preferred to hear it from your own mouth rather than play this stupid game of hide-and-seek."

"I'm sorry, Tess. I wanted to tell you more, and sooner, but Bob and the others vetoed that. They thought you weren't ready... And when I see the look your receptacle is giving me right now, I have the feeling they weren't completely wrong."

"I don't like being manipulated."

"Nobody does. It's just that, sometimes–"

"You don't have a choice, is that it? I've heard that excuse before, so find something else!"

James coughed into his fist. "Sorry to interrupt the family reunion, but we don't have all day to complete this mission."

"That's right," Razovski agreed. "We need to hurry."

"So, are you our 'agent on site'?"

"Exactly!"

Dominika tapped Razovski's arm. "How did you manage to arrive here in your original form?"

"Magic."

"Huh?"

"Be nice, let me keep one or two secrets in my bag of tricks."

The insolent smile reappeared, accompanied this time by a wink, and then, in a quarter of a second, his face became completely serious.

"I know this place... You were going to the temple, weren't you?"

The four companions nodded.

"You're headed in the right direction, but I'm going to show you a shortcut. Follow me."

Razovski led the team into a maze of narrow streets as crowded as those of a Turkish bazaar. Tess trailed them, feeling groggy, as if she'd received a knockout blow.

Just like every time I meet my–

No, she definitely had difficulty with the idea. It was still too fresh. Too disturbing.

Just like every time I meet Razovski!

It was better like that.

She had many questions for this man. Had he loved her mother? Or had he been acting on orders? How much time had they spent together? Had they seen one another again, after the zombies episode? Was their relationship a secret? Or known only to a part of the agency? Just Bob and Laura?

Tess advanced looking straight ahead, her eyes fixed on the back of this strange person in a worn robe, this stranger who was at the origin of her own existence... Could any answers he provided relieve her of her doubts, of this state of constant rebellion that stirred within her? She had the impression that she was living in a house whose walls were developing widening cracks. All the certainties she once believed were solid were crumbling. She was tired of being the plaything of forces that were beyond her ken, but she was also fed up with being the permanent hostage of her own anger. Rage was a powerful fuel. But it consumed from the inside and left her drained.

She surprised herself by dreaming of a peaceful relationship with a father she had never had. Did he really exist, this being who could offer her benevolent, unconditional love? Instinctively, her gaze turned toward Dominika, who was walking beside her with a martial stride.

James, who was still keeping an eye on the timer, announced, "We only have fifty minutes remaining."

"That should be enough, if we don't dawdle," Razovski assured them. "And if we're lucky."

"That's a lot of ifs," Dominika muttered.

They arrived at a sort of small park that had been created at the foot of the hill. After passing through a gate, they were now walking on lanes lined with lawns. Well-trimmed bushes burst with multicoloured flowers. There were far fewer people here than in the city streets. One could hear the sandals of the temporal agents crunching on the gravel, a sound mixed with the music from the fountains. One of these fountains represented a strange creature, a hybrid with the tentacled head of an octopus and body of a fish. Water gurgled from its mouth. *"The god exiled to Antarctica?"* Tess suggested as she interrogated the residual consciousness of her receptacle. She felt a burst of adoration rise within her, like a blaze of desire.

Contemplating the crudely sculpted statue revived memories buried at the periphery of her zone of mental control. It was an unhealthy form of veneration, tinged with fear, that tickled her neurons. Tess sensed vaguely (no, she knew it for a fact!) that sacrifices had been made in honour of this hideous monster.

The ascent of the stairway proved long and laborious, as there were hundreds of steps and most of them were uneven, but once they reached the top, the view was worth the ordeal. The city stretched beneath them, a labyrinth swarming with human ants crossing in the streets, circulating in unpredictable currents, like oil stains creating an ever-changing picture. Once they had their fill of the view, they turned around. The temple stood on the promontory, preceded by a row of obelisks. Behind the building, like a border between land and sea, the giant wall of water glittered with a thousand small fires in the sunlight.

The double doors of the temple were wide open, but two guards were blocking the entry.

"You need to make an offering before going inside," murmured Razovski from beneath his hood. "A few coins will suffice."

He demonstrated by tossing some small coins (rectangular, and struck with an Atlantean seal) into a sort of niche set in a hollow of one of the obelisks. His companions drew coins from their purses and did likewise.

The guards stepped aside. They weren't dressed like the soldiers hosting the temporal agents. No doubt they belonged to an order that was more religious than military in nature, evidenced by their long red robes, the same colour as the cowls surrounding the grille-like masks which hid their faces. Leather straps crisscrossed their torsos, and they were armed with long, fearsome spears.

Razovski and the team held their breaths before penetrating the deep silence of the temple.

CHAPTER 10

Advancing at a measured pace, the group moved along a corridor lit by torches. Bowls containing plants were suspended in the air by chains. The torch-holders seemed to be forged from the same metal as the bowls, something akin to bronze. Rich tapestries and frescos painted onto stone covered the walls on either side. They looked something like Egyptian hieroglyphs. The naïve-looking fresco told a story: worshippers prostrated themselves before an enormous creature with obscene aquatic twists, the same creature depicted in the sculpture they had seen earlier at the fountain below. People were offered as sacrifices to the monster (this image confirmed the diffuse impression Tess had picked up from her host), while tornados and luminous convolutions like the one that appeared over the Grand Banks filled the skies...

"Quantum disturbances?"

The next panel (Tess almost felt like she was reading a comic book) showed four warriors attacking the living god with bows and arrows...

"That was one hell of a fight," commented Razovski in a low voice.

"Were you there?"

"Yeah. And old Bob was also part of our commando unit. We had a hard time, let me tell you." He tapped his finger on the fresco. "That goddamned creature did everything it could to thwart us. It took us at least ten runs before we cornered it so we could take it..."

The five time travellers emerged from the corridor into an oval space ringed with arcades. In the middle of this room there was an altar surrounded by a smoke that hid its exact form. Aromatic torches had been arranged around it. The sweetish scent emanating from the fumes was somewhat heady, and Tess told herself that if she breathed it for long she might become nauseated.

A sinister-looking figure officiated behind the altar.

"Is that him, the famous high priest?" asked Rr'naal.

"Yeah," replied Razovski, with a note of disgust. "He's named Aktur. A real piece of work. But we're not here for him."

Aktur was not very tall, about five feet three inches. It was difficult, on the other hand, to evaluate his girth, masked by the long floating trains of his ceremonial dress. He wore a necklace of teeth and a horned headdress by way of a helmet. Bright stripes decorated his shoulders. His forearms and his face were covered in tattoos and scars. The glow from the torches gave him the gaze of a madman, intense and bright. Tess could not see Aktur's feet but would not have been surprised to see goat hooves peeping out from the dark folds of his robes.

A dozen of his followers were prostrated in front of the altar, hands flat on the floor. They began to sing in chorus a throbbing chant, with harmonies that were unpleasant to the human ear. The chant swelled and fell, its tone rising and descending, but the fervour of the believers seemed to remain constant. Aktur intoned the responses when the choir marked a pause. His voice was impersonal and yet it commanded respect. No one seemed to notice the five intruders. Nevertheless, they prudently kept their distance, remaining hidden in the shadows of a gallery. All energy seemed to be concentrated on the priest.

There was something unhealthy about the ceremony taking place. Tess expected at any moment one of the believers would take a knife from their tunic in order to stab themselves in the chest or slit open their throat while gargling a final oath of fanatical loyalty. After a plaintive interlude, the chant reached a climax. Powerful, demanding, it expressed a growing passion and even monstrous unfulfilled desires.

"No use hanging around here," muttered Razovski.

No one dared to contradict him, and the four novice agents followed him further into the shadows. They soon came to a series of lateral corridors. Tortured demons appeared in relief, sculpted on the walls. The group passed in front of a hideous face endowed with fangs and pointy ears. The place looked like something you might see on a ghost train ride at the fun fair. All that was missing were the spider webs and the howling of werewolves in the background.

Razovski pressed his hand to the grimacing face. There was a click and the wall slid aside with a long stony scraping sound. A spiral staircase descended into the depths. It seemed endless.

"Watch out, the steps are slippery," warned Razovski, still leading the group.

The foursome started down the stairs after him, and the wall panel slid back into place, making the same sound as a tomb being closed up.

The further they descended into the entrails of the earth, the more the humidity grew, becoming oppressive in its omnipresence. It impregnated the air with an icy dampness. The stairway was badly lit, with a torch every thirty feet or so. There seemed to be a more generous source of light somewhere below, but they still needed to reach it. Faint sounds, difficult to identify, rose from the underground spaces. Was it the rustling and squeaking of famished rodents? Running water on stone? The whistling of an air current seeking a way out of this labyrinth? The three different noises combined to produce a dismal cacophony.

At the end of several long minutes, the agents arrived at the last level. Here, the torches crackled with a fiercer energy as they burned, and a strange sulphurous smell floated in the air. A corridor dug by human hands opened before the group. Tess turned back toward the stairs, already discouraged.

"Are we going to have to climb all the way back up on the return journey?"

"Yes, I'm afraid so," her father replied.

They were walking on a muddy floor, punctuated in places by stagnant puddles. Drops fell one by one from the ceiling, seeming to count off the seconds. Algae had colonized a fetid, silty puddle where a few bizarre fish lay dying, their mouths gaping. Razovski pushed them away with his foot. Masses of slimy seashells encrusted the walls. Small crabs scurried hither and thither. There was a feeling of abandonment, as if the creatures who normally inhabited this space had fled, disturbed by the human intrusion.

The tunnel soon divided into two branches, and then there were more crossings at regular intervals. Razovski obviously knew the way. He took a left turn, then a right. He barely paused at all. At one point, he signalled to the others to duck into a recess. He'd heard something. Tess pricked up her ears and could make out the sound of footsteps splashing across the muddy floor. A patrol of five guards wearing red robes passed in front of the adventurers without seeing them. With their hoods and mesh masks, it was impossible to differentiate between them. This detail only intensified their menacing character. They had voluntarily sacrificed all individuality when they joined the sect that protected the temple's security. The implacable manner of their progression and the absence of any hesitation in their movements indicated they were ready to fight and to die, if necessary, in case of an armed confrontation.

The rhythmic steps faded in the distance. Tess and her comrades emerged from their hiding place. Their exploration resumed, seemingly erratic, and yet Razovski knew where he was going. Arriving at a bend in the tunnel, he halted, indicating to the rest of the group with a peremptory gesture that they imitate him, and then he risked a glance around the corner at the tunnel that lay beyond. This passage ended thirty feet further on, at an intersection unlike the previous ones. Firstly, this one was guarded by four cult members in red dress, one for each branch of the tunnel. And secondly, a ray of light descended from the ceiling, forming an immaterial column at the very centre of the crossing.

Razovski retreated and gathered his troops for a brief huddle. "We've arrived at the location of the cube, but there are guards. Four guys. We can take them."

Tess felt the blood of her receptacle boiling. The prospect of combat did not frighten him; on the contrary, the soldier who vegetated inside her seemed eager to put his skill with weapons to the test.

"We're going to have to charge thirty feet across open ground, which means we'll lose the element of surprise," Razovski continued.

Tess shrugged her shoulders, as if to signify: "Makes no difference to me."

Besides, she'd already bared her sword. Rr'naal had done the same. Dominika had removed her dagger from its sheath.

James said, "We have less than a quarter of an hour left."

Razovski drew forth a short sword from the folds of his rags. He also possessed a knife, tucked into a sheath tied to his ankle. He gave it to James, the only member of the group without a weapon.

"Ready?"

He sounded like a coach delivering a pep talk to a sports team in the changing room before a match.

They nodded their heads.

Razovski charged forward, screaming like a thousand banshees, and his companions followed suit, running closely on his heels.

The guard posted at the other end of the corridor, just before the intersection, was taken by surprise, but he quickly directed the point of his weapon toward the band of furies bearing down on him.

Dominika threw her dagger without slowing. The blade planted itself into the guard's chest, almost to the hilt. The man fell to his knees. He hadn't had time to use his spear. The three other guards joined the fight at a run. One of them threw his spear toward the assailants. With a resounding *cling*, Razovski deflected the fatal trajectory with a backhanded blow of his sword. The next instant, he was in direct contact with the enemy, slamming into the guard with a metallic clash.

The three guards possessed both experience and plenty of courage, but they weren't as good as their opponents. There was a flash of steel, and Tess severed the spear held by the cult member facing her. Rr'naal impaled him upon his sword. Razovski opened the belly of another adversary, whose guts fell into the mud in warm coils.

The last guard standing retreated slowly. Attacked on two fronts at the same time, he nevertheless managed to keep Rr'naal and James at a distance. Meanwhile, the guard who had fallen to his knees, with the dagger in his chest, took out a sort of trumpet which resembled a hunting horn and blew on it until his veins nearly burst. Tess slit his throat without hesitation. He dropped his instrument and raised his hands to his neck. The blood spurted in crimson cascades between his fingers before spreading, red on red, down the front of his robe. He tumbled to one side, face in the dirt. Tess was panting, filled with an intense feeling of satisfaction... which was completely unlike her. Killing gave her pleasure; no, it was stronger than that: it gave her joy.

The remaining guard stabbed James in the arm. The Englishman had been a little too bold and paid for it with a wound; a minor one, to be sure, but a hindrance for further combat. Razovski nudged Rr'naal and James aside, and then advanced toward the survivor, twirling his sword rapidly. The guard retreated further, until his back touched the damp wall behind him. In a burst of rage mixed with terror, he launched a final, desperate attack, his body thrusting forward. Razovski evaded the blow with the grace of a bullfighter, stepping aside at the last moment and spinning around to plant his blade in the back of his adversary's neck. The point reemerged in the man's wide-open mouth, like a second tongue. A cold, hard metal appendage.

James had rushed over to the light pouring down in the middle of the intersection. The beam was quite visible, its outline clearly defined.

"Hey?!!"

The Englishman was stopped dead in his tracks and then projected backward. He fell on his behind in a puddle of saltwater. Dominika meanwhile tried to place her hand inside the beam, but it resisted her attempt. It was like an invisible wall, or rather some kind of inviolable elastic membrane.

Razovski addressed his daughter: "Tess, I guess it's all up to you."

"Hurry," added Rr'naal, "because there are more people coming this way."

The Ganymedian had turned toward one of the four corridors. He could already see vague silhouettes moving toward them through the inky black shadows.

Tess felt a prickling in the hollow of her belly and within her chest. It felt like the stage fright of an actor before the curtain went up. It was as if all the threads of her existence were converging on this particular point in space and time.

"Go on, what are you waiting for?" Razovski urged her.

She really wanted to put him in his place, this father of hers. And what if she wasn't the "Chosen One" after all? Would her life still have any meaning? She had been conceived for this moment, like a part made in a factory. It was her function, her utility. In theory, at least. There was still no proof that the genetic programming would work.

Tess stepped into the light.

CHAPTER 11

As Tess crossed the boundary of the luminous beam, she closed her eyes. A brief tingling sensation ran down her body, from the roots of her hair to the arches of her feet. She had the impression of being swept from top to bottom by the beam of a scanner, and it penetrated to the depths of her soul.

The beam perceived the young woman hidden inside the body of the warrior, the agent within the receptacle. The tingling faded. Tess reopened her eyes. She needed a few seconds to become accustomed to the light level. She was at the heart of the ray. She lifted her head. Above her, a vertical shaft, as wide as a person, rose toward a large phosphorescence, a green-and-blue circle. She lowered her eyes. Her friends in the tunnel were now mere silhouettes, their outlines blurred by the curtain of light. Each agent was posted at the opening of one of the four corridors. They had taken up combat positions, waiting. Tess knew that they would protect her for as long as they could, but she needed to be quick.

Suddenly, she felt herself being lifted into the air by an irresistible force. She had taken off and was ascending toward the surface with the speed of a rocket. In the blink of an eye, she had emerged from the earth and was being propelled upward through a vertical tunnel of water, a liquid gullet. She was *inside* the giant wave they had seen. She had entered a dreamlike world. It was truly astounding. All around her, strange aquatic creatures seemed to have stopped moving their fins and were examining her with sinister expressions. It was the kind of bestiary one expected to see at the bottom of the oceans' trenches. A nightmare bestiary. Here, there was a sort of manta ray, but even bigger than the standard. Over there, she saw a fish with globular eyes and long scarlet whiskers. And elsewhere, there were crustaceans armoured with barbed scales. All these beasts were immobile, like insects imprisoned in some kind of amber with green reflections. The wave was riddled with green veins. This luminescence shifted about, crawling like something living. In places, the liquid element gave way to a gelatinous substance.

The hollow column climbed, further and further, until it ended in a kind of bubble, like a small cave in the heart of the tsunami. The cube floated inside it. It was a bizarre object, seemingly weightless, about the size of a small box. There were blinking squares on its surface, sometimes white, sometimes a dark grey. It vibrated with an energy that was barely contained.

Tess floated too, light as a feather, her heart racing like mad. Her mouth was dry. She stretched out her hand slowly and held her breath.

Contact.

There was an electrical discharge.

Tess gave a start. Her hand closed. She took possession of the cube, just as the cube took possession of her.

Bluish spores appeared in the form of swarms, dancing around the warrior in zero gravity. The fragments multiplied, teeming. Each of these spores contained a memory from the past. They went back ten generations at least. Tess saw images first seen by the ancestors of her receptacle. She shared their fears and their secret hopes... Another flashback... There was once a time when Atlantis was much vaster... the city was located inland, and not on the coast... The sea level appeared to be lower, and, of course, the giant wave did not exist... One of the young warrior's ancestors had been enslaved... A flashback revealed him carving the steps of a big stairway, using a hammer and chisel. Tess felt the vibrations travel up her arm, as far as the shoulder, with each blow... A leap in time: now she was another enslaved person, but this time a man working underground along with hundreds of other wretches. They were carrying sacks of stones or pushing wagons. Metal picks clinked against the rock. Tess recognized the tunnels dug beneath the temple. Another flashback: a vendor cooking marine animals on a wood fire... Tess smelled the scent of fish, filling her nostrils and throat. This ancestor would be robbed and killed one evening, as he was closing his stall... A generation later: she was a woman assigned to work in the fields... She had felt the lash of the whip on her back, leaving indelible bites... The memories of all these people poured into Tess's mind. She suddenly felt like a jar so full that she was about to explode. It was the same effect as when she took possession of a receptacle... but to the power of ten. The communion was brutal, and the shock phenomenal.

Everything halted. Suddenly.

The spores vanished and Tess, barely conscious, felt the force of gravity returning.

She descended, gently at first, then at an increasing rate. She penetrated the ground and, when the muddy bottom finally approached, she was nearly falling free.

Tess bounced off a puddle of water. She was dazed, but she hadn't let go of the cube. She struggled to regain her bearings. She no longer knew who she was, or where she was...

She looked all around her. Beyond the curtain of light, silhouetted figures were fighting.

Her friends!

This thought was like a bucket of water thrown in her face. She stood up, her legs still shaky, and then she put the cube into the satchel she was wearing over her shoulder.

She emerged from the beam. Her father turned his head toward her, and that second of distraction proved fatal.

"Tess!"

An enemy spear hit him in the lower belly and went straight through him. He found himself pinned to a wall, grimacing with pain. Tess unsheathed her sword and lunged at the guard. The latter withdrew his spear from Razovski's body, causing a geyser of blood to spray forth. Razovski screamed as the metal ripped through his flesh again. The enemy raised his weapon to protect himself, but Tess's blade cut right through the wooden shaft and, pursuing its trajectory, sliced his skull open, like an axe splitting a log.

Razovski pressed a hand to his wound, and his features contorted like a tortured gargoyle. The haemorrhage looked serious. He was so white that it seemed as if all his blood was being pumped out of him.

"Do you have the cube?"

"Yes."

Tess was having difficulty recovering her weapon. She had to press the body of the guard with one heel in order to pry it free. The blade came out with a glutinous sound.

Meanwhile, Dominika and the others were finishing off their respective adversaries. Tess heard some brief cries, mixed with the noise of corporal impacts, one or two death rattles, and then she saw bodies falling in the puddles or curling up on themselves.

Tess blinked twice. The timer appeared, showing that they had five minutes remaining.

"We're getting out of here," said Razovski.

"Can you walk?"

"I can even run, if I have to."

The column of light started to blink. The greenish phosphorescence it had been giving off was fading. It vibrated and flickered.

"What's going on?" asked Rr'naal.

"Without the cube to maintain its integrity, the stasis gel is going to dissolve."

"Huh? That means that–"

"The wave is going to fall, yeah."

Images instantly took form in Tess's mind. She saw the colossal liquid wall crashing down on the island in an apocalyptic tidal wave. The temple was the first building in the city to be shattered when tons and tons of water poured over it. The high priest did not even have time to utter a final prayer. The water burst through the walls in torrents that nothing could stop. Blocks of stone shifted around like children's building blocks. Pillars that looked solid enough to support mountains were broken. The waters spread through the streets in furious torrents, carrying everything before them. Merchants, soldiers, citizens, slaves, and animals spun around in an aquatic dance of death. The sea smashed down doors and invaded palaces and hovels alike. Young or old, men or women, no one was spared.

The vision vanished and Tess found herself back in the tunnels. She turned to her father. "You didn't warn me about this!" she said furiously. "You didn't tell me that taking the cube meant signing a death warrant for all these people."

"If I'd told you, you wouldn't have taken it," replied Razovski, and he spat bloody phlegm on the floor.

Once a manipulator, always a manipulator. Tess felt her anger growling inside her.

"We'll settle this later, if you don't mind," suggested James.

The survival instinct of their receptacles was urging them to save themselves. Overcoming her rancour, Tess passed her father's arm over her shoulder and started to walk. Razovski continued to play the role of a tough guy, but he was hurt badly. He stumbled every few feet and struggled to keep moving at a decent rhythm. The three others walked ahead of the father and daughter. They cleared the path whenever one or more guards tried to block their advance.

Dominika dodged an assault and skewered a man in red. Another adversary leapt out of the shadows: this time, it was Rr'naal who took care of him. But Dominika was worried. She glanced frequently over her shoulder to make sure that Tess and the wounded man were still following them. The pair of them were lagging further and further behind.

Three minutes left.

Razovski groaned. "Stop…"

"What?"

"I'm hurting too much."

His usual boastful tone had been replaced by real suffering. He was having difficulty breathing. His legs gave way and he slid to the ground.

With one hand, Tess pulled aside a layer of his torn clothing. He had no protective armour underneath. The raw flesh looked like the pulp of blood oranges, and the two edges of the wound, gaping open, did not bode well. Razovski was trembling from head to foot. His gaze already seemed distant, and his lips formed a sad little smile.

"I'm sorry," he said, taking Tess's hand in his.

"About what?"

"About everything…"

He tried to master his pain, but it was a lost cause.

"Tess… we need to leave!" Dominika implored, standing a few feet away.

"Go ahead, I'll catch up with you," Tess replied, knowing full well she would never have the time.

She felt the tears welling up inside her. She detested this man who was dying right in front of her. And yet, she also loved him.

Her father.

She had fantasized so much about their meeting when she was younger. She had dreamed about it so often. She wasn't able to tear herself away from him, even if, deep down, he really was a first-class bastard.

She pressed on the wound with her hand, but it wasn't enough to stop the bleeding.

"I'm happy to have known you, even a little bit," murmured Razovski.

His voice was gradually weakening, as if he were falling deeper into an abyss. The mask of pain had been replaced by a much softer expression. His hand caressed Tess's cheek, leaving a red streak there, like war paint.

There was a final tensing of his body, and then nothing more.

Tess bit her lower lip, as if doing so would help her hold back the tears. Her throat was so knotted that she could barely breathe.

"It's over," said Dominika.

The Russian forced her to stand up. Tess turned her head: her friends were still there. They hadn't left. They were waiting for her.

"It's over," Dominika repeated. "We have to go."

Tess yielded. With a heavy heart, she let herself be dragged away. Dominika towed her along by the wrist.

"Quickly!"

While trying to move faster, Tess turned around and looked one more time at the body of her father... which was undergoing a change.

Tess blinked her eyes, but, no, she wasn't dreaming: the skin of the deceased Pete Razovski had turned pale blue, and his hair had turned white! She was unable to see his features clearly, but it seemed to her they had become finer.

An incredible metamorphosis!

Tess wanted to make sure of this. She tried to slow down, but Dominika gave her arm an energetic jerk. "Move!"

"We need to try to find shelter for our receptacles," said Rr'naal. "It's the least we can do for them."

A dull roar came in reply to the Ganymedian's words. The noise intensified. In the tunnel that seemed to extend to infinity, the light from the most distant torches was extinguished, like candle flames being blown out one by one. The walls started to vibrate.

"The wave," croaked Rr'naal.

Adrenaline surged through the blood of the receptacles. Tess and the three others started to run as fast as they could. The roar of the waters was deafening. A pitiless tidal wave had invaded the labyrinth. The fugitives' race against death seemed hopeless. They felt the damp breath of the tsunami on the back of their necks, licking at their heels. Its foamy snout pushed everything before it: debris, stones, bodies... The corpse of Razovski was swept away like a rag doll, taking with it the secret of its new ethereal appearance.

When she felt herself being lifted from the ground and shaken by an irresistible force, Tess closed her eyes, abandoning herself to a white-and-green death, and then–

CHAPTER 12

Excerpt from Tess Heiden's diary:

When I opened my eyes again, the cube was in my hands... By what quantum miracle had this happened? I have no idea. The ways of space and time are inscrutable! All I know is that Bob and company succeeded in teleporting the artefact at the same time as our minds. One strange detail: the object had "shrunk in the wash," if you'll allow the expression. It was now no bigger than a thimble. Bob stood before me. He gave me a discreet sign of complicity (a simple nod of the head, nothing more). The transparent lid opened with its usual slowness. I staggered as I got out of the capsule, and Bob caught me. It wasn't merely a thoughtful gesture on his part. I felt his hand slip into the hollow of mine and take the cube, a sleight of hand that went undetected. Bravo, Bobby!

I glanced over the shoulder of the master instructor: Commander Sand was there. His SSU watchdogs did not accompany him, this time, but he still seemed to be pissed off. Laura was speaking to him, no doubt trying to distract him. He listened to the hologram while keeping an eye on us, my comrades and me. The other members of the team were emerging one by one from their respective capsules, their legs unsteady. I often suffered from stuffed-up ears after a transfer. Probably a question of pressure. My hearing gradually returned to normal, and I could hear Laura trying to make excuses full of technical jargon:

"The death of the high priest provoked an incident... Tachyonic interference... We could not have predicted it, but there was something like a quantum pile-up... The whole island was erased from the map!"

I gritted my teeth, feeling disgusted. Because of me, a giant wave had ravaged an entire population. The word "genocide" came into my head with the force of a tsunami... And then, I thought of Razovski, without managing to settle on any precise emotion. Did I love him? Did I hate him? I guess I had mixed feelings. But what was that business at the very end, with him turning into some sort of blue elf?!

Sand cut short Laura's explanations. "I want to interrogate them personally," he said, pointing at me and my friends.

We were taken to the debriefing room. Bob accompanied us. On the way, he whispered in my ear, "The official version is that the tsunami was the direct consequence of the high priest's death... A spell that went wrong, OK?"

I nodded discreetly to show that I'd understood.

There was no time to get into more details. We delivered our report. The SSU commander grilled us, playing "bad cop." Bob and Laura were the "good cops." I set the tone by feeding him a pretty story that carefully left out the role of the cube in this shadowy affair. There were no cortical recordings: I could say whatever I wanted, and my comrades backed up my statements. When I evoked the death of Agent Razovski (damn, I still can't bring myself to say "my father"), my eyes grew misty with tears, and I wasn't faking it. I sensed that Dominika was resisting a furious urge to take hold of my hand and say something comforting.

But she managed to restrain herself. It was a good thing she did...

I believe I'm falling in love with her... OK, now we're starting to turn this into a teen girl's private diary, full of mush, but how else can I put it into words? Sometimes, you need to call a spade a spade. I can't stop thinking about her. When she isn't here, I miss her, and whenever I see her, my chest feels like it's going to explode.

A bunch of clichés, you say? Yeah, well, to hell with you!

So, now we're back in our quarters. "And now?" asked James, when we left the elevator and were about to go our separate ways. We couldn't speak openly and talk about what we'd just experienced, but the looks we exchanged said a lot.

We formed a circle and held hands in silence. It was very intimate and very beautiful, because something strong emanated from the four of us. It was a closed circle and yet at the same time open to the rest of the universe. My friends! Now that's a word I no longer have any hesitation about using. I've felt the warmth of their blood which has become mixed with mine. I have FRIENDS! *It's a new emotion for me, and frankly, almost a little frightening. For years now, I've been used to thinking and acting on my own. And now I'm part of an ensemble, a group. Me, who once hated the idea of owing something to someone, now realize that not only does this not bother me, but I actually find it... liberating!*

Creating bonds... Damn, I had to travel four centuries into the future to learn how to do that!

Yeah, "and now?" as James would say.

I think I'm going to

Someone was knocking on the door of the cabin. Tess saved her text, closed her file, and stood up, feeling uncertain. It was late. Who would come bother her at this hour? She hoped it was Dominika. Her heart started racing while a long shiver ran down her spine, a promise of delights to follow. She went to the door and opened it…

And found herself face-to-face with a bearded old man dressed in an eccentric purple robe.

Professor Ronn, in person.

"Good evening, Tess. May I come in?"

The young woman remained open-mouthed for a couple of seconds.

"I… I mean… Yes, of course…"

She stepped aside to let the old man enter, and then she closed the door, but not before glancing out into the empty corridor. Ronn was definitely here alone. She wondered: what did he want?

"I… Would you like something to drink?"

"No, thank you."

There was an awkward silence.

"But I would like to sit down," the old scientist said with a small smile.

He caressed his long beard. It was longer than had been in the snapshots she'd seen on the Infosphere. It was as if, with the passing years, his Dr Freud look had gradually given way to a Merlin returned from the ancient past.

The young woman and the scientist sat together on a bench, facing a big oval-shaped porthole looking out on space. A sun, a majestic scarlet star, was burning in an infinite black sea.

Tess asked, "Can we speak? I mean… really speak?"

She made a vague gesture that encompassed the rest of the cabin. Ronn responded with a sign indicating that he understood.

"Yes," he said. "This conversation will remain between just the two of us. Strictly confidential. Laura has made sure of that."

The scientist drew in a long breath. He twiddled with his beard. Evidently, he didn't know where to begin.

"I've been observing you for a long time, did you know that?" he said by way of an introduction. When Tess made no reply, he continued, "I'm aware that you've undergone some difficult ordeals lately... I feel responsible and I would like to apologize for that."

"Responsible?"

"This whole complicated plan, aimed at saving the agency... I'm the principal mastermind behind it. Bob, Laura, your father... They were merely carrying out my directives. So, if you need to feel angry with someone, it should be me."

Tess had trouble swallowing. She wasn't too sure what she was feeling. She was just extremely tired. Perhaps that was what people meant by "letting go"?

She sighed. "How could you?"

"What are you talking about?"

"About Atlantis... About its population being sacrificed on the altar of your plots, your schemes."

"The island was doomed in any case. There was no impact on the historical scale."

"Is that the only thing that counts, in the end? Preserving the integrity of your frigging timeline?"

Ronn said nothing, like a defendant taking refuge in silence to protect himself.

But Tess still had questions: "My role is over, isn't it? I was supposed to serve as the key to unlock the system protecting the last cube and... Hey, by the way, what happened to the cube?"

The old man displayed a timid smile. But also a crafty one. One sensed that cunning had become second nature for him. "It's in a safe place. Thanks to you."

"So now that I've done what I was genetically programmed for–"

Ronn raised his hand to signify that she should stop right there.

"You weren't 'programmed', as you put it. You have free will. At any time, you could have told us to go to hell and jumped ship. But you didn't do that."

"Oh yeah? From where I stand, I don't have much choice at all."

She shot him an accusing look.

He did not turn away, but replied, "We always have a choice."

Tess scowled. She wanted to bite her nails, but restrained herself.

"OK," she conceded grudgingly. "But that doesn't answer my question..."

"Which was?"

"What do you expect from me now?"

"Lots of things. Thanks to you, we've won a battle–"

The young woman snorted derisively. "But not the war, is that it? Let me guess: the struggle between the forces of good and evil is endless?"

Tess could not prevent her words from taking on a bitter note. What was she doing here, on a space station, discussing the fate of the universe with a phony Dumbledore? It was a surreal situation. One more to add to a growing list.

Ronn gave her a patient look. "Yes, that's exactly how things stand," he said very calmly, without the slightest hint of irony. "Our enemies are powerful. I think the great confrontation has simply been postponed."

As he uttered these words, the old man let his gaze drift toward the porthole, and the infinite space that lay beyond the clearsteel. There were two ways of seeing this cosmic panorama. Each small light, even the furthest one, was a star that shone with a warm, friendly fire. Or else one could consider the immense void as a bottomless well, full of latent menaces. No doubt in this precise instant Ronn was leaning toward the second option, because a veil seemed to darken his sparkling eyes as he lost himself in contemplation of the Sculptor Galaxy. His bushy, steely grey eyebrows practically merged into one as he frowned.

"We don't know when the next assault will come, nor what form it will take," he sighed. "But the clash is inevitable."

"These enemies. If they aren't the Syaans... Who are they?"

"Believe me, I'm not deliberately withholding information from you, this time... We really don't know much about them. They were around before humanity. And since they're immortal, their perception of time is very different from our own..."

"Immortal? Great... makes it super-easy to fight them! So, they're sort of like gods, aren't they?"

"In some ways. But they can also take on human form. They don't need machines to travel in time, as opposed to the members of our agency..."

"My father could do that too, huh?"

"Yes."

"That face with the blue skin and fine features that I thought I saw, just after his death... Was that his real appearance?"

Ronn nodded. "The Syaans are metamorphs. Since the beginning of this age-old struggle they've been engaged in, they've adopted the habit of not exposing their true faces. On the other hand, when they die, they revert to their original form... Your father was the first to extend a helping hand to we humans. He made the link between our two species... and you're the living proof of that."

"But... I don't have blue skin!"

"A Syaan can control which part of their genetic capital they pass on to their children. I imagine that Pete wanted to spare you, let's say, some teasing at school."

Once again, the old man's voice and gaze became cunning. He just couldn't help himself...

Tess frowned. "Our common enemies, do they have a plan? Any precise objectives?"

"We think they want to return to primordial chaos, the beginnings of our universe..."

"The Big Bang?"

"Something like that, yes."

Tess let out a long sigh. Suddenly, she felt discouraged. "To sum things up, we're in big trouble... And please don't answer that with something along the lines of: 'Where there's life, there's hope.'"

"Yes, we're in big trouble, as you say," the scientist agreed with a melancholy smile. "Once again, the choice belongs to you. You can continue to help us, or you can stand there with your arms crossed and watch the end of the universe as a mere spectator. It will be one hell of a show, believe me…"

"I don't doubt that."

"But I have the feeling that you won't stand by with your arms crossed, will you. That's not your style."

"We'll see… I would have liked a break from active duty, even so."

Ronn chuckled and stood up.

"I'm going to take my leave now, if you'll allow me, dear."

The old man was polite.

He'd get on well with James, Tess thought.

She stood up and accompanied her guest to the door, which opened with its characteristic hiss.

"Ah, I almost forgot…"

But Tess's intuition told her that he never forgot a thing, and that this envelope he took from the violet folds of his robe, he'd been intending all along to give it to her now, at the end of their interview, and not before.

"For you."

Tess took the envelope.

"You can open it."

She unsealed it and discovered a photo.

An old photo in which her father, Pete Razovski, was holding her mother, Marcy Culligham, in his arms. They posed together in a forest with tall trees, perhaps sequoias, in front of a cabin which looked like a hunting lodge. You could almost smell the perfume of fresh earth and resin. They were smiling. They looked happy.

Tess's heart and the throat were both knotted up.

"I liked your father very much," Ronn said. "We had our

differences. He was impossible to control, he liked being a maverick, and meddling in things... but he was a dear friend. I know that Bob is very sad, this evening. At this hour, he's probably in the Red Light, downing drinks in Pete's honour..."

"Thank you," Tess articulated with difficulty.

Ronn nodded with his beard and turned around. "I'll see you soon, Ms Heiden."

The door closed behind him.

Tess remained alone with a yellowed snapshot in her hands and a bunch of emotions ready to burst in her chest.

This photo was perhaps her last link with the past.

And that past is behind you, she thought. *It might be time now to turn to the future.*

Ronn had not been mistaken. Bob was indeed in the *Red Light*. Tess caught sight of his big back hunched over the bar. It was late, and the place was emptying out, the bartender busying himself polishing and putting away glasses. Tess looked around like a wary cat, searching for any SSU members or other undesirable elements. But there was no sign of Commander Sand's men, and not many people at all on the dance floor.

Tess advanced and put her hand on the arm of her master instructor. He turned around, looking older than usual. Sadder too. Another point that Ronn had gotten right.

Tess pointed with her chin at the half-empty bottle of hooch in front of Bob.

"Buy me a drink?"

Bob nodded his head and motioned toward the stool next to his. The gesture was clearly an invitation, and she accepted it without further ado.

A wistful smile had appeared on Bob's face. He ordered a cocktail from the bartender, who swiftly mixed it and slid it across the bar to Tess, before resuming his cleaning.

Elbow still placed on the bar, Bob lifted his glass to make a toast with the young woman.

"I'm going to tell you about your father," he said.

And his smile grew wider and more affectionate.

CHAPTER ONE

A spectral apparition shot overhead on rotten vulture's wings.

Edmund Templeton, perched atop a rusted orange gantry crane some eight or nine stories above sea level, folded up the map he'd been inspecting and tucked it into his black double-breasted suit jacket. Good. The mercenaries must be further inland. If he were them, he would have kept his distance, too.

He glanced over his shoulder at the faint, fog-softened outlines of crumbling towers that rose across the brackish waters of the sound. It was a skyline that should have been familiar – it was New York City, after all, or had been – but the Wizard War had changed that. Now the only constant was the dark spire that loomed over its lesser and ever-changing brethren, auroras crackling from its peak.

It was worse than Boston. He hated being this close.

He climbed back down to the crane's cabin, holding onto his top hat. The evening wind tore at his opera cape, but he'd just replaced the buttons: it would hold.

His first official assignment since 2013, and it had to take him within thirty miles of New York. He'd lost friends in New York. He'd lost Grace in New York.

He was the Hour Thief, the oldest and one of the most powerful agents of the wizard's cabal that now tried its hardest to be a government, and he had been put out of commission for almost eight years by New York.

He shook his head, admonishing himself. Not now.

Focus on those mercenaries. Their mysterious employer. The artifact smuggling that the Twelfth Hour had so far failed to keep in check.

Focus on 2020.

The apparition wheeled back into sight. It circled once, streaming contrails of barbed wire, and then alighted on the gantry above him with a booming rush that sounded like distant artillery.

"I'm in the cabin," Edmund called, unfolding the map again. Less wind down here. He retrieved a thin marker and noted changes to the coastline. There had been a small enclave of survivors here, last he knew, but they seemed to have left in a real hurry some time ago.

And about those gouges on the beach...

A ghost swung down onto the cabin catwalk.

It was a man, bespectacled and broad-shouldered, wearing an army uniform tunic, field cap, and leg wrappings of a style not sported since 1916. Austro-Hungarian. The First World War. A medic's cross banded one arm. He might have resembled a hawkish clerk, with broad cheekbones and a hooked nose, if the burn scarring that twisted the left side of his face into a ruined mockery of a grin hadn't countered that impression. Barbed wire coiled at his feet.

Istvan Czernin. Best surgeon in the world, and one of the most dangerous entities the Twelfth Hour had ever captured. He was *des Teufels Arzt*, the Devil's Doctor, the legendary apparition who had haunted battlefields across Europe and Asia for decades, leaving a trail of blurred photographs, tight-lipped veterans, unofficial unit insignia, and mysterious gashes in the wreckage of tanks and aircraft.

He'd tried to kill Edmund once, a long time ago. Edmund liked him better as a friend.

"I found the convoy," the ghost began in a cadenced Hungarian accent more than reminiscent of Dracula. "Four tanks, just as Miss Justice said, and they're having a terrible time trying to conceal their exhaust."

Edmund marked "krakens" off the shore. "I believe you."

"It's the coal, you know. I don't know what they do to refine it." The ghost peered over his shoulder. "Is that a map?"

"Someone has to do it."

"But the satellites–"

"–aren't wizards, don't know what to look for, and I don't trust their accuracy. Besides, I thought you liked my maps." He brandished it. "Which road?"

Istvan hesitated. "I liked you making use of your naval cartography," he said.

"Gee, thanks. Which road?"

"The bridge," Istvan said, reluctantly. He pointed at the stretch marked across the sound. "They've taken the bridge."

Edmund took a deep breath. This kept getting better. "The bridge."

He looked back towards the shore, where the latticed bracing of a steel cantilever bridge jutted into the water and stretched impossibly for miles, with no evident endpoint save the distant downtown skyline. Below it bobbed a tangle of floating piers, shipping containers cut apart and bolted to them, and a mess of abandoned rafts and canoes, and likely worse things.

"They are carrying Bernault devices," Istvan pointed out, "Twenty of them. Edmund, the bridge is the shortest route. With a cargo that dangerous–"

Edmund put the map away. "I know."

Twenty Bernault devices. Palm-sized spheres that were perfectly safe until jostled too hard, at which point they jostled back in a wildly uncertain radius of radiant destruction. The things had a habit of materializing in the middle of former city centers, where the worst of the fracturing held rein, and if there was a pattern to when and where, no one had found it.

One of the many, many new problems that had come along with the Wizard War.

On August 31, 2012, Mexico City dropped off the map. Torn apart. Sunk beneath a lake that had been drained long ago. Survivors insisted that there had been a monster made of stone, that it had come from below.

The news flashed around the globe. Governments expressed their concern, pledged to send aid, and promised that the matter would soon be resolved. Everyone else worried about the unknown: conspiracy, aliens, ancient curses, cosmic alignments, mass transcendence, the wrath of God.

Seven days later, she struck.

No announcement. No name. No one knew her name. Even the Persians had called her by title. The Arab mystics who defeated her in the Dark Ages had merely appended one of their own.

Shokat Anoushak al-Khalid. Glory Everlasting, the Immortal.

She targeted cities. Only cities. All cities.

2012 was a year of magic revealed after millennia of secrecy. A year that saw every major population center in the world ripped out of normal existence, drowned in the impossible, walled off by impassable spellscars hundreds of miles deep. A year of armies, of mockeries of machines with scything mandibles, twisted beasts of vine and earth and fire, skyscrapers shredded by steel claws and drawn upwards, tornado-like, new spires accreting on new skylines emerging with a roar from solid stone.

Fifteen hundred years of preparation. Long enough that even most wizards had never heard of her. Long enough to utterly divorce her from anything human.

The Wizard War lasted only eleven months.

Sometimes, most often at night, Edmund wondered if she were truly dead.

"Big East" now ran from Boston to Washington DC, a gaping wound in reality populated by structures and inhabitants torn from a thousand elsewheres and elsewhens, a crumbling patchwork of survivors' enclaves and petty fiefdoms surrounded by broad swathes of anarchy and ruin. It wasn't the only fracture – Greater Great Lakes and Fracture Atlanta were the nearest two others – but it was the only one clear of monsters. It counted among its many battlefields the former city of Providence, where Shokat Anoushak fell.

No one went to Providence.

Edmund had never thought of leaving. Not once. Home was here, and the Twelfth Hour was here, and the survivors who poured into the remote areas of the continent wanted nothing to do with wizards. She had been one, after all, however far removed from the knowledge and practice of her modern-day descendants.

He could still wish for an assignment further inland.

"You know, I could see to the mercenaries," offered Istvan. He plucked at his bandolier, turning his head to hide the worst of the scarring as he did. "I'm sure that's why I was permitted to come along; you don't have to go out there."

Edmund shook his head. "I'll be fine."

"You're certain?"

"I'm certain. I appreciate the offer, but I'm the Hour Thief, remember? I have a reputation to consider."

He tried a smile. It fit into place like a well-used shoe.

Istvan regarded him a moment. He was impossible to fool – Edmund knew that – but they both had a job to do and Edmund was stubborn.

Finally, the ghost sighed and looked away. "They're some miles out, still," he said. "I'll show you to them. Do mind the wind, won't you?"

Edmund nodded. "I'll be fine."

He ran through his habitual checks. Shoes tied. Tie straightened. Cape properly fastened, buttoned to his suit jacket so it would tear off rather than choke him if something caught it. His Twelfth Hour pin, two crescent moons together forming a clock face marking midnight, shone at his lapel: as close to a police badge as it came in Big East.

Istvan had never understood why he added the cape to his ensemble, much less the aviator goggles or the fingerless gloves, but at least the other man could appreciate the conceit for what it was: an effort to disguise the truth as something more palatable. Mystery men were heroes, no matter their methods.

Magic didn't care for morality. Magic demanded, and if disrespected it would simply take. Magic, and the ancient immortal wielding it, had destroyed civilization as most knew it in a single night and day.

Edmund had been thirty-five for seventy years.

He retrieved his pocket watch. It was brass, attached to one of his buttons with a sturdy chain, with an embossed hourglass on the front that was starting to wear off again. "Right," he said. He flipped open the watch. "Lead the way."

Istvan vaulted over the catwalk railing.

Edmund eyed the bridge. The roadway seemed clear, but with mercenaries around, he wasn't about to trust a visual inspection.

He waited for the sight of vulture's wings hovering near one of the upper spars.

Then he convinced himself that he was the center of all universes, just as he simultaneously convinced himself that the center was in fact the bridge spar, which would have been a useless mental exercise if he hadn't made sure some time ago to catch the attention of someone or something (opinions differed) that cared about these things and didn't like such a disjointed affair as two centers at once. An offering of cartographical calculations, based on a cosmological model proven comprehensively wrong long ago, and–

Edmund snapped his pocket watch shut.

He stood on the spar. The wind tried to yank him into the sea. He grabbed at his hat before it left his head, hastily eyed the next spot along the bridge, and repeated the same mental gymnastics as before, focusing on the smooth metal between his fingers. The flick of the wrist. The snap of hinges.

Again. And again.

That old model was wrong, sure, but compelling – an idea that worked wonders in its own blinkered context, and there was a power in ideas, if you knew how to ask them. If you didn't mind how sharply-honed they were. If you had the discipline to sincerely believe multiple worrisome and contradictory notions and the stubbornness to not get nihilistic about it.

It helped to have a guarantee from another power that he wouldn't spatter himself across the heavenly spheres if he slipped up. Teleportation was tricky like that.

Edmund covered what had to have been three miles of bridge in less than thirty seconds.

The structure seemed to be getting larger: broader, or more reinforced. Some parts of it were covered, clad in vast sheets of iron.

A skeletal hand grabbed his boot.

"Down here," hissed Istvan. Tattered feathers tumbled into the murk below and vanished. The sun was too low, now; the fog getting thicker.

Edmund caught his breath. Great.

He peered over the edge, searching for hand-holds amid the metal latticework, and discovered that Istvan had led him to a ladder. He tucked his pocket watch away and swung himself down.

This section was covered, out of the wind, and he gave thanks for small favors.

He climbed.

The ladder stretched away below him. Iron cladding rose up around him. Red bulbs guttered along rusted beams. The bridge creaked with the wind, more claustrophobic by the minute, saturated with the smells of paint and grease.

He focused on breathing.

It felt like thirty stories to the bottom. It might have been five.

The ladder reverberated with the sound of engines. Headlights flashed below them.

"All right?" asked Istvan from somewhere further down.

Edmund paused where he was, holding tightly to the rungs. "I'm fine. How far away are they?"

Istvan dropped to the roadway. He turned towards the headlights, shaded his eyes, then called back up, "Not far."

A burst of machine-gun fire ripped through his chest.

"I think they've seen us," he added.

Edmund straightened his hat, only half-deafened. He fingered his pocket watch. Took a breath. Smiled. "Wholly possible," he said.

Then the Hour Thief let go of the ladder.

Another burst, fired from a weapon he couldn't see. He twisted out of the way – he couldn't see the bullets, either, but that didn't matter – and snapped his pocket watch.

He reappeared next to Istvan.

Plenty of time. Bullets were fast, but they couldn't cheat causality, couldn't fit an extra moment between moments, couldn't rely on the protection of something best left unsaid. Focus, and he could outspeed anything he was aware of, no matter how implausible. Even if something did hit him, it wouldn't kill him.

Nothing could kill him. Nothing but running out of time.

That was the agreement.

"Thank you for the warning shot," he called above the dull roar of engines, "but I prefer to negotiate. Give me some time and I'm sure we can work something out."

No return fire.

Edmund waited. They had to know who he was. Just about everyone in Big East did.

Or used to, anyway.

"The Herald recognizes your right to parlay," boomed a voice from past the headlights, distorted by some kind of electronic filter. The accent suggested a native language somewhere between Russian and Japanese: nothing Edmund knew, which these days was no surprise. "Keep well-leashed the unquiet spirit you command and make good account of yourself."Acknowledgment. Agreement. Implicit acceptance of the bargain. What they'd said about Istvan wasn't strictly true, but that part didn't matter.

Edmund nodded, relieved. "Thank you," he said. He dropped his watch into a pocket, stolen moments secured and added to his collection. He hadn't chosen "Hour Thief" as his moniker for no reason. "I'm glad you see the value in learning the whole score."

A hatch clanked open.

Istvan neatened his bandolier and the ornamental buttons beneath it, brushing away the last of the bullet holes like they were stains. "Machine-guns," he sighed.

Edmund squinted at the headlights, trying to make out the machines attached to them. They seemed to have filigree along their sides. Spikes. "Don't take it too personally."

"Have they no sense of history?"

"Less than a full dollar."

Istvan winced. "Must you?"

Edmund realized he was grinning. Gratified at this turn of events. Harboring some genuine hope that his first run in a long time might turn out OK. "Sorry."

"You're not sorry."

"You're right."A man clad in a cross between archaic plate armor and nineteenth-century military finery stepped into view, sharply back-lit: the shadow of a long coat, loose pants tucked into armored boots, an exposed breastplate that glittered gold. A scarlet cape fluttered from spiked shoulders. An elaborate crest crowned his helmet, fully enclosed, embossed cheek guards sweeping upwards to meet a visor that flickered with internal lights. A saber hung at his side.

A sharp inhale to Edmund's left. Istvan. The ghost didn't breathe anymore, really, but habit was hard to break. The barbed wire at his feet looped bright and bloodied: a sign of eagerness he couldn't hide and that Edmund wished he didn't recognize.

This was going to be something, all right.

The man before them was a mercenary of Triskelion. A member of a stranded army from an alternate history, rarely seen but widely feared. Edmund knew that Istvan had never fought one before.

With luck, today wouldn't be his first chance.

The mercenary thumped a fist on the emblazoned eagle of his breastplate. "I am the Armsmaster," he boomed in his distorted timbre. "What is it at this late hour that you seek?"Edmund smiled. "We received word that you're carrying twenty Bernault devices for one of your clients," he said, keeping his voice carefully even. "Someone called 'the Cameraman,' I believe?"

The mercenary stared down at him. "We do not give up names, Hour Thief."

"I understand."

An ominous clanking came from beyond the lights. Edmund tried to estimate how many men it would take to handle four tanks. Five to a machine? Four?

Fewer, if they were automated?

He kept talking. "I'm sure you're aware of the Twelfth Hour's stance on the sale and export of artifacts from deep fracture zones, particularly Bernault devices, so I won't remind you." He tapped his lapel pin. "I'd like to come to a mutual arrangement, if at all possible. This doesn't have to become a problem."

Flashes of red. Dark outlines moving through the shadows.

Istvan touched his shoulder, a chill that instantly numbed. "Edmund..."

The world lit up like the sun.

Edmund threw himself sideways, expecting a hail of gunfire any second. He spent a moment to blink away blindness. Couldn't outrun light. Spots danced before his vision.

A popping burst around him. He spun around –

– and then the area flooded with mist.

He sucked in a lungful of it before he could stop himself.

Sputtered. Coughed. Waved an arm in a futile attempt to clear the miasma, trying not to breathe, a familiar and unwanted panic rising in his throat.

Gas. Tear gas.

The light slanted in a swirling haze, shafts and strange shapes. The roadway rang with running feet. The seals of his goggles held, but his lungs burned. Not enough air. Not enough air, and outside there was nothing but water. Water and krakens.

Drowning. Not again.

He staggered away, face buried in a sleeve.

A jagged shape rushed at him. It held a saber in one hand.

Edmund fumbled for his pocket watch.

"Come now," said a voice like Dracula, "you aren't finished with me, yet!"

Steel met steel. A trench knife; skeletal fingers; a bloodied sleeve. A death's-head, grinning, incongruously wearing an antique field cap and glasses. Vague figures stumbled through a stinking haze of bitter mustard and chlorine.

"You know," said Istvan, mud-spattered and bullet-riddled, "I was once told that a man wielding a knife would always lose out to a man wielding a sword."

The mercenary hesitated.

Vulture's wings flared in the mists, vast and rotten, tattered feathers tangled with trailing loops of barbed wire. Istvan shrugged a rustling shrug. "I suppose that only holds if both combatants are men, hm?"

The mercenary bolted.

Edmund scooted away, shaking, as Istvan laughed. Outstretched feathers passed through him. Poison swirled around blood-smeared bone.

He was used to it – used to the sudden cessation of flesh,

the smell, the cold, the phantom blast marks and bullet holes that appeared on every nearby surface – but he would never be comfortable with it. Never.

Istvan was the ghost of an event as much as the ghost of a man. A soul torn to pieces and reconstituted by disaster. A member of a class so vanishingly rare that Edmund had heard of only three others: one tied to the Black Death, one to the Shaanxi earthquake of 1556, and the last to the atomic bombing of Japan.

A sundered spirit.

Istvan was tied to the First World War. He was by far the most active, the most combative, and the most far-ranging of his kind, and Edmund was the only survivor of an earlier attempt to capture him in 1941. In a very real way, he was violence.

He couldn't help himself.

"Istvan," Edmund tried to say, but his throat wouldn't work.

He couldn't breathe.

The horror that was now his closest friend leapt into an oppressive hover that scattered mud and wire all over the roadway. "I'll deal with this," he called, "Don't you worry, Edmund!"

He shot away. The memory of artillery boomed and flashed in his passage.

Something else responded, blowing a hole in one side of the bridge.

The roadway shook.

"Go on," Istvan shouted, still laughing, "God is on your side, isn't he? Doesn't he play national favorites?"

Wind screamed through the gap. Spray. Saltwater.

Edmund fled.

•••

Istvan chased flashes of men through smoke and fire. Stray bullets zinged from the bridge supports. Grenades burst around him: flashes, more gas, a few that exploded with a sharp snap and roar. The mercenaries shouted in a language he didn't know. The wind tore at his wings. The memory of pain – Edmund's pain, chemical fire clawing at the wizard's innards – tingled in his awareness like the afterglow of a fine wine, spiced with a more present, broader terror.

So familiar. So delightful. A meager trickle compared to the old days, but more than enough to make it all worth it. He couldn't kill anyone – not chained as he was, not without direct order – but the chase...

Oh, the chase!

Triskelion mercenaries. Members of the only real army for a thousand miles. Fierce enough to occupy the spellscars, dangerous even in small numbers, coordinated and disciplined and so very splendid.

He'd hoped this would happen. He hadn't said anything – but he'd hoped.

It would have been perfect if the mercenaries didn't keep vanishing.

A shell exploded on one of the overhead spars. Istvan swooped through a jagged hole in the bridge cladding and then back around and up through another blown in the roadway. Torn bolts and lengths of shrapnel pattered through him like ghastly hail.

One of the men ducked the wrong way.

Istvan pounced on him.

The mercenary slapped at his right gauntlet. The air contorted about him, gas coiling into mathematical patterns with a clanging, ripping sound, like a bullet through iron – and then he disappeared.

Gone. Teleported.

"That's cheating," Istvan shouted. Edmund cheated, as well, but he was Edmund; he was permitted. No one else Istvan had ever encountered could disappear like that.

Three more men vanished from his awareness. Istvan whirled about.

One of the tanks sat there, squat and square and belching smoke from gilded stacks. Spikes jutted from its sides. Scorch marks marred its barrel. It was the only tank that had fired so far.

The tanks couldn't teleport, probably.

Istvan darted for it. The Bernault devices were in there, if they were anywhere, and what else had he come for if not to help secure them? How they hadn't burst already he had no idea – the things were terrifically temperamental – but that didn't matter.

Edmund would move them, of course. Later. Once Istvan cleared the way for him, and he had recovered.

Poor, dear Edmund.

The hatch of the tank was open. Istvan swung inside –

– and discovered a tangle of wires attached to at least a dozen ominous bundles stuck to the interior walls.

"Oh," he said, "That's clever."

Fire.

Once, in life, he'd survived a near-miss by British artillery. The Boer War. That was where he'd ruined part of his face, his left arm, most of his left side, scorched and partially paralyzed... and that was what had landed him, for the next few years, in a prisoner-of-war camp in Ceylon.

Now, of course, explosions mattered less. He couldn't recall how many times he'd been struck since the Great War, but it was a great many.

It still hurt.

Istvan found himself floating dazedly just outside the bridge. Smoke billowed from the rents in its armored sides. Sunset cast orange blazes across the sky. No hint of the mercenaries – that wonderful well-masked terror – or anything else living.

He traced two fingers across where his dueling scars had been, scorched phalanges against bare bone. A cursory wingbeat revealed that more of his feathers than usual were still missing.

Well-played.

Oh, they would have to do that again.

Istvan wheeled about and made for shore as pieces of tank and pieces of roadway fell, burning, into the sea.

He found Edmund back at the gantry crane. Hat off. Goggles off. Sitting down, back to the cabin, staring less at and more in the general direction of the bridge. The terrors still lingered but he wasn't breathing too hard, which was a good sign.

Istvan had been forty-four on his last day of life and looked older, scarred and weather-beaten. Edmund, on the other hand, boasted an elegance almost feline in quality, dark-haired and dark-eyed, his narrow face framed by a trim goatee and sideburns. He looked every bit the thirty-five he insisted he still was... save for the near-permanent weariness of his expression, and the gathered shadows under his eyes.

He smelled powerfully of tear gas.

Istvan alighted beside him, folding wings that evaporated into wisps of wire and chlorine. "Edmund," he said, breathlessly, "it's quite all right now."

The reply was flat. "They're all gone, aren't they?"

"They are. Teleported, of all things. I didn't know they could do that – I think this is only the third time in a hundred years I've encountered an enemy who can do that. It's so rare." He sighed, savoring what he knew he oughtn't. "Don't they say you always remember your first?"

"Something like that."

"You know, I don't think they had the Bernault devices," Istvan continued, dropping down companionably beside him, "The entire bridge would have burst, if they had. Did you know that they wired one of their tanks? I think they were expecting us."

Edmund stared down at the barbed wire twining around one of his shins. "Great."

"Where do you suppose they learned to teleport?"

"Why don't you ask one of them?"

Istvan paused. "Edmund, they've all gone."

Edmund sighed. Then he sneezed.

Istvan patted his shoulder. Tear gas was nothing, really. It didn't destroy vision or burn flesh or drown victims in their own bodily fluids or anything of that nature, after all. The poor man would be perfectly fine.

"What did it look like?" Edmund asked once he'd stopped coughing.

"What, the teleport?"

"Yes."

Istvan considered. "Lines in the smoke," he said. "And a sort of clanging. A rush, like a train. Do you know it?"

The wizard shook his head. "You're sure the devices aren't there?"

"If they were, they would have burst by now." Istvan glanced at the horizon, which hadn't gone up in a blue-white conflagration, and then shrugged. "I truly don't think they had the devices with them in the first place."

"Go make sure."

Istvan nodded. He swung himself up onto the catwalk rail. "Edmund?"

"Yes?"

"The Magister isn't going to be happy about this, is she?"

Edmund retrieved his pocket watch. "Not at all."

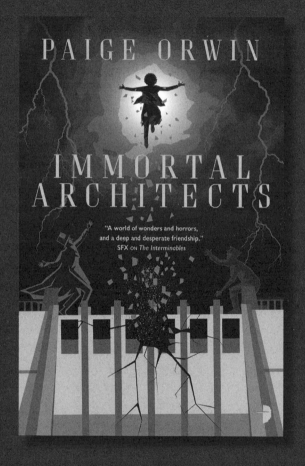

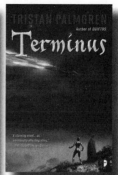

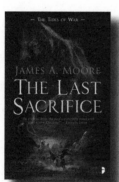
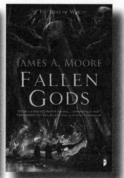
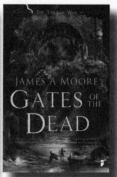

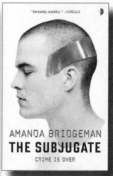

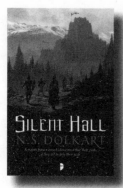 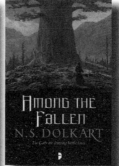 
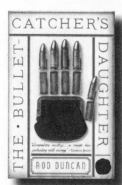  

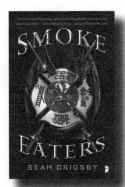

We are Angry Robot

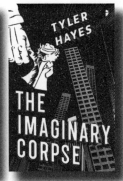

angryrobotbooks.com

  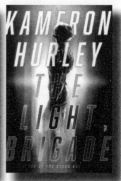